Murder Can Rain on Your Shower

A Desiree Shapiro Mystery

Selma Eichler

Thorndike Press • Waterville, Maine

This is a work of fiction. Names, characters, places, and incidents either are the product of the author's imagination or are used fictitiously, and any resemblance to actual persons, living or dead, business establishments, events, or locales is entirely coincidental.

Published in 2003 by arrangement with NAL Signet, a member of Penguin Group (USA) Inc.

Thorndike Press® Large Print Mystery Series.

The tree indicium is a trademark of Thorndike Press.

The text of this Large Print edition is unabridged. Other aspects of the book may vary from the original edition.

Set in 16 pt. Plantin by Christina S. Huff.

Printed in the United States on permanent paper.

Library of Congress Cataloging-in-Publication Data

Eichler, Selma.
Murder can rain on your shower : a Desiree Shapiro mystery / Selma Eichler
Waterville, ME : Thorndike Press, 2003.
p. cm.
ISBN 0-7862-5566-8 (lg. print : hc : alk. paper)
1. Shapiro, Desiree (Fictitious character) — Fiction. 2. Women private investigators — New York (State) — New York — Fiction. 3. Showers (Parties) — Fiction. 4. Overweight women — Fiction. 5. New York (N.Y.) — Fiction. 6. Large type books. 7. Humorous fiction. 8. Mystery fiction. I. Title.
PS3555.I226M86 2003
813′.54—dc21 2003050783

Murder Can Rain on Your Shower

Also by Selma Eichler in Large Print:

Murder Can Cool Off Your Affair
Murder Can Kill Your Social Life
Murder Can Singe Your Old Flame
Murder Can Stunt Your Growth

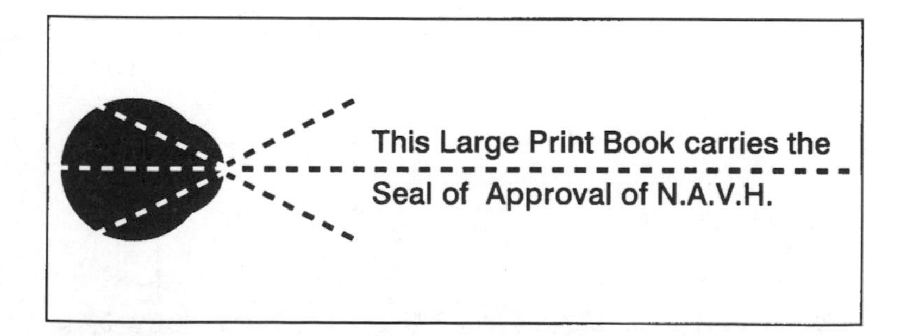

To my husband, Lloyd Eichler,
who contributed greatly to this book
with his helpful critiques,
constant encouragement,
and willingness to eat leftovers.

As the Founder/CEO of NAVH, the only national health agency solely devoted to those who, although not totally blind, have an eye disease which could lead to serious visual impairment, I am pleased to recognize Thorndike Press as one of the leading publishers in the large print field.

Founded in 1954 in San Francisco to prepare large print textbooks for partially seeing children, NAVH became the pioneer and standard setting agency in the preparation of large type.

Today, those publishers who meet our standards carry the prestigious "Seal of Approval" indicating high quality large print. We are delighted that Thorndike Press is one of the publishers whose titles meet these standards. We are also pleased to recognize the significant contribution Thorndike Press is making in this important and growing field.

Lorraine H. Marchi, L.H.D.
Founder/CEO
NAVH

Acknowledgments

Many thanks to:

Major Alan G. Martin of the New York State Police, whose willingness to answer a million questions on law enforcement continues to lend authenticity to my story lines.

Martin Turkish, MD, for helping me see to it that my dying victim received the proper medical care.

David Gruber, Esq., of Lehman and Gruber, who provided important legal information.

My editor, Ellen Edwards, who read this manuscript with such a perceptive eye.

Prologue

Ellen's bridal shower.

It has to be really, really special, I'd been reminding myself from the instant the planning began. After all, this was a very important day in the life of my favorite (and only) niece.

And special it was.

This, however, had nothing to do with the ambience — although you couldn't have asked for a setting lovelier than the Silver Oaks Country Club. With its stately Colonial-style mansion set high up on a sweeping, impeccably groomed front lawn, the place looked like something straight out of *Gone with the Wind*, for heaven's sake.

It had nothing to do with the food, either. Even though my cohostess and I had agonized over the menu options for hours. And every dish — from the filet mignon and salmon Florentine to the three dessert choices — was, I expect, very tastefully prepared. The fact is, as it turned out, our painstaking efforts and the kitchen's expertise went equally unappreciated.

And it certainly wasn't the gifts that made this event so memorable. All of that extravagant silver and china and crystal, in company with the requisite cookware and toaster ovens (there were three of these), remained in their beribboned wrappings, unopened. Not destined to catch so much as a single light ray on this sunshiney mid-August afternoon.

No.

What *did* make this an affair that no one who attended is likely to forget was something horrific, chilling — *unimaginable*.

It happened right in the middle of the salad course.

Suddenly, the woman seated directly across from me dropped her fork and pitched forward on her elegant, damask-covered chair, uttering strange, guttural sounds and snatching frantically at her throat.

And at that moment Ellen's bridal shower turned into a death watch.

Chapter 1

I'd been practically wired on my way over to Ellen's that Sunday morning. I mean, I wanted so much for her to be surprised by the bridal shower that Allison Lynton — mother of the bridegroom — and I were throwing for her. And of course, there was a better than even chance that some blabbermouth had already managed to give the whole thing away.

As soon as Ellen got in the car, though, I could tell from her expression, which was more or less placid — for Ellen, anyway — that she had no idea what had been planned.

Weeks ago Allison's future sister-in-law, Bobbie Jean — a member of Silver Oaks — had telephoned her, ostensibly to extend an invitation to lunch at her club. "We have to start getting to know each other," the woman had declared — they'd met only once before at a gathering of some kind. "After all, in a few months we'll be family. And speaking of family, your future mother-in-law — she'll be there, too, of course — tells me you have an aunt in Manhattan you're very close to — a private investigator, she said. I'd like to have her join us if she can make it."

And now, here we were, driving out to Forsythe, Long Island — and Ellen's surprise.

In spite of her comparative equanimity when we'd greeted each other, it didn't take long before she began to fret. Which was predictable. I swear, Ellen wouldn't be Ellen if she didn't continually find ways of inflicting herself with *agita*. "I hope Bobbie Jean likes me — she's Mike's only aunt," she murmured, Mike being Ellen's almost-husband.

"Why wouldn't she like you?" I countered.

"I don't know — chemistry maybe. You never can tell about those things." After about five seconds of silence, which were accompanied by a couple of barely audible sighs, she was able to find something else to pick away at. (And believe it or not, Ellen is really much less of a worrywart than she'd been before love came into her life.) "Maybe I should have stuck with the brown."

"What brown?"

"The brown two-piece linen," she responded in a voice that told me she'd expected me to *divine* what brown. "I tried it on before the turquoise this morning. And I really liked the way it looked on me — when I first get into it, anyway. But then five minutes later, you would have thought I'd been sleeping in it for a week."

Oh, I see. We're talking about a dress. "What you're wearing is perfect," I responded, reaching over and patting the cotton suit skirt. "Turquoise is a wonderful color for you."

"Do you really think so?"

"Absolutely."

"It's as flattering as the brown?"

I gritted my teeth. "More so."

Now, why my niece is so unsure of herself I'll never be able to figure out. Listen, if *I* were the one who looked like Audrey Hepburn I'd thumb my nose at the world and wear orange with purple polka dots if I felt like it.

As it was, though, I had on a conservative powder-blue A-line. I mean, not having been blessed with Ellen's bone structure and being a little more than a little overweight, I consider it only prudent to forgo orange outfits with purple polka dots.

A good ten seconds passed before Ellen became anxious again. "I really don't know

Allison — Mike's mother — all that well, either."

"But you did say that she's a very nice woman."

"She seems to be. Still . . ."

"And I'm sure she *is* a very nice woman. So will you please relax for a few minutes and stop driving us both crazy?"

"I'm sorry. It's only that I do want Mike's family to like me."

"And they will." I smiled encouragement. "How can they help it?"

For most of the rest of the trip Ellen was pretty quiet. While it couldn't have been easy for her, I think she finally ran out of nervous-making material. At any rate, it was just past noon when we drove up the magnificent front driveway of the Silver Oaks Country Club.

"Wow," Ellen murmured, craning her neck to take in all she could. "Wow," she said again.

A minute or two later the parking attendant relieved us of my Chevy. Ellen was still glancing around as we walked toward the front door. There was something akin to reverence in her tone when she murmured, "What a beautiful place. I'll bet lunch here will be quite an experience."

How right she was.

Chapter 2

I was reaching for the doorknob when the door swung open from the inside.

"We're joining Mrs. Morton for lunch," I told the smiling, well-groomed strawberry blonde with her hand on the knob.

"Of course. Right this way, please."

We followed the woman down a winding corridor, at the end of which was a richly burnished wooden door. She pulled it open, then stepped aside. I gave Ellen a little push over the threshold.

"SURPRISE!" exploded around us.

We were in a long, somewhat narrow rectangular space just off the closed dining room. And seventy-three enthusiastic ladies with good, strong voices had gathered here to fete my niece. But it took some time before this registered on Ellen. I could almost hear her thinking *Surprise? What surprise?* Then Allison rushed over to embrace her, and after that a pretty fair portion of the other women present closed in on her, pecking away at her cheeks and squeezing various parts of her person and demanding to know if she'd suspected anything. And somewhere along the line she got the message that she was the guest of honor, that this was *her* surprise.

Ellen was still attempting to collect herself when her mother-in-law-to-be removed a glass of champagne from the tray of a passing waiter and pressed it into her hand. "You look like you can use this," she announced. "You, too, Desiree." She snatched up a second glass for me and then one for herself. "Let's not forget the mother of the groom."

For a few minutes Ellen continued to hold court, although her loyal subjects were already proving themselves to be not all that loyal. Doubtless because in addition to the champagne, there were now trays laden with mini crabcakes, tiny potato puffs, and bite-size quiches to compete for one's attention. A number of Ellen's friends and coworkers at the store — Ellen's a buyer at Macy's — had just disengaged themselves from the group when Bobbie Jean joined us.

An attractive, if somewhat flashy platinum blonde, Bobbie Jean was on the short side and quite thin, although very buxom, her stretchy lime green V-necked top barely managing to make it across her chest. I wondered idly what kind of bra she had on. I mean, the thing pushed her breasts up practically to her chin. Obviously, Bobbie Jean didn't have any qualms when it came to showing off her gift from Mother Nature. Which, I conjectured, might have contributed in some small way to the lady's having acquired three husbands — so far.

"Bobbie Jean — who's soon to be your *Aunt* Bobbie Jean — worked very hard to make today a success," Allison apprised Ellen.

Ellen gushed her thanks, and the four of us visited for a couple of minutes. Suddenly Ellen was enveloped in an enthusiastic bear hug, courtesy of the good buddy she always refers to as "Ginger, who lives in my building." (I don't recall my niece's ever mentioning Ginger without tagging on that part about the building; it appears to have replaced the girl's last name.) Anyhow, it seemed that Ginger had appointed herself the event's unofficial photographer, and she quickly began clicking away and barking commands at our little foursome as if she were Steven Spielberg or somebody. After about half a dozen photos — and with no end in sight — Ellen and I tried to persuade her that she had enough pictures of us.

Whereupon Bobbie Jean, taking advantage of this slight delay in the action, made her escape. Two more photos followed, and then Ginger finally marched off to spread her talent around — but not before we'd extracted her promise to restrict herself to candid shots from now on.

Moments later I had a chance to exchange brief pleasantries with a few friends of my own: Pat Martucci (only she's not Pat Martucci anymore, having recently become Mrs. Burton Wizniak) and my neighbors Barbara Gleason and Harriet Gould. All of whom have known Ellen for years.

Allison must have been waiting for me to free up, because the instant I became available she took my arm. "C'mon, Desiree, there are a few people I want to introduce you to."

She propelled me toward two women who were standing and whispering together a short distance away. My first thought was that they seemed almost conspiratorial, which I considered more or less borne out when, on seeing us approach, they stepped quickly apart. And if that wasn't telling enough, two bright red spots put in an immediate appearance on the cheeks of the younger of the pair.

"Meet my good friends Robin Fremont

and her daughter, Carla Fremont. Robin and I also live next door to each other," Allison informed me.

"*And* we're cousins — if a few times removed," Robin interjected.

"That's true, too. This is Ellen's aunt Desiree," Allison went on. "Mike raves so much about this future aunt of his that I'm getting a little jealous. In fact, I seriously considered slipping some arsenic in her drink before." Both Fremonts tittered politely, and Robin extended her hand to me. It would have been quite a feat, however, if Carla had managed to do the same, considering that she was presently holding a glass of champagne in her right hand and a napkin with a small stash of hors d'oeuvres in her left. She smiled apologetically. It wasn't much of a smile, because Carla, poor thing, had large yellow teeth. Maybe someone should have clued her in on porcelain veneers. I got the impression, however, that it probably wouldn't have made any difference if they had. Judging from her rumpled yellow cotton dress and crinkled stockings, Carla wasn't really that into appearances.

Robin, on the other hand, was fashionably turned out in an obviously expensive black moiré suit. Large boned and very substantially built, Robin Fremont wore her thick salt-and-pepper hair brushed away from a face that vaguely resembled Allison's but lacked the other's delicate features. (Have I mentioned how lovely Ellen's prospective mother-in-law is — with a slim figure, beautiful silver hair, and the most gorgeous green eyes?)

At any rate, in between bites of stuffed mushrooms and sips of champagne, Allison and I chatted with mother and daughter for a short time. After which we were off for more introductions.

Even from a distance I'd been intrigued by one of the women I met — well, almost met, if you want to be technical — this almost-meeting captured on film by our zealous, although now very unobtrusive photographer, Ginger. Anyhow, the lady was tall to begin with. And in her skinny spiked heels she had to be well over six feet, towering above everyone else in sight. She was dressed entirely in black and white, in a too-low-cut print top and matching too-short skirt. She had on white gloves that reached midway up her forearms, the left-hand pinkie of which was adorned by a huge — and I mean *huge* — topaz ring. When it came to jewelry, though, this woman didn't seem to know the meaning of restraint. In addition to the ring, she sported long topaz earrings and three gold neck chains, plus a very large gold, sapphire, and pearl pendant, which I believe was supposed to be an abstract representation of some kind of flower. (Trust me, "hideous" would not have been too strong a word to describe that piece.) An enormous black picture hat that managed to conceal about half her face completed the outlandish outfit.

Before Allison had a chance to get out so much as a single syllable, the woman confronted her. I might as well not have been there. "Did you see her come up to me before?" she demanded, viciously spearing a cucumber canapé from the tray of a haughty-looking waiter and popping it into her vivid red mouth. And now, her voice still more strident: "Well, did you?"

"No, I didn't," Allison responded softly.

"She was actually trying to make nice to me!"

"Uh, listen, Lorraine, it's been so many years, and I —"

At that moment an elderly lady leaning heavily on an ornate cane stopped to speak to us, and Allison broke off abruptly. Then while Lorraine was occupied with the newcomer, Allison took the opportunity to slip away, yours truly in tow.

"Don't mind Lorraine," she said. "She's

really a very good person. It's just that there's someone here today that she's terribly upset with — and understandably so. Pretty paper, isn't it?" she observed almost in the same breath, most probably in order to change the subject.

"Very." The wallpaper rising above the four-foot-high wooden wainscoting that encircled the room was a floral in beautiful, muted pastels reminiscent of a Monet painting.

Allison took a brief detour to the powder room at this juncture, following which she was back to determinedly squiring me around to acquaint me with the other guests. We paused to greet a pair of late arrivals, and then we walked over to a short, waiflike woman with dark, lifeless hair and a sallow complexion. Like Lorraine, she also appeared to have an archenemy at the shower. I got the idea that it could be the same archenemy, too.

"I figured that I'd be able to handle seeing her again," she said, frowning. "But when she came over to me before and acted as if nothing had happened . . . well . . . that was too much."

"I wish I could have spared you this, but —"

"I didn't mean . . . It's certainly not *your*

fault, Allison." Suddenly the woman became aware of her failure to acknowledge me. "Oh, I'm so sorry. My manners are as rotten as my disposition is today. I'm Grace Banner."

"And I'm Desiree Shapiro." I took the hand she held out. It was icy cold.

What was going on here anyway?

"You're Ellen's aunt!" The tone had me feeling like a minor celebrity. "I've heard so many nice things about your niece. I'm looking forward to getting to know her. Ellen's mother — is she here, too?"

"No, she'd planned to come — she's living in Florida now — but two days ago she broke her ankle, so she wasn't able to make the trip."

"That's a shame."

"Yes, isn't it?" I agreed, hypocrite that I am. What else could I say though? That I was delighted that an act of God — Margot had fallen off her kitchen step stool — had spared me her company today?

"Ellen must be so distressed that her mother isn't able to share such a happy occasion with her."

I bristled inwardly at the observation. After all, it wasn't as if I'd *willed* Margot to take the header, for heaven's sake. (This sister of my much-loved late husband, Ed, was, as you must have gathered, not exactly dear to my heart.) I was spared any further need to defend myself to myself, however, because just then the double doors that led into the adjoining dining room opened wide.

Lunch was about to be served.

Entering the spacious, high-ceilinged room, I glanced around me with a deep sense of satisfaction. The ten round tables were covered with white lace cloths and set with white-and-gold china, gleaming gold-and-silver flatware, and sparkling glassware. Each table had a different floral arrangement as a centerpiece, all of them quite magnificent. A bottle of red wine and a bottle of white had been placed on either side of the centerpieces.

It was really more like a wedding than a shower, I decided happily. And so what if, even sharing the expenses with Allison, I could conceivably be in hock for the rest of my natural life. I mean, how often did my only niece get married? Besides, if I didn't spend the money on this I'd just wind up wasting it on things that would give me a lot less pleasure — like rent and utility bills.

I crossed the room to the table closest to the front, which a small white sign identified as table #1 and which I would be occupying along with Ellen, Allison, Bobbie Jean, and three of Allison's young cousins, sisters from Connecticut. I located my place card; it was between Ellen's and one of the Connecticut sisters'. But before my bottom even touched the chair, I checked out the corner a few yards to my left, where the gifts had been stacked. There was a veritable mountain of packages here, I was gratified to note, each one more extravagantly wrapped than the next.

Our salads were already awaiting us when we sat down, so everyone began to eat pretty much at once. I don't believe I'd had more than four or five bites when I happened to look over at Bobbie Jean. I could tell immediately from the way her eyes bulged that she was in great distress. A second later, her fork clattering onto the table, she grabbed for her throat. She attempted to speak, but all she was able to produce were the god-awful gurgling sounds of utter desperation.

I half-rose, thinking she could be in need of the Heimlich maneuver.

Allison put a hand on my shoulder, restraining me. "Where's Karen?" she shrieked. "We need a doctor here!"

A cacophony of nervous babble ensued, the collective outpouring of just about everyone present. Then, from somewhere behind me, a commanding voice cut through the clamor. "I'm coming! Please, everybody, stay where you are." A scowling, matronly-type individual marched quickly over to Allison. "What's wrong?"

"Oh, Karen, thank heaven." Allison nodded in Bobbie Jean's direction. "It's my sister-in-law. She . . . you'd better see to her." But Karen was already crouching beside the stricken woman. "Karen's a physician — my neighbor," Allison murmured to me.

"Move away, will you?" the doctor snapped to those of us sharing the table with Bobbie Jean. And as we hastily vacated our seats and scurried off to the side: "Somebody call 9-1-1!"

"I'll do it," Amy, one of the Connecticut sisters, volunteered, fishing her cell phone from her purse.

"I'm going to need help getting her on the floor!" Karen hollered.

A nearby waiter, who must have weighed upward of two-hundred-fifty pounds, hustled over. "I'll take care of it."

With Karen barking instructions, he effortlessly lifted the petite victim from her chair and carefully laid her on the floor, placing her on her left side.

And now, as the physician knelt alongside her patient, a hush descended on the room, with only the terrible sounds of Bobbie Jean's retching intruding on the silence.

Swiftly, Karen unhooked Bobbie Jean's bra, loosened her clothes, and pulled off her panty hose. Then, taking Bobbie Jean's pulse, she called out, "Allison, does your sister-in-law have any sort of health problems? Epilepsy, diabetes, severe allergies — anything that could account for this?"

"No, nothing."

I suddenly realized that I was holding my breath, in apparent empathy with Bobbie Jean's respiratory difficulties. As I began to breathe normally, I glanced at the doctor's face.

What I saw there sent a chill through me.

At this point, obviously alerted by one of the staff, the smiling strawberry blonde who'd greeted us at the door rushed in. But she wasn't smiling anymore.

"How is she?" the strawberry blonde asked Karen.

"Not good, I'm afraid," the doctor replied grimly. "Not good at all."

Chapter 3

"Gangway!" one of the paramedics shouted.

As they propelled the gurney out of the rear door, they were only a few feet in front of me. And I caught a glimpse of Bobbie Jean lying there motionless, the only sign of life the rapid blinking of her eyes.

I reached for Allison's hand and squeezed it. She acknowledged the gesture with a small, sad smile.

Our entire party was presently clustered at the back of the room, politely ordered there by the young policeman (and I'm talking barely old enough to have acquired peach fuzz, for heaven's sake), who had shown up immediately following the arrival of the EMS. And now, almost simultaneously, Allison and I swiveled our heads in his direction. We watched Baby Face hold a whispered consultation with the strawberry blonde, then secure both the rear and side entrances to the dining room. After which he shifted his attention to the shower guests.

"We're going to need some information from all of you," he announced in a nervous, high-pitched voice. "So please, everyone, take your belongings and follow Ms. Kramer. And please don't touch anything, okay? I'll be with you as soon as I take care of a coupla things."

Ms. Kramer, a.k.a. the strawberry blonde, shepherded us through the double doors that led into the rectangular space — the Minerva Room, it was called — where this ill-fated party had originated.

"The police would like to keep this section of the house cordoned off," she explained, "so please, come with me." She led us through an archway at the far end of the room, then down a long hallway to a large, open sitting area. It was furnished with some handsome, highly polished mahogany tables, a number of which displayed a selection of magazines, with two of the tables containing a telephone, as well. Most prominent here, however, were the upholstered pieces, which consisted of half a dozen overstuffed chairs and three plump sofas, all covered in the same fabric — a cheerful, floral chintz that contrasted sharply with the mood of our gloomy little gathering.

Ms. Kramer addressed us somberly. "I can't even express to you how sorry I am that Ms. Morton has been taken ill like this. She's *such* a lovely person — all of us at Silver Oaks are extremely fond of her. I know our entire staff will be praying for her speedy and complete recovery.

"I do apologize that there isn't enough seating in here to accommodate everyone, but this is the best option we have available right now. Please make yourselves as comfortable as you can. The police officer will be with you in a few minutes, and he assured me you won't be detained for very long. I'm going to have to leave you, but if I can be of assistance to anyone, just pick up one of the phones. I'm on extension five — Janice Kramer." And now, true to her word, the woman, after favoring us with a faint smile, turned and left.

The available seats were instantly preempted by the swiftest of our company. Naturally, I remained a standee. I was leaning against a table, absently riffling through an *Architectural Digest*, my mind occupied with unwanted thoughts about the improbability of our ever seeing Bobbie Jean again, when Harriet Gould came up alongside me and touched my arm. "Do you think she'll make it?"

I censored myself. "I hope so," was as much as I said.

At that moment we were joined by the rookie cop, who immediately busied himself with taking down names, addresses, and telephone numbers, at the same time establishing everyone's relationship to the victim.

A little more than a half hour after Bobbie Jean had been dispatched to the hospital — and only a few minutes after the young policeman had finished collecting his information — we were joined by the Forsythe chief of police himself, along with another of his officers.

The chief was rather attractive. I mean, he had good features, a full head of wavy gray hair, and a tall, lanky physique. His tan uniform was neatly pressed and an excellent fit. In fact, only a slight potbelly — and it was borderline, at that — disqualified him from being considered a hunk. Presupposing, of course, that you'd rate anyone a hunk who was most likely on the less desirable side of fifty.

"I'm Chief Porchow," he apprised us, "and this is Sergeant Block." He indicated the short, portly man who'd accompanied him and who was standing with arms folded and feet apart, gazing ceilingward with a scowl that appeared to be a permanent part of his face. "I assume you've already met

Officer Smilowitz." The chief inclined his head toward the rookie. A pause followed, after which Porchow cleared his throat. "I'm very sorry to have to tell you this, but Ms. Morton was pronounced dead on arrival at the hospital."

There were gasps and outcries and murmurs of sorrow from the assemblage.

"Can any of you shed some light on what happened here this afternoon?" he asked. "How did the deceased seem earlier today?"

A mingled response of "fine," "okay," "good," "all right."

One of the women inquired about the cause of Bobbie Jean's demise.

"We don't know yet," he said tersely. "Anyone have any idea if she'd been ill recently?"

The replies included a lot of head shaking and a smattering of negatives.

At this point Officer Smilowitz came over to confer with his superior, handing him a notebook and jabbing his finger at one of the entries, which prompted Porchow to call out, "Where is Ms. Allison Lynton?"

Allison held up her arm. "Here I am." The chief nodded and walked toward the back of the room, where a very unnerved Allison and I had been talking quietly for the past five minutes.

"I understand Ms. Morton was your husband's sister."

"Yes, that's right." There was a barely perceptible quaver in her voice.

"What about other close relatives? Was she married?"

"Widowed."

The questioning continued for a brief time: Had the dead woman currently been living with anyone? Did she have any children? Were her parents still alive?

Allison answered with a string of no's.

"Well, are *you* at all familiar with her medical history?"

"I am. And she'd always been in very good health."

"Would you, by any chance, have the name of her physician?" Porchow put to her then.

"Bobbie Jean and I have — we *had* — the same primary physician. His name is Dr. Anders Krauss. His practice is in Connecticut — Greenwich. I can give you the phone number, if you like."

"I'd appreciate it."

His interrogation of Allison concluded, Chief Porchow spoke to the room in general. "There's a possibility I may need to talk to all of you again. But right now you're free to leave. And drive carefully, ya hear?"

* * *

Allison, Ellen, and I waited at the front door to see to it that everyone got off okay. There were plenty of hugs, some tears, and a lot of words of sympathy exchanged.

Grace Banner seemed to be riddled with embarrassment when she took Allison's hand and told her, "I despised Bobbie Jean. I won't deny it. But I hope you don't think I wanted something like this to happen."

"No, of course not."

"I'll talk to you tomorrow, Allie," Grace said softly, looking grateful. "In the meantime, if you need anything, give me a call. Will you do that?"

"You can count on it," Allison assured her.

"Good. And please extend my condolences to Wes." Grace bussed her friend on the cheek, standing on tiptoe in order to accomplish this — a requirement that at a scant five-two I could definitely relate to.

A few minutes later Allison's friend Lorraine entered the vestibule. Predictably, she made no such attempt at civility. A small smile played at the corners of her crimson-colored mouth. Peering up at her, I observed that the lipstick extended well beyond the natural contours of her too-thin lips in an attempt to make them appear fuller. Which only served to remind you of just how thin they actually were. Still, there was something quite attractive about this Lorraine — maybe part of it being that there was so much of her. "So Bobbie Jean finally got hers," she proclaimed.

"She just *died*, Lorraine," Allison scolded mildly.

"And it couldn't have happened to anyone more worthy." Lorraine turned to Ellen. Reaching over, she brushed my niece's face with long, slim fingers, the topaz ring leaving a bright red mark on Ellen's cheek. "But it's a shame that whoever did this decided to extract her pound of flesh at your shower, little Ellen."

Lorraine had removed the white gloves, probably when she sat down to eat. And now I took note of the woman's nails. Painted the same shade as her mouth, they were so long and pointy as to qualify as lethal weapons. Assuming they were the real thing — and I had serious reservations there — this sweet lady must consume enough calcium to keep the milk companies in business.

Ellen was stoical. "Under the circumstances, my shower isn't that important."

Lorraine scowled. "Don't be silly. Of course it is."

"Wait a minute," Allison commanded. "Did I hear you right? What do you mean, 'Whoever did this'? What makes you think anyone *did* anything?"

"There's this rumor going around that your beloved sister-in-law was poisoned."

"*Poisoned?* I don't believe it."

"Then we'll just have to wait and see, won't we?" Lorraine turned to Ellen again. "Anyhow, I hope you made out like a bandit with your gifts. Where are they, by the way?"

It was Allison who answered. "They're still in the dining room. I imagine we'll be able to pick them up during the week sometime." She glanced in my direction. "Oh, and Lorraine, this is —"

"I hope there are lots and lots of Tiffany boxes," Lorraine told Ellen.

Well, how do you like that! I mean, the woman was starting to make me feel invisible, for crying out loud. And I'm much too big — width-wise, at any rate — to even come close.

"I guess I'll be on my way," she was saying. "As soon as I get home, I'm going to haul some Brie out of the refrigerator and pour myself a king-size shot of bourbon. I feel I should do *something* to commemorate Bobbie Jean's passing. Oh, and you *will* let me know when the funeral will be. That's one event I don't intend to miss."

Allison's eyes were shooting curare-dipped darts at her friend. "Listen, I understand why you feel the way you do. But I wish you'd try to exercise some restraint right now. This *is* my husband's sister you're referring to. And as you're aware, he happened to love her."

A chastised Lorraine didn't respond immediately. And when she did, her voice was so low you had to strain to catch the words. "I'm sorry, Allie. I can be such an ass sometimes. Forgive me?"

"You're forgiven," Allison replied good-naturedly.

"I'll call you tomorrow, okay?"

The two women embraced, following which Lorraine adjusted her umbrella-size hat and tottered out of the building on those skyscraper heels of hers — without, of course, having uttered one word to me.

Robin and Carla Fremont were among the last to leave. "What can I say, Allison?" Robin murmured. "It's terrible. Just terrible."

"You're sounding hypocritical, Mother," Carla pointed out dryly.

Robin flushed. "Carla, please," she

snapped. "Stop always passing judgment on me. I'm not saying I feel bad about Bobbie Jean. But it's awful that something like this occurred on what was supposed to be such a lovely occasion for Ellen here. To say nothing of what his only sister's death will probably do to Wes. You understood how that was meant, didn't you, Allison?"

"Yes, I did."

"I had no doubt you would." And to Carla: "Come on. I'll call you in a day or two, Allison."

As they headed for the exit, Robin went back to chastising her daughter. "And for your information, Miss Mouth, even if I *were* being hypocritical — which I wasn't — it's in very poor taste to . . ." The door closing behind them muted the rest of the lecture.

Ellen and I were both concerned about Allison's driving home to Connecticut alone. After all, she had just lost a family member. But she insisted she'd be fine. "If you want me to be perfectly honest, it hasn't actually sunk in yet that Bobbie Jean is gone, so I'm pretty numb on that score. What really does bother me is having to break the news to Wes."

"I gather your husband and his sister were close," I said.

"Very. In spite of the fact that over the years she'd lived abroad a great deal of the time." And now, her eyes filling up, Allison added, "Bobbie Jean mattered very much to Wes."

"Umm . . . about Mike," Ellen brought up here, her voice tentative. "Would you like me to tell him, or would you rather do it yourself?"

"I'm not going to put that on you. I think it's only right that I do it. I'll call him as soon as I get to the house."

We walked outside then, and Allison put her arms around Ellen. "I'm so sorry, dear. Your aunt and I wanted this to be such a special day for you, too. I'll make it up to you, though."

"There's nothing to —"

"Don't argue with your future mother-in-law," her future mother-in-law commanded. Then she sighed. "Well, I can't speak for the two of you, but I've had enough of this place to last me forever. So what do you say we get our cars and get the hell out of here?"

Chapter 4

Over Ellen's protests, we stopped off at a diner on the way home.

"I couldn't eat a thing, Aunt Dez," she'd insisted. "Not after what happened. Do you think Bobbie Jean might actually have been . . . that somebody p-p-p-poisoned her?"

Now, it is only when Ellen's nervous system is on the verge of collapse that she begins to stutter. Of course, it seems to me that witnessing a death, especially the death of someone you're acquainted with — your almost-aunt, no less — can do that to you as well as anything. The truth is, I wasn't exactly in control of my emotions, either. Anyhow, at that point I really couldn't say whether Bobbie Jean was a murder victim or not. But in deference to my niece's nervous system, I answered with, "Well, I suppose it's possible, but it's far more likely that she suffered a heart attack. Or maybe a stroke."

"D-d-do you honestly think so?"

"Yes, I do."

But I didn't. I mean, there were at least four ladies at the Silver Oaks Country Club that afternoon who would be very unlikely to carry a hankie to the dead woman's funeral. More than that, though, from the depth of the hatred she seemed to inspire, there was a better than even chance that someone at that shower had seen to it that Bobbie Jean would soon be enjoying the peace and quiet of Shady Lawn. Still, she *could have* died of natural causes. But I was definitely skeptical.

At any rate, once I persuaded Ellen that she'd feel better if she got some food in her — and God knows *I'd* feel better if we both had a little sustenance — she did herself proud. I swear, Ellen doesn't eat like a truck driver; she packs it in like a pair of them. And where she manages to hide it all is the million-dollar question. The truth is, my *thumb* is bigger than that girl's waist.

Just listen to this. We both started the meal with good-size shrimp cocktails. These were followed by hot open roast-beef sandwiches served with carrots and mashed potatoes, with Ellen ordering a humongous salad on the side. For dessert, I had a slice (more like a sliver, really) of rhubarb pie, while my niece elected to have a hot fudge sundae, with three — count 'em, *three* —

scoops of ice cream. And don't forget she was off her feed at the time.

I dropped Ellen off at her apartment around seven, then headed back to my own place.

Unfortunately, I hadn't bothered to put on fresh lipstick before leaving the diner. Also, by the time I arrived home, my dress could have matched Carla Fremont's wrinkle for wrinkle. Plus, my glorious hennaed hair looked like I hadn't run a comb through it that entire day. Which I hadn't. So who was coming out of the elevator at the precise moment I was about to get in?

Nick Grainger.

That same Nick Grainger who had recently moved into my building, and who, every time I saw him, caused my knees to buckle under me — just like I was a damn teenager!

Now, before I go into any physical description of Nick, I suppose I should prepare you by admitting that my taste in members of the masculine persuasion is slightly on the unconventional side. In fact, it's been rudely suggested — and by more than one person — that it's just plain weird. You see, I have this thing for pathetic-looking little guys, the kind who give the impression that they're in desperate need of plenty of good home cooking accompanied by a generous share of TLC. It's been further suggested that I gravitate toward men like this because I have this nurturing nature and Ed and I never had any children. Anyhow, I have no more idea of the reason for my preference than the next person. Besides, it doesn't really matter, does it?

I was going to tell you about Nick, though. . . .

As you've no doubt already surmised, a Mr. Macho he isn't. What he *is* is small and skinny and slightly balding. On the pale side, too. Plus — and be still my heart — his teeth are slightly bucked. I mean, Nick Grainger is so much my type that I might have had him made to order — appearance-wise, at any rate. I was, however, still trying to figure out how to actually get to know the man. And so far I'd made zero progress.

He was looking particularly dapper just then — even today's tragedy couldn't prevent me from noticing that. (After all, it's not as if I'd suddenly gone blind.) And it didn't take an Einstein to conclude that dressed as he was in a navy blazer, white shirt, and red-and-navy polka-dot tie, Nick was not on his way to a poker game with the boys. “Hi, Desiree,” he said, holding the elevator door for me. “Haven’t seen you in a while.”

And whose fault is that? I challenged. But only to myself. Aloud, I was a tad less combative. “Uh, yes, I suppose it has been some time.”

He smiled warmly. “Well, it’s always nice to run into you.”

It’s always nice to run into you, I mouthed as soon as the elevator door clanked shut. I couldn’t stop myself from giving that door a little kick. And naturally, I hurt my toe.

Practically the first thing I saw when I walked into my apartment was the flashing light on the answering machine. I had one message.

“Hi, Dez, it’s Mike. Please give me a call at Ellen’s when you come in.”

I got back to him immediately.

“I spoke to my mother this afternoon,” Mike said softly. “She phoned about . . . about my aunt.”

“Yes, she wanted to be the one to break the news to you. I’m so sorry, Mike.”

“Thank you.”

“How is your dad taking it?”

“I’ll soon find out for myself. Ellen and I are driving up to Greenwich a little later on this evening. I don't expect him to be in very good shape, though. Bobbie Jean was his only sibling. Also, her death has to be an awful shock to him. She was a very healthy woman — at least, we all assumed she was. Besides, she was considerably younger than my dad is. And for this to — Well, it must have knocked him for a loop."

"I'm sure your presence there will help."

"Luckily, I'm working nights all of next week" — Mike's an MD, a resident at St. Gregory's — "so I'll be able to spend most of tomorrow with my folks, too. But tell me something. I understand Bobbie Jean became fatally ill at the table while she was eating her salad."

"That's right."

"Did she appear to be okay earlier?"

"As far as I could see, she appeared to be fine."

Now, as the conversation progressed, Mike's tone had more or less returned to its normal level. At this point, however, he lowered his voice again. "Do you suspect that . . . and I hate to even think this might be the case . . . but do you suspect she may have been poisoned? Ellen says you told *her* it was most likely a heart attack, but I figured that might have been just to reassure her."

"You figured right. Which doesn't mean

that *I'm* right. We may learn that Bobbie Jean died of a heart attack after all."

"Maybe. Uh, listen, Dez, my aunt had her share of faults, probably more than her share. She did some things to people that were . . . that I consider . . . that I imagine *most* people would consider just about unforgivable. But while I didn't always approve of her actions, I *was* fond of her. Even if I hadn't been, though, I wouldn't want anyone to get away with murdering her — if that's what happened. So — and please don't take this wrong — what I'm trying to say is, I'd like to hire you."

"To *hire* me? You want to *pay* me to check into your aunt's death?"

"Yes, I want to pay you. That's how you earn your living, isn't it?"

"Not by taking money from my family, I don't." (*And not these past few weeks, either, for that matter — when I'd handled a grand total of one lousy insurance investigation.*)

"You're jumping the gun a little, Dez," I was reminded. "I'm not family yet."

"And *you're* splitting hairs, Mike Lynton. Look, I have every intention of learning what happened to Bobbie Jean. The only thing is, if you insist on bugging me about taking money, I won't keep you posted on my progress."

"Okay, okay, you win," Mike conceded with an anemic little chuckle.

I grinned at the receiver. "Of course I do. But you said that your aunt had done some terrible things to people. What people? And what things?"

"I'm not sure exactly what transpired with everyone. My mother could undoubtedly fill you in on the details. But there was something with Carla Fremont. And I seem to remember that prior to this, Bobbie Jean had some sort of altercation with Robin, Carla's mother. There was also some nasty business with Lorraine Corwin. And a Grace somebody-or-other. And I don't know who else."

"Those women you mentioned — are you aware that they were all at the shower?"

"Yes," Mike said gravely. "That's what's so troubling."

At this precise moment I realized that the surprising thing wasn't that Mike's aunt had died today.

It was that Bobbie Jean Morton, formerly Connell formerly Polansky formerly Lynton, had lived as long as she did.

Chapter 5

When I walked through the office door on Monday morning, I was all but accosted by Jackie, my one-third secretary. (I share her services with the two principals of — are you ready? — Gilbert and Sullivan, the law firm that rents me my space here.) "Well? How did everything go yesterday?" she demanded. Unfortunately — or fortunately for Jackie, as it turned out — a cousin's wedding had prevented her from attending Ellen's shower.

"It wound up being a *real* surprise."

"I don't like the way you said that. What happened?"

"Mike's aunt — the one who arranged for the affair to be held at her country club? She became ill — *deathly* ill — while eating her salad. The paramedics were called, and they rushed her to the hospital. But she was gone by the time they got her there."

"Oh, no, how terrible! Heart?"

"My guess would be poison. Although right now that's all it is: a guess."

"But you *believe* that somebody slipped something into her salad." (Jackie is nothing if not persistent.)

I hunched my shoulders. "Or possibly her drink. Who knows? I doubt if the cause of death has been established yet, though. So it could turn out to be her heart or her liver — or whatever — after all. But I'll tell you this: That lady would never have won a popularity contest — even if no one was competing against her."

"Do you suspect anybody in particular?"

"Christ, Jackie! Give me a break, will you? The body's hardly cold yet."

"But you do have a tendency to jump to conclusions," Jackie very thoughtfully pointed out. Suddenly her eyes narrowed. "Say, did you telephone your dentist on Friday? That was the third reminder you've gotten from him."

"I intended to, honestly. But it slipped my mind." From the expression on her face I could tell that Jackie wasn't buying into this little falsehood. The fact is, I was really in no mad rush to schedule an appointment to have someone poke away at my gums until they bled. "I'll get to it later, I promise."

"You are so lax, Desiree. Right this minute I'm picturing you without a tooth in your head, and take my word for it, you could give someone nightmares. If you don't call — and today — I'll call for you. I'm not kidding."

Is it any wonder that I frequently have trouble remembering who works for whom?

Nevertheless, while Jackie can be so overbearing that at times I've daydreamed about stapling her lips together, at other times I realize how important she is to me. And not only in her capacity as my one-third secretary, either. She's also a valued friend.

I had already started to head for my little cubicle, but Jackie wasn't through with me. "Why don't you phone the dentist as soon as you get to your office? That way you won't forget."

I pretended I didn't hear her.

As soon as I sat down at my desk I proceeded to set up a folder on Bobbie Jean. It was a pathetically thin folder, of course. I started by typing up a brief description of her sudden illness. And then I added what I could remember of the remarks made about her at the shower by the four women who so obviously — and passionately — despised her.

Following this, I went through my overdue bills and wrote out checks to those companies that seemed most likely to either cut off an essential service or send somebody over to break my kneecaps.

These things having been dealt with, I went to lunch. Now, in view of yesterday's trauma, I felt entitled to a little treat. So I made a beeline for Little Angie's, where you can gorge yourself on *the* most delectable toppings on the world's thinnest, crispiest pizza crust. Exactly how good are those pies? All I can tell you is that if I should ever get the death penalty (for murdering my sister-in-law, Margot, maybe?), my last meal will be a slice or four of Little Angie's pizza. Probably with anchovies.

As soon as I got back from lunch I stopped off at the water cooler. (Anchovies will do it to you every time.) Elliot Gilbert — one of the partners in the aforementioned Gilbert and Sullivan — was just tossing away his paper cup. I noticed instantly that this sweetheart of a man didn't look like himself today. The usual smile was absent from his cherubic face, and his eyelids were almost at half-mast.

"Are you okay?" I asked.

Elliot managed to spread his lips in a smile. "It's that obvious, huh? The truth is, my daughter and son-in-law dropped off their three kids at our house on Friday —

they had some kind of function in Maine this weekend. And much as I love them, those grandchildren of mine are a handful. On Saturday morning Mitchell, one of the twins — they're two — drank some dishwashing detergent and we rushed him to emergency."

"Dishwashing detergent?"

"I know. What can I say? The boy has lousy taste." He grinned, then followed this up with a yawn. "Thank God he's all right, though."

"Still, that must have taken a lot out of you."

"Oh, that wasn't even the half of it. Bradley, the eleven-year-old, is suddenly into music — drums, with our luck. And he brought his set along so he could practice. And practice he did, day and night and night and day." Elliot grimaced as he said this. "You may not believe it, Desiree, but those sounds are still reverberating in my head." I was about to offer a few words of commiseration at that point, but Elliot hadn't wound down yet. "And then poor Florence, our cocker spaniel, began acting strangely — she went around whimpering all the time. We still wouldn't have any idea what the problem was if my wife hadn't caught Mitchell shooing Florence away from her dish this morning and then polishing off the rest of her Alpo himself. And" — suddenly Elliot brightened — "I almost forgot," he said. "Jackie told me the other day that you were giving your niece a shower on Sunday."

"Uh, that's right."

He forced another smile. "Well, I'm glad *somebody* had a pleasant weekend, anyway."

Chapter 6

Call it self-defense.

I didn't have a smidgen of a doubt that Jackie would make good on her threat to get in touch with my dentist herself if I let things slide any longer. So before leaving work on Monday, I contacted Dr. Lutz's office to arrange for an appointment. At least this way I'd have some input about the scheduling. Anyhow, I was in luck. There were no openings before three weeks from this coming Wednesday. Figuring I owed myself a two-day grace period, I set something up for that following Friday.

Ellen phoned after ten P.M. She'd gotten home only a short while ago, having taken time off from Macy's so she could spend the day in Connecticut with Mike and his parents.

"How is Mike's father?" I asked.

"Not too good. Wes is finding it very hard to accept that Bobbie Jean went just like *that* — out of the blue. He kept shaking his head and saying over and over again that she'd been in perfect health. Mike told his dad that he, of all people — he was referring to Wes's being a physician — had to be aware of how often men and women die without any warning. I'm not sure Mike actually believes that that's true in this case, though. But he realizes how m-m-much more p-painful the alternative would be for his father." Ellen's voice caught in her throat. "I mean, that someone . . . that someone . . . p-p-p-purposely took her life."

Anxious to pull Ellen away from the topic of murder, I hastily moved on. "What kind of service are they having for Bobbie Jean? Do you know?" I was aware at once that I might have picked a less emotionally charged option.

"I understand Bobbie Jean always said she wanted to be cremated," Ellen responded tremulously. "But before they do . . . *that* to her, the family's arranged for a viewing. That *is* what it's called, isn't it — a viewing?" She didn't seem too interested in having this confirmed, however, because she went on without taking a breath. "It's going to be at the Frank E. Campbell Funeral Home here in Manhattan on Wednesday evening, and then the cremation will take place on Thursday morning. You'll be coming to the viewing, won't you?"

"Of course." After all, in December Bobbie Jean and I would have become practically related.

"Uh, Aunt Dez?"

"What?"

"Do you really, *honestly* agree with Mike — about what caused Bobbie Jean's death? Because the more I think about it, the more skeptical I am. Look, I can see how he'd decide that Bobbie Jean's dying of a heart attack or something would be a lot easier for his father to cope with than her having been murdered. But Mike's been giving *me* the same story — that's how I've begun to look at it, incidentally, as a story. And I've been thinking that he may not want to level with me unless it should become necessary because he considers me so fragile." And now, her tone defiant: "But I'm no shrinking pansy, Aunt Dez."

"Violet. Shrinking *violet*," I automatically corrected — only silently. Then aloud: "No, you're not." As you can gather, I don't consider it any crime to fudge the truth a bit when warranted.

"Maybe you have your doubts, too, though, about my being able to handle things," Ellen accused. "Maybe that's why you told me the same thing Mike did."

"That isn't the case at all. So far there's been nothing to indicate that a crime was committed," I pointed out. "And —"

"But the thing is, Bobbie Jean *had* been in very good health. And in light of the way those women spoke about her at the shower — they seemed to have so much hatred toward her — well, I'm finding it harder and harder to accept that one of them didn't, umm, you know. . . ." It was obvious she found the thought too disturbing to complete.

"Bobbie Jean could have been as robust a specimen as . . . as Xena, Warrior Princess, and it still wouldn't rule out a sudden, fatal heart attack."

"You're not just trying to spare me?"

It was time for a bit more truth-fudging. "If I thought Bobbie Jean had been murdered, I'd say so, Ellen."

Now, I was expecting her to demand that I swear to this — my niece being very big on oaths — but, to my surprise, she let it go at that. No doubt because I was so convincing. (Listen, it wasn't for nothing that I was the shining light of my high school thespian society.) I was about to attempt to wind up the conversation when she asked, "When do you think they'll get the autopsy report?"

"There's no way to be sure."

"I hope they find out she died of natural causes," Ellen said almost prayerfully.

"So do I, Ellen. So do I." But the small knot that, as of yesterday, had taken up residence in the pit of my stomach disputed the likelihood of this.

The phone was barely back in its cradle when it rang again.

I glanced at my watch: ten fifty. *Now, who could be calling at this hour?*

The voice was accusatory. "I just spoke to my daughter."

Crap! My sister-in-law, Margot!

"I'd been trying to reach Ellen since last night," Margot went on. "I couldn't wait to find out about all the lovely gifts she'd received. And here she tells me that she hasn't even *seen* them yet. She informs me that they're still sitting at that Silver Oaks Country Club" — with the tone she employed, Margot might have been talking about some rat-infested hovel — "because one of the guests died in the middle of the shower."

I have no idea how she managed it, but Margot made it sound as though Bobbie Jean's death were my fault. Worse yet, she even had me experiencing guilt pangs about it.

"Uh, how are you feeling, Margot? How's the ankle?" I inquired politely. The truth is, I was hoping to hear that she was in a lot of pain.

"That's not important now. I'm terribly sorry about the dead woman, of course." (*What a crock!*) "But unfortunately there's nothing I can do about that. The reason I'm calling is that *somebody* has to check and find out when Ellen will be able to retrieve her presents. You wouldn't mind following up on that, would you? You know how busy Ellen is at the store."

And I suppose I spend my time glued to the TV watching all those judge shows. That is, when I'm not lunching at Le Cirque and exchanging snippets of gossip with ladies decked out in Armani.

I bit back this snotty retort, however, which was on the very edge of my tongue, substituting a bland, "She'll be able to get them anyday, I'm sure."

The fact is that I hadn't given a thought to those gifts since yesterday. Not with a probable murder to occupy my mind.

"I'd like to think I can count on you to make certain of that," Margot persisted.

"All right," I told her resignedly.

"Good. I'll take you at your word then. Well, see you at the wedding."

"I've been just fine, Margot," I grumbled, slamming down the dead receiver in my hand. "Thank you ever so much for asking."

As is usual following one of my infrequent chats with Ellen's mother, it took me a few minutes to calm myself. Which is ridiculous. I should have been able to just shrug her off — her and these irritating little conversations she never fails to initiate. After all, ours is a contentious relationship of many years' standing.

Listen, from the second she first took a look at me — no, even before that face-to-face meeting — Margot was not pleased with Ed's selection of a future spouse. And she didn't do a helluva lot to conceal it, either. Mostly her antagonism stemmed from the very strong feelings she held about the members of her family marrying within their religion. Her expectations of her brother's swapping vows with a nice, Jewish girl, however, wound up in the junk heap when he told her about his (nonpracticing) Catholic fiancée.

So why, you might ask, had she refrained from throwing a few tantrums over Ellen's choosing a Protestant for a mate?

Had she come to acknowledge that individuals — and this would include her daughter — are entitled to make their own decisions about a matter this vital? Or could it be that she now regarded religion as less of a criterion in selecting a mate?

Uh-uh, to both of the above. Mike escaped Margot's displeasure because my sister-in-law has a kind of . . . well, let's be nice and call it *flexibility.* All it took to convince her that Michael Lynton was the perfect man for Ellen was the MD after his name. Listen, tag one of those things onto "Desiree Shapiro" and I could have been a (practicing) Buddhist, and Margot would have clasped me to her bosom. She'd even have been willing to overlook that on my person is a lot more weight than she deems it seemly to schlep around. Plus, I'll bet she'd also have closed her eyes to my having had countless suppers at her home without once making a fuss over her potato pancakes.

Anyway, I intended to check into those shower gifts. But not because I told Margot I would. In spite of it.

I didn't sleep well that night.

I was feeling incredibly frustrated.

You see, under normal circumstances, if there's any indication that I might be dealing with a homicide, I don't hang around waiting for the autopsy report to confirm it. By the time that happens — I've known the toxicology findings to take as long as a couple of months — the trail could be colder than Margot's attitude. (I can't help it; after every exposure to that woman, it's a while before I'm able to expel her from my head.) Not that I intended to leave my investigation in limbo until I got the official word in this instance, either, you understand. But unlike my usual practice of plunging right in, I'd allowed an entire day to go by without making a single inquiry into Bobbie Jean's death.

The trouble was that I needed to talk to Allison in order to learn something about the motives of those four suspects I was zeroing in on. She might even be able to offer up a few other possible assassins that I wasn't aware of. As antsy as I was to speak to Allison Lynton, however, I hadn't felt that today was the ideal time to phone her. After all, she had to handle the arrangements at the funeral home; also, she had a freshly grieving husband to attend to. Actually, it would probably be best to put things on hold until after Wednesday night's viewing.

But patience never having been one of my virtues, this just didn't appear feasible. So at the risk of being considered insensitive by the family of my nephew-to-be, I planned on getting in touch with Allison tomorrow.

I mean, it would really be asking too much of myself to continue cooling my heels like this.

Chapter 7

As soon as I was settled in my office on Tuesday, I phoned Ellen at the store to find out if, by any chance, she'd contacted the country club about her shower gifts yet.

"Oh, didn't I mention it to you last night? There was a message from Silver Oaks on my machine when I got home from Greenwich — they wanted me to call back so they could arrange to have the gifts delivered to me. They have an employee who lives in Manhattan, and this person volunteered to drop off the packages at my apartment. Isn't that nice?"

"Very. But apparently you didn't relay that information to your mother."

"How do you know?"

"I heard from her right after she spoke to you. She requested that I follow up on the gifts."

"Oh. I wish she hadn't bothered you. The thing is, I never had a chance to tell her about that message. She asked how the shower was, and I told her what happened. She felt terrible about Bobbie Jean, of course." (*Yeah, yeah.*) "But she said that she hoped I'd at least received some nice presents, and I said that I hadn't seen them yet, that I had to leave them at Silver Oaks for a couple of days. She started to carry on about the club's having no right to confiscate somebody's property like that. Well, I tried to explain that since the presents had been stacked up in the room where Bobbie Jean had taken sick, the police hadn't wanted them removed until they'd finished going over everything.

"My mother has a one-track mind, though. She didn't care why those gifts were being held there; she just wanted them released. Anyway, before I could get out that they were being delivered to me, she'd hung up. I love her very much, Aunt Dez, but that woman can be absolutely impossible sometimes."

Give me credit; I didn't utter a word. After all, Margot *is* Ellen's mother.

"She really hasn't been herself lately, though," Ellen added protectively.

"What do you mean?"

"Her ankle. She's in pain a lot of the time."

Now, although I've never wished for anything *dire* to happen to Margot (well, only on a couple of rare occasions), it did my heart good to hear that she was suffering *somewhat,* at least.

So while I said, "Gee, that's too bad," I was grinning like crazy when I said it.

I dialed Allison Lynton shortly after Ellen and I hung up. We talked for a few minutes about how many people had reached out to the family in the less than two days since Bobbie Jean's death. "Dozens of friends and neighbors have called and stopped by," Allison told me. "And we received so many beautiful bouquets that I ran some of them over to the hospital a bit earlier."

A fruit basket instantly replaced the flowers I'd planned on sending that afternoon.

"And how is Wes feeling?" I asked then. I had met Mike's father only once, but I'd taken an immediate liking to him. You really couldn't help it; he was such a gentle, soft-spoken man.

"He's extremely depressed," Allison confided, sounding pretty depressed herself. "I was hoping that having all those visitors would divert him — for a little while, anyway. That hasn't happened, though. Not yet."

"Well, the tragedy is still awfully fresh."

"You're right. And I realize these things take time. But it hurts me to see Wes like that."

"You'll give him my best, won't you? Please convey how very sorry I am for his loss."

Allison murmured that she'd do that, after which I asked if she'd heard anything from the Forsythe police.

"No, but Dr. Krauss telephoned yesterday. He was Bobbie Jean's physician — he's mine, too. Anders — Dr. Krauss — is also a family friend; he and Wes went to medical school together. At any rate, Chief Porchow contacted him about Bobbie Jean's medical history. Anders told him basically the same thing I did, that she'd always been in good health — at least, to the best of his knowledge. As I believe I mentioned to you, Bobbie Jean did live abroad for a time. Nevertheless, Dr. Krauss is still reasonably certain she'd never been seriously ill."

"The doctor must have been very surprised to learn of her death."

"He was shocked." There was what I'd describe as a pregnant pause here. And from her next words, I can only gather that Allison had been trying to make up her mind whether or not to share more of her conversation with the physician.

"Anders has known Bobbie Jean for many years," she went on at last. "*Had* known, I imagine I should say. And being fairly familiar with her past, he's aware that she sometimes engaged in rather . . . uh . . . thoughtless behavior, which didn't exactly endear her to a number of people. Well, in the course of our talk I told Anders that a few of those people had been at the shower. Incidentally, one of them — Grace Banner — is even a patient of his. As I started to say, though, once he heard that four of Bobbie Jean's — it's probably not a stretch to call them enemies — were right there on the scene, he asked if I considered her death to be suspicious."

"And do you?"

A protracted silence followed, after which Allison said quietly, "I suppose I have to concede that it *is* possible she met with foul play, although I don't believe that's actually the case." And now she seemed to be struggling with herself. "Still, even before Lorraine claimed to have heard something of that nature on Sunday, it crossed my mind that Bobbie Jean might have been murdered. But then again, this would mean that the person responsible was one of my very good friends, and I can't even imagine any of them *poisoning* somebody." A few moments went by before she made another admission. "I'm also terribly concerned about how Wes might react if it should turn out that someone *did* do away with Bobbie Jean. Perhaps that's another reason I tend to reject that theory."

"It sounds to me as if the doctor himself may regard her death as suspicious."

"I think you're right, although he didn't offer an opinion." I was about to bring up another matter when Allison hit me with, "You know, Desiree, if Bobbie Jean *was* murdered, I'm afraid I could be at least partially responsible."

"Why would you say a thing like that?"

"I might have set the stage for it to occur. Look, it wasn't my idea to have Ellen's shower at Bobbie Jean's club. In fact, I fought it. But Bobbie Jean was absolutely determined. In the end she went to Wes, and he persuaded me to go along with her. My husband was always extremely supportive of his sister, which had a great deal to do with her childhood. But that's another story entirely. Anyhow, I shouldn't have listened to Wes. I recognized instinctively that allowing Bobbie Jean to . . . well . . . in a way, act as hostess wouldn't exactly be appreciated by certain of the guests. It was almost as if they'd be attending the shower at her sufferance. Do you understand what I mean?"

"I think I do. But listen, Allison, there was no way you could predict that Bobbie Jean would be poisoned — if, in fact, that's how she died. Or be sure that her death could have been avoided if the affair had been held somewhere else."

"I'd like to think that's true."

"It is. But tell me this. Is it your opinion that your sister-in-law wanted the shower at Silver Oaks in order to make it uncomfortable for these particular ladies who so obviously hated her?"

"No, it's not. Bobbie Jean wasn't especially concerned with what people thought of her. I'm fairly positive that the only reason she was so keen on her country club was because it's such an elegant setting. And she figured that by arranging for the function to be held there, she'd be doing something nice for Mike and his bride-to-be. But I'm not at all sure the women involved would agree with this assessment.

"In any event, I did try my best to explain to Bobbie Jean that because of the bitterness existing between her and some of the guests, it might be advisable to have the shower at a more neutral location. But she shrugged off my objections."

"Incidentally, I presume we've been talking about Lorraine, Grace, and the Fremonts — mother and daughter."

"Yes," Allison said softly.

"Well, why didn't any of the four just decline the invitation if they were troubled by the Silver Oaks thing?"

"A good question. Particularly since I assured them I wouldn't be offended if that's what they decided to do. But Lorraine said she had no intention of giving Bobbie Jean the satisfaction of staying away. Besides, Lorraine had attended a shower at Silver Oaks about a year ago and evidently she was very impressed with the food. She told me she refused to allow Bobbie Jean to deprive her of a meal like that. The others insisted — and I really don't quite accept this — that the situation didn't bother them that much. All four of them ~~of them~~ also said that they wouldn't dream of missing a shower for my future daughter-in-law."

"Aside from those women, was there anyone else at Silver Oaks that day who harbored a grudge against your sister-in-law?"

"No one I'm aware of. But it *is* conceivable, with a track record like Bobbie Jean's. I should really give it some thought, shouldn't I? Thanks, Desiree."

"For what?"

"For the reminder that even if it should be determined that Bobbie Jean was poisoned, this wouldn't necessarily mean one of those four had a hand in it."

"No, it wouldn't. And I certainly intend to explore additional areas, as well. Nevertheless, it's important that you and I go over the grievances your friends harbored against Bobbie Jean."

I fully expected that Allison would put me off until the end of the week. Which she sort of did. And which, in view of the circumstances, was understandable. But then she inquired hesitantly, "Our talk *can* wait, can't it?"

"Yes, I guess it can. But —" I cut myself off.

"But what?"

"If there *has* been a crime committed here, the more promptly I begin my investigation, the better my chances of apprehending the perpetrator. As time goes by, memories fade, perceptions change, evidence —"

"So you're saying that we should get together as quickly as possible."

"Pretty much, if you can possibly arrange it. We can do it anywhere that's convenient for you, Allison. Naturally, I'll be glad to come up to Greenwich if that would be best."

"That wouldn't be necessary. I happen to be coming into Manhattan this afternoon — I have to attend to some business at the funeral parlor today." Then, with more than a hint of reluctance: "If you really believe my meeting with you this soon could make a difference, I suppose I can stop by your apartment before driving back."

"I believe it could make a critical difference."

"All right," Allison agreed. "I should be able to get there by six thirty or so. How does that sound?"

"Perfect. Listen, why don't you stay for dinner?" Not known for my speed — not even in the kitchen — the instant I extended the invitation I was half out of my chair, poised to head for home and start putting together a meal of some kind.

"I'd really love to, Desiree, but I'm anxious to return to Connecticut as early as I can. My brother and sister-in-law will be keeping Wes company, but still — Listen, this won't take very long, will it?"

"I promise it won't."

Now, this is a promise I make with regularity. And break with equal regularity.

But I vowed to myself to keep my word this time. Even if I had to pull out my tongue to do it.

Chapter 8

Allison phoned at around twenty to six.

Damn, I muttered to myself the instant I heard her voice. But almost immediately I took heart. It seemed she wasn't calling to cancel after all.

"I finished at the funeral home before I figured I would. Would it be all right if we had our meeting ahead of schedule?" she asked, her voice tentative.

"Sure."

"If I leave my car parked where it is and hop a cab over to your apartment, I could probably be there in ten minutes."

"That's fine."

"Oh, I'm so relieved. That way I can be back in Greenwich a bit sooner. I didn't want to just burst in on you, though."

Now, how do you like that? I mean, if there's one thing that irks me more than a person's being late for an appointment, it's a person's showing up before they're expected. Listen, I can't tell you how many times some damn early bird has caught me either half-dressed or half-coiffed. And once, a couple of years ago — and I can still hardly bear to recall it — I even had to go to the door with a totally naked face.

I already liked Allison Lynton, but after that call she shot up about a thousand points in my estimation. Never mind that I happened to be fully clothed, combed, and made up when she telephoned. Like they say: It's the thought that counts.

I sat in one of the club chairs. Allison was directly across from me, perched on the edge of the sofa, sipping coffee. (I'd tried to persuade her to switch to tea — my coffee being a few steps down from sludge. But she wasn't a tea drinker. The proffered options of wine, beer, and soda were also scratched. So, really, my conscience was clear.)

Anyway, she looked tired, drawn. I had set out a plate of cheese and crackers, along with an onion tart that had been stored in the freezer for emergencies. Aside from the coffee, though, it was fairly plain that Allison wouldn't be touching a thing. This meant that I had to ignore my own stomach, which was threatening to commence gurgling its complaints at any minute. But, listen, I didn't want Mike's mother to think I was a glutton or anything.

"How are you feeling?" her appearance prompted me to inquire.

"Worried." She smiled wanly. "About my friends, of course, in the event Bobbie Jean's death should turn out to be what we're all praying it wasn't. But mostly about Wes. I knew his sister's passing would be tough on him, but I had no idea he'd take it *this* badly. He's barely had anything to eat since Sunday." And then about three seconds later, she tagged on, "Naturally I'm also terribly sad about Bobbie Jean."

Well, this mention of the dead woman was so obviously an afterthought that I commented, "I have an idea you weren't too fond of Bobbie Jean."

"What makes you think that?" I was attempting to firm up an answer, but Allison held up her palm. "Never mind." For a moment her lips stretched into another sad smile. "My sister-in-law was intelligent and witty, even generous. Actually, she was better company than most people I know. There were times I was fond of her in spite of myself. I say 'in spite of myself' because she was almost completely lacking in any sort of moral code. The truth is, she didn't care who she stepped on — or how hard — in order to get what she wanted."

"I imagine, then, that she must have alienated an awful lot of people."

"She had quite a talent for it. And speaking of that, something occurred to me after our conversation this morning."

"What's that?"

"I wouldn't be surprised if Bobbie Jean had had a few altercations with some of the staff at Silver Oaks. She could be very demanding. Maybe one of *them* . . . ?"

"Maybe. But tell me, have you come up with anyone else at the shower who was on less than friendly terms with her? Among the guests, I mean."

"I've been racking my brain for some additional . . . I suppose I should call them 'suspects.' But if there *were* other enemies of Bobbie Jean's at the shower — and with my sister-in-law that's a very real possibility — I'm not aware of it."

"I take it she didn't confide in you."

"Not normally, no. But there were occasions when she realized that I had to have learned of her most recent transgression, and she was worried that I might tattle to Wes. So she'd initiate a heart-to-heart talk with me — or I should say, her version of one — in order to defend her actions. You see, her brother was the only person in the world whose opinion really mattered to Bobbie Jean. She needn't have been concerned, though. I avoided discussing her with Wes. Her behavior not only upset him greatly, but we almost invariably wound up in an argument. However, when your conduct is that blatant, that *dreadful*, the word is bound to get around. So in spite of my keeping quiet, I'm afraid my husband wasn't spared very much."

"He found out what had occurred between Bobbie Jean and those four friends of yours?"

Nodding, Allison set her cup on the table between us. I looked down. She couldn't have taken more than four or five sips. Which, come to think of it, is more of my coffee than most people can manage.

"And I take it he was disturbed by whatever it was she did to them?"

"He was appalled. He even persuaded her to see a therapist a number of years back — for all the good that did. Nevertheless, my husband constantly ended up making excuses for her. He attributed his sister's actions to the circumstances of her childhood, and evidently her analyst concurred. Whatever the cause, though, the fact of the matter is that Bobbie Jean was a sexual predator."

"*A sexual predator?* What was so wrong with her childhood?"

"Their mother — hers and Wes's — passed away when she was only five. And apparently Bobbie Jean was devastated — she'd been devoted to the woman. The father was a wealthy businessman. He died less than a year after Wes and I were married, but I can certainly confirm my husband's contention that he was an extremely cold person. Also, it seems that when the children were growing up, the man was so consumed with making money that he had very little time to spare for them. And to make matters worse, Wes, who was ten years older than Bobbie Jean, was away at prep school and then college during most of her formative years. She was raised by a series of nannies, and from what I understand, she never really bonded with any of them.

"According to Wes — and here again the analyst reached the same conclusion — his sister, feeling as alienated and unloved as she did, developed very low self-esteem." Something closely resembling a sneer crept into Allison's voice as she said, "Her emergence into the sort of woman she eventually became was supposedly the result of a desperate search for love."

Now, granted Bobbie Jean's early life fell

short of being idyllic. But as far as I was concerned, that didn't earn her any God-given right to be a bitch for the rest of her days. I have this thing about our being responsible for our own actions, regardless of the baggage we carry around. "Listen," I remarked, "maybe the Boston Strangler wasn't blessed with such a hotsy-totsy childhood, either. And who knows what kind of parents Fidel Castro had. Or how much affection was lavished on little Josef Stalin, for that matter."

"Exactly. But long ago I gave up trying to make that point with my husband. I'm certain he blames himself to a great degree for having been away from home so much of the time when Bobbie Jean was little. He did approach his dad about attending a college here in New York, but his father was adamant that he go to Yale."

"Are you sure I can't get you something else to drink?" I said then. "Something cold, maybe?"

"Thanks, but I'm fine." Allison glanced at her watch. "And I do have to be getting back to Connecticut."

Well, I realized I'd promised both Allison and myself that our meeting would be brief. But at this juncture we hadn't even touched on the topic I considered most crucial to my investigation. "I won't detain you much longer. But if you could just fill me in on the nature of your friends' grievances against Bobbie Jean . . ."

Allison's expression communicated that she was not exactly delighted to comply. "You know, it occurred to me during the drive to Manhattan that I wouldn't be able to give you a truly accurate picture of what actually transpired in any of those cases. None of the events were that recent, and I've no doubt forgotten many of the details. I think it would be best if you spoke to the women themselves. I'm sure they'd have no problem revealing to you precisely how Bobbie Jean messed up their lives."

"But *you* do? Have some problem with discussing these matters with me, I mean."

"It isn't that. I really don't recall just what went on."

Naturally, I was skeptical — to say the least. I figured Allison was disinclined to relate information that might conceivably give one — or all — of her buddies a strong motive for doing away with the deceased. Plus, some of her reticence could also stem from a desire to avoid besmirching the memory of her dead sister-in-law — any more than she already had, that is — mostly, I felt, out of loyalty to Wes.

Still, if I was able to convince Allison to

provide me with even a vague idea of what dire deed Bobbie Jean had done to each of my suspects, it could prove helpful. Suppose, for example, that one of these ladies was resistant to meeting with me. I could come back at her with something like, "You might as well talk to me. I've already discovered that Bobbie Jean defrauded you of a million dollars." Or whatever. What I'm trying to say is that anything I learned today might provide me with some leverage in the future.

However, being that I regarded Allison Lynton as a decent sort of person who was in a very uncomfortable position, I was reluctant to badger her. But I managed to overcome the reluctance. "Look, I'll be frank. I'm hoping I'm wrong, but I'm now pretty much convinced that Bobbie Jean's death was premeditated murder. If you would just tell me the *kind* of thing she pulled in each instance, it could make a difference in my investigation."

"Kind of thing?" Allison echoed.

"Did your sister-in-law, the sexual predator, wreck any marriages? Seduce a boyfriend or two? Or what? It isn't necessary that you go into the nitty-gritty. You can speak in general terms." And here I threw in what must have been the clincher: "I'm sure your husband's primary concern right now is to find out what happened to his sister."

Allison didn't say anything immediately, probably because she was still wrestling with herself about how much she *should* say. But at last she murmured, "I may as well start with Lorraine. You remember, she's the very tall woman with the big hat."

Yeah. The one who was so taken with me, I thought sarcastically. But I merely nodded.

"Bobbie Jean made a play — a successful play — for Lorraine's fiancé. Actually, the two of them even moved in together for a while."

"I gather that ended the engagement."

"It did," Allison said flatly.

"What happened with Robin Fremont?"

"Bobbie Jean set her sights on Carla's husband. And before long Roy became Bobbie Jean's husband number two."

"I suppose that's also the reason Carla felt as she did about Bobbie Jean."

"Can you blame her?"

"Of course not. Bobbie Jean and Roy eventually divorced, though."

"No, he was killed in a car crash less than a year into the marriage."

"Umm, Mike mentioned that there was something else Robin held against your sister-in-law, apart from Bobbie Jean's wrecking her daughter's marriage."

"Oh, *that*. In light of all of Bobbie Jean's other transgressions, it's really pretty minor." Allison hesitated for a moment before adding resignedly, "I imagine you want to hear about it anyway, though."

"Please."

"Well, when Bobbie Jean was in her twenties, she claimed that she caught Robin in a ménage à trois with the Fremonts' gardener and pool boy. Robin, however, insisted that it was Bobbie Jean who was part of that precious trio."

"I assume you believed Robin's version."

"Considering my sister-in-law's past, it was no contest."

Naturally, I could see where Robin would have been furious at Bobbie Jean for fabricating a tale like that. But angry enough to commit murder? And over something that took place so long ago? Uh-uh. I moved on. "Incidentally, whatever happened to Bobbie Jean's first husband?"

"Lyle Polansky? The marriage lasted less than three months. That was twenty-five years ago, and she hadn't seen or heard from him since. Bobbie Jean used to say that she realized it had been a big mistake from the instant they said their I-do's." Allison peered at her watch again. "I really must be going."

"I understand. But I'd appreciate it if you could spare just a minute or two to tell me about Grace Banner."

She heaved a deep sigh. "All right. But I definitely have to be on my way after that."

"Thank you," I murmured.

"For a short time Bobbie Jean and the Banners — Grace and her husband — co-owned a restaurant. After about a year Bobbie Jean got this notion that the other two had been engaging in some financial hanky-panky. And she took them to court. She lost, but Grace and Karl felt that the action against them had caused irreparable damage to their reputations, so they sued Bobbie Jean for slander. They also lost."

"Is there a chance your sister-in-law was right, that there *was* something fishy going on?"

"None. She was mistaken. Grace and Karl Banner are good people, *honest* people. Anything questionable that was going on at that restaurant was strictly in Bobbie Jean's head."

And with this, Allison reached for the handbag on the seat cushion alongside her, obviously preparing to rise.

Now, I hated to detain her any further, but

I felt I had no choice. "Just one more question," I put in hurriedly, experiencing, even as I said this, what must have been guilt pangs. (Unless, of course, they were hunger pains.) "What became of husband number three?"

"Geoffrey Morton had a heart attack six months ago and made Bobbie Jean a widow for the second time," Allison informed me tersely.

"How many years had they been married?"

"Close to three. They separated three or four months before he died, though — a 'trial separation,' they called it."

"So they might have gotten together again."

"There was that possibility."

"You sound skeptical."

"I was hoping they could work things out. I even thought that a stable relationship might put an end to my sister-in-law's destructive behavior. But I can't really say that I was overly optimistic about a reconciliation."

At this juncture Allison very purposefully picked up her handbag. But before she was able to make her escape, I managed to squeeze in a few other questions. "Why is that?"

"Because there was so much friction in the marriage."

"Friction?" I repeated, keeping my fingers crossed that she'd expand on this.

"Geoffrey was British," she added then, "and at first Bobbie Jean attributed all their difficulties to living in England. She didn't care for it there."

"But there was more to it than that?"

"Apparently." I wasn't at all sure Allison would say anything further. However — and you could tell this was almost against her will — she went on. "Bobbie Jean convinced Geoffrey to ask for a transfer to his company's New York office. And two years before his death they pulled up stakes and moved to Long Island. Unfortunately, though, the move wasn't the cure-all she'd been counting on."

At last a determined-looking Allison got to her feet.

"I appreciate all the time you've given me," I said sheepishly. "It wasn't my intention to keep you here this long, honestly."

"Well, at any rate, now you have an idea of what transpired between Bobbie Jean and those friends of mine." She screwed up her mouth. "Although some friend I turned out to be, right?"

I didn't think a response was expected,

and anyhow, I didn't know what to say to this. "Umm, I'm going to need the telephone numbers of those women from you," I brought up instead. "I'll be contacting them to schedule appointments. And, Allison? It would be really helpful if you'd phone them and request that they agree to see me. Uh, and if you could do it as soon as possible . . . ?"

"I'll make the calls in the morning."

Minutes later we were standing at the half-open door.

Allison looked so forlorn that, for her sake, I forced myself to voice what I'd been refusing to allow myself to so much as think about since Sunday.

I broached the subject with, "It might be worthwhile if you tried coming up with the names of other people who have had problems with your sister-in-law. I'm referring to people who didn't attend the shower."

"I don't understand."

"Well, we'll probably know more when the autopsy report comes in, but there's always the chance that a slow-acting poison had been administered to Bobbie Jean days or even weeks earlier."

In a case like that, of course, the list of suspects could be practically endless. And this was particularly true when you had a victim like Bobbie Jean Morton.

But Allison brightened. "I'll do that," she said, sounding upbeat for the first time that evening.

I, on the other hand, was — for obvious reasons — not at all happy with this theory.

In fact, I was feeling pretty damn queasy as I closed the door behind her.

Chapter 9

I had to give Allison time to contact those four suspects and pave the way for me. So somehow I managed to keep my itchy forefinger away from the telephone dial all of Wednesday morning.

However, at precisely two o'clock — which is when I got back from lunch — I couldn't contain myself any longer.

I kicked off with a call to Lorraine Corwin, mostly because I wanted to get that one over with. I mean, not only did I have a decidedly negative impression of Ms. Corwin, but I figured her to require some heavy-duty persuasion when it came to scheduling an appointment with me.

I was so wrong.

After reminding her we'd met at the shower (I couldn't say, "almost met," could I?) and that I was Ellen's aunt, I explained that I was a PI looking into Bobbie Jean's death.

"I remember you. You're the woman with the beautiful red hair."

I almost fell off the chair.

"Well, thank you. Uh, I suppose you've spoken to Allison today," I said, as, almost of its own volition, my hand went to my head and began playing with my sticky, oversprayed coiffure.

"No, why?"

"She was going to request that you get together with me to talk about Bobbie Jean." I hastily threw in the usual lie: "I won't take up much of your time."

"Could be Allison did phone. I've been out of the office all day — I just this second walked in — and I haven't had a chance to check my messages yet. When would you like to have this talk?"

"As soon as you can make it."

Lorraine's tone was regretful. "I can't do it today anymore. Is tomorrow okay?"

"Fine. What time?"

"I live here in the city, so I'm pretty flexible. I'd really prefer it if we could make it around eight o'clock, though, if that's all right with you."

"Sure."

"We could meet for coffee," she suggested, mentioning a coffee shop on West Fifty-second Street, near her workplace. "They make a great cuppa, and they don't care how long you sit around."

"Sounds ideal. Well, see you tomorrow night."

The receiver was more than halfway to its cradle when Lorraine shouted something.

I quickly brought it up to my ear again. "What was that?"

"I meant eight in the *morning* — before work."

"Oh. That's even better."

But I hung up grousing to myself. *Eight in the morning? Who sets something up for that hour, anyway?* (Listen, I'm lucky if I can drag my behind out of the apartment in time to get to the office by nine thirty. Which only happens on my good days.)

Well, I did say that I wanted to get together as soon as possible.

Still, my initial dislike for Lorraine Corwin momentarily flared up again. I mean, *eight A.M.?* The woman had to be crazy! Regardless of her appreciation of my glorious hennaed hair.

I reached Grace Banner at work — she was a salesperson at a leather goods store in Greenwich. She'd already been contacted by Allison and would have no problem telling me whatever I wanted to know about her relationship with Bobbie Jean.

"But do you really think she was *poisoned?*" she ventured timidly.

"It hasn't been ruled out. And the thing is, if it should turn out that she *was* murdered, it's more likely that the killer will be identified if the investigation begins now, while the evidence and everyone's recollection of that day are still fresh."

"I understand. Do you have any idea when we'll find out for sure what happened to her?"

"It's hard to predict. It could be today; it could take months."

"Oh, my."

"Listen, would it be possible to arrange something for tomorrow? I could drive up to Connecticut."

"You don't have to do that. As it turns out, Thursday's my day off, and for weeks now I've been looking for an excuse to come into Manhattan for some shopping."

It was agreed that Grace would be at my office at three thirty.

That's three thirty *P.M.*, of course.

Robin Fremont wasn't home, and I elected not to leave word on her answering machine. As difficult as it is to believe, not everyone is so pleased to hear from me that they're motivated to return my call. I would try her again later.

* * *

I had better luck with Robin's daughter. She was between patients when I dialed the Manhattan dental office where she was employed as a hygienist.

Replying to my question, the girl told me she'd just been handed a message slip with the notation that Allison had phoned her at around eleven. But having been tied up until about five minutes ago, Carla hadn't gotten back to her yet. "To be truthful, I was a little surprised that she telephoned me here; we don't really talk that often."

"I was under the impression that in addition to being distant cousins, you're also good friends."

"Oh, we are. We're just not in constant touch, that's all. Allison and my mother are *very* close, though — dating from when I was still toddling around in diapers — and the two of them are always yakking on the phone."

I explained the reason Allison was attempting to contact her.

"Is it definite then?" She sounded excited, almost ghoulish.

"Is what definite?" I inquired, just to be certain I hadn't misinterpreted the question.

"That Bobbie Jean was poisoned?"

"No, it's not definite, but it is pretty likely." And I proceeded to go into my spiel about how important it was that I start checking things out before too much time went by.

Well, Carla was more than willing to sit down with me. In fact, unless I was very much mistaken, the word was "eager." No doubt she was unable to resist this opportunity to rant to a brand-new set of ears about the woman who'd appropriated her husband.

The only problem was that Carla's job prevented her from meeting with me during the day. And she already had previous engagements for both tonight and tomorrow night that she didn't feel comfortable canceling. Plus — delaying things even further — she would be going out of town for the entire weekend when she finished work on Friday.

We left it that she would stop by my apartment on Monday at seven P.M.

Just before five I gave Robin another try — no answer yet. After which I headed home.

Then, following a quick supper, I dressed for that evening's sad event.

There must have been a couple of hundred people gathered at the Frank E. Campbell Funeral Home to attend the viewing. Most of them wore dark clothes and somber expressions and spoke in hushed tones. But I had my doubts that more than a handful of them truly mourned the deceased.

Standing on tiptoe, I was searching for someone I knew in the jam-packed room when I spied Wes Lynton about ten yards away. He was having a conversation with a short, squat man and a shorter, squatter woman. I was just about to start planting my elbows in some ribs in order to reach him when suddenly the crowd between us dispersed for two or three seconds, and Wes spotted me, too. He held up his forefinger, which I read as, "Be with you in a minute." And after a few words to the people he was standing with, he made his way toward me.

"Desiree," he said, his arms outstretched, "how nice of you to be here." I gave him a brief hug and mumbled my condolences.

Now, the one other time I'd met Mike's father, I'd been instantly struck by his aristocratic good looks. A tall man and slender, his only slightly thinning hair was a beautiful silver, like his wife's. His brown eyes were warm and intelligent, his Roman nose the perfect fit for his arresting, angular face. I recall thinking at the time that if I had to cast a wealthy and successful physician of sixty or so, I'd do my damnedest to snag Wes Lynton for the role.

Tonight, however, it appeared that he'd lost a good ten pounds and aged about ten years. Even his shoulders were stooped.

You had merely to be aware of how Bobbie Jean's demise was affecting her brother to appreciate why — in spite of Allison's revelations yesterday — I continued to regard the woman's untimely end as a tragedy. Besides, even though she was certainly no prize package, she had to have *some* redeeming qualities. (Hadn't Allison mentioned her generosity?) As I saw it, Bobbie Jean certainly merited some payback pain in her life, but this didn't give anyone the right to snuff out that life completely.

Wes and I chatted for a brief time about the state of each other's health (with Wes insisting that he was "coming along"). Then he told me how grateful he was that I was looking into Bobbie Jean's death. This, as was only natural, led to an attempt to question me. "Desiree, do you believe that my sister was mur—"

Well, it didn't take a Rhodes scholar to figure out where he was heading. Fortunately, at that precise moment Mike and Ellen materialized alongside us, which took me off the hook.

Mike was apologetic. "I hoped we could make it before now, Dad. I switched shifts with someone so I could have tonight off, but there were three emergencies and —"

Wes patted his son's shoulder. "That's all right. Those things can't be helped. Bobbie Jean is laid out in the other room, Mike. I'd like to go in again and see her one last time. Would you care to come with me?"

"Yes, I would. You stay here with Desiree, Ellen. We won't be long."

Ellen watched the two men walk away and get swallowed up in the crowd. Then, moments later, looking perturbed, she murmured, "Maybe I should have gone with them."

"What, so you could pass out cold?"

She shot me a black look. "Don't be silly. I —"

"Look, Ellen, Bobbie Jean was practically a stranger to you, even if she was Mike's aunt. And anyhow," I pointed out, "it's evident that neither Mike nor Wes expected that of you."

Ellen was relieved. "I guess," she responded softly, immediately following this with the demand that I fill her in on what I'd learned about the deceased.

"If you're talking about the cause of her death, absolutely nothing. But if you're referring to what I found out about her character, I discovered that it wasn't exactly sterling."

"Mike more or less indicated that. He was still fond of her, though."

It was at this juncture that Ellen caught a glimpse of Allison, who was not more than an arm's length away from us. "There's Mike's mother," she informed me. Unaware of our presence, Allison was attempting to squeeze through the wall-to-wall people, Robin Fremont close behind her, clutching her hand. They had already passed us when Ellen, leaning over, managed to grab Robin's shoulder.

"Ellen! I've been looking all over for you!" Allison exclaimed as the two women approached us. "And Desiree. I appreciate your coming." She bussed us both on the cheek.

"Allison tells me you're anxious to meet with me about Bobbie Jean," Robin said after the hellos.

"Yes, I am."

"Well, I'll be very happy to accommodate you."

"That's great. Suppose I drive out to Greenwich on Friday? Any time you say."

"Come at twelve thirty — for lunch."

"Have you seen Wes?" I overheard Allison put to Ellen now.

"He and Mike went to view the bod— To say good-bye to Bobbie Jean."

"Something I can't bring myself to do," Allison admitted sheepishly.

Tapping my niece on the arm, I shot her a "You see?" kind of look.

A few minutes later Robin was quizzing Ellen about her honeymoon plans, which, as of last week, had been narrowed down to eight locations — count 'em, *eight*. At about this same time, Allison apprised me that she'd already begun preparing a list of Bobbie Jean-haters who weren't at the shower on Sunday.

Yesterday's queasy feeling instantly resurfaced, but I hurriedly suppressed it. "Your other three friends — are they around somewhere?"

"No. Carla told me that in light of her negative feelings toward Bobbie Jean, she didn't think it would be appropriate for her to attend." Ahh. I'd been wondering if the viewing could be one of the "previous engagements" Carla had spoken of.

"Her mother doesn't appear to share that sentiment," I remarked.

Allison glanced affectionately at Robin. "She insisted on being here — for Wes and me, she said. As for Lorraine and Grace, they were planning to show up, mainly out of respect for Wes. But I convinced them he'd understand if they didn't." She waited a second or two before adding, "To be truthful, I was relieved by the decision."

Before I could ask why, Allison smiled mischievously. "I'd be absolutely mortified if Lorraine wound up dancing on the coffin."

Chapter 10

I was still brushing the sleep from my eyes when I walked into the Monte Carlo Coffee Shop at eight A.M. This Lorraine Corwin was a damned sadist, I groused to myself.

I spotted the lady in a booth toward the back — you'd have had to be blind to miss her. Even sitting down, she had the advantage height-wise over every other female in the place. And most of the men, too. She was wearing a very large, wide-brimmed hat — which I was beginning to think was a trademark of hers — this one in navy straw. And while I couldn't see all that much of her sleeveless navy dress, there was sufficient décolletage to cause a four-car pileup. As for this morning's jewelry, she had on six rings, three on each hand. Plus, I counted seven bracelets on her left forearm — one of them really chunky — and three on her right. It's a wonder the woman was able to raise her arms! She didn't neglect her neck, either. It was adorned with a gold, amethyst, and pearl chain and a turquoise pendant. Oh, and let's not forget the gold-and-pearl earrings, which came close to brushing her shoulders.

As soon as I was alongside the booth, Lorraine set down her lipstick-rimmed coffee cup and welcomed me with a smile. She looked wide-awake and disgustingly chipper. "I hope this isn't too early for you," she chirped, as I took a seat opposite her.

"Oh, no. Not at all." (I did mention before that I'm an accomplished liar, didn't I? — something that should be a requirement in my profession.)

"That's good." Another smile, and then she turned serious. "Allison tells me I owe you an apology, that I really dissed you at the shower. The only defense I can offer is that I wasn't myself. Bobbie Jean and I had quite a history — in case you haven't already gathered as much. And being in her company again — which I'd been able to avoid for many years until this past Sunday — was bad enough. But when she acted as though we were old *friends*, well, I went positively bonkers."

I opted to be generous. "I understand."

"Thanks, Dez. Okay if I call you Dez?"

"Please do."

"Listen, let's have ourselves something to eat, huh? My treat."

"Sounds like a good idea, but I'll be doing the treating. I was the one who asked for this get-together, remember?"

Lorraine opened her mouth, obviously to protest, then shut it again and shrugged. After which she signaled the waiter, a large, middle-aged man with a substantial stomach, a moon face, and about six strands of dyed black hair. He waddled over immediately. "How ya doin', Lorraine?" He permitted himself a quick glance down the front of her dress. "Youse two know what you're havin', or you wanna see a menu?"

"I think we'd better see a menu, Rocky."

"Sure thing." And with this he removed the two menus that had been tucked under his arm and handed one to each of us. "Be back witcha in a few minutes," he declared as he lumbered off.

"What'll it be, Dez?" Lorraine asked when I'd finished studying the breakfast specials.

"I'm going to have number four."

"Me, too." She glanced around for Rocky, who was hovering next to an empty table not more than five or six feet behind us. A crook of her finger brought him over faster than I'd have thought possible.

Lorraine gave him the order, and as soon as he left us she had a question, one I felt she could barely wait to put to me. "I figure that if you wanted this meeting, you must be fairly certain that someone other than the Almighty sped Bobbie Jean on her way. Am I right?"

"Let's just say I strongly suspect that to be true. Incidentally, on Sunday you said something about a rumor that Bobbie Jean had been poisoned. Who told you that?"

"Nobody, actually; I overheard two women talking. But no doubt they were merely speculating. Listen, those of us who really knew Bobbie Jean always figured that the chances of her dying in her sleep someday were pretty piss-poor."

"Would you mind telling me who the women were anyway?"

"Not at all — only I have no idea." My skepticism must have shown on my face. "Honestly," Lorraine maintained, "I'd never set eyes on either of them before."

"All right. Well, did you, by any chance, notice anything suspicious that afternoon?"

" 'Fraid not."

"Let me ask you this: Who among your friends and acquaintances had cause to want Bobbie Jean dead?"

"Enough of them, trust me."

"That would include Grace Banner and the Fremont ladies."

"That would include a lot of people," Lorraine responded evasively.

"Were any of the others at the shower?"

"Look, if you want me to supply you with names, forget it. All I'll say is that Bobbie Jean spread her special brand of sweetness around. And if there wasn't anyone besides me at that affair who'd have liked to see her laid out on a slab, I'd be very much surprised."

"You hated her a great deal, didn't you?"

"Like poison — if you'll pardon the expression. If I'd had this same opportunity thirty-three years ago, which is when she screwed me over, I can't swear I wouldn't have been responsible for her consuming something lethal. As it is, though, while I'm still angry as hell when I think about what she did to me, I just don't think about it that much anymore. And I can't remember the last time I shed any tears over it."

"I know this can't be pleasant for you, but I'd appreciate your filling me in on what happened between you and Bobbie Jean. All right?"

"That's the reason I'm here, isn't it?"

"I hope so," I responded with an insipid little chuckle.

"Okay. I should begin by telling you that Allison and I were roommates at college — until Allie dropped out of school because she was with child. Mike, as it turned out." Suddenly Lorraine's eyes opened wide. "Oh."

"Is anything wrong?"

"Maybe Allie would have preferred me to keep that to myself. It was ages ago, though. Besides, she and Wes were already gaga about each other by then, and they had every intention of getting married way before she became pregnant."

At this point our food arrived, courtesy of Rocky. We continued to talk about the dead woman while we ate, Lorraine having vetoed my suggestion to table any further discussion about Bobbie Jean until we finished breakfast. "I can't stay long," she'd apprised me. "Something came up after we spoke yesterday, and I have to be at work soon."

Well, this is the kind of thing I try to avoid. I'm referring to having murder-related conversations during a meal (even if, as in this instance, murder is only a strong — albeit a really strong — possibility). I mean, they certainly don't do much for a person's appetite. But what choice did I have?

"Allison and I have been the best of friends since our Radcliffe days," Lorraine was saying now. "So I got to know Bobbie Jean early on — in fact, while she was still a teenager. In the event you haven't been informed, she went to live with Allison and Wes when her father died, which was soon after they were married. At any rate, when I visited them, Bobbie Jean would frequently be there, too. And we became pretty close, Bobbie Jean and I. That's what makes me regard what she did as such a betrayal. I actually saw myself as a sort of big sister to the fucking little bitch." She interrupted her narrative to ask whether I was offended by her language.

To make her feel comfortable, I assured her that when the occasion warranted, I'd been known to use a few expletives that could induce a longshoreman to put his fingers in his ears.

Lorraine grinned. "Listen, I'm always interested in expanding my vocabulary, so maybe you could teach them to me sometime, okay? Unless, of course, they're already a part of my everyday speech — which is more than likely. But to go on . . .

"During my senior year in college, I fell completely, insanely, *stupidly* in love with a man named Kevin Moore, and within three months we were engaged. Then right after the engagement, Kevin's firm transferred him to San Francisco, and in June, with college over, I got a job out there to be with him. We intended to make it legal in the fall — until Bobbie Jean showed up."

"Just like that?"

"Oh, no, I invited her — her and a girlfriend of hers. Bobbie Jean had just graduated from high school, and she wrote to tell me that in August she and this Michelle would be coming to California for a month. For most of the vacation they'd be bunking with an aunt of Michelle's living in Oakland, which, as you're no doubt aware, is just outside Frisco. Anyhow, in her letter Bobbie Jean asked if it would be all right if she stopped by to say hello. And I — being totally non compos mentis — practically insisted the two of them spend a few days with Kevin and me. And that's all that goddamned nymph needed — a few days."

Pressing her lips together, Lorraine shook her head. Even after all these years, it appeared that she still hadn't forgiven herself for this unfortunate gesture of hospitality. "I suppose I have to take my share of the blame for what happened that summer. The truth is, I'd heard plenty of gossip about Bobbie Jean by then; I just hadn't wanted to believe it.

"But don't get me wrong. I'm not excusing Kevin for having his brains between his legs. Not for a minute. I'd bet my last dollar, though, that Bobbie Jean was the one to seduce *him,* something I base on her extensive history of similar situations.

"At any rate, to sum it all up, the engagement went *pfft.* Less than a week after the girls went back to stay with Michelle's aunt, I came in from work one evening to find Kevin — and all his stuff — gone. There was a note on the kitchen table informing me that it was over between us and that he'd gotten his own place. Down the line I discovered that Bobbie Jean had moved in with him the day he left me."

"Were they together long — Kevin and Bobbie Jean?"

"Don't be silly. She dumped him three weeks later and went home to Allison and her brother, Wes, both of whom had been under the impression she and Michelle were on an extended visit with Michelle's aunt all that time she'd been playing house with Kevin."

"When did they learn the truth?"

"When I did. A mutual acquaintance of Kevin's and mine laid the whole thing on me when I ran into her at the beginning of September. Until then I hadn't a clue that while that little nymph was *my guest,* she'd been out to hook the man I was planning to marry."

"And you let Allison know about this?"

"You betcha."

"I imagine she must have been terribly disturbed by what Bobbie Jean did to you."

"She was. From what Allie said, even Wes — who's always been so damn protective of Sister Dearest — reamed her out pretty good. And she acted *terribly* remorseful — although the way she told it, *she'd* been a victim herself, Kevin being so much older and more sophisticated than she was. How's that for chutzpah? I ask you. At any rate, she claimed — tearfully, of course — that he'd refused to leave her alone, phoning her day and night when she returned to Oakland. According to Bobbie Jean, that awful man had been so persistent that for a while he'd had her convinced that this was true love. She came up with another doozie, too. Supposedly Kevin confided to her that he and I had been having problems well before she entered the picture and that he'd been trying to work up to calling it quits with me anyhow."

"*Had* you been having problems?"

"That was plain bullshit," Lorraine said heatedly. "Either Kevin lied to Bobbie Jean about us or — and this is far more probable

— Bobbie Jean lied to Allison and Wes. It really didn't matter to me what the truth was, though. The only thing that mattered was that my fiancé had suddenly become my *ex*-fiancé."

"Uh, did you ever see or hear from him again?"

"I got a brief letter from him sometime in October saying that he was sorry — *sorry!* — and that his lawyer would be contacting me about his financial obligations — you know, with regard to the apartment lease, things like that."

"You never considered calling *him?*"

"In the first place, I didn't have any idea how to reach him. Not initially. But more than that, I was too anguished, too *raw* to even think about picking up a phone — especially once I got wind of the Bobbie Jean connection. The only way I could deal with the situation was to convince myself that I was better off without the louse — which was undoubtedly true. A couple of years later, though, I went to a concert with a girlfriend. I spied Kevin in the lobby at intermission, and I'm sure he spotted me, too. He was with another man, and I debated with myself about going over to him. But while I was still trying to make up my mind, he turned his head, whispered something to his buddy, and they both walked away."

"You're positive he saw you?"

"*Absolutely* positive." Lorraine had a bite of toast and washed it down with a sip of coffee before concluding with a lopsided smile, "So that was the end of that." And picking up a piece of bacon with her fingers, she nibbled on it slowly.

I didn't know what to say. I could have cried for the woman. I was searching my sluggish brain for another topic when she took me off the hook. "You want to hear what finally got me past the Kevin/Bobbie Jean thing, Dez? My job."

"What is it you do?"

"I'm a talent agent. I changed careers and went into the biz eighteen years ago, getting my feet wet with a small outfit in San Francisco. My work gives me a *tremendous* amount of satisfaction. And I'm good at it, too — I opened my own office a year ago, six months after moving back to New York."

"Who do you represent? Anyone I'd know?"

"I would hope so. My clients include the cream of today's rock artists. People like the Spastics, Irish Rachel Bernstein, and the Head Cases," Lorraine announced proudly.

I tried to sound impressed. "No kidding."

"I assume you've heard of them, then."

"Uh, hasn't everybody?" I equivocated.

"Listen, I'd better shake my keister and get on over to the office." And before I could stop her, she grabbed the check that Rocky had deposited on the table moments earlier (at the same time — as long as he was in the neighborhood — taking another peek down her dress). Seconds later Lorraine lowered her voice to the point where I had trouble making out the words. "I'm expecting a call this morning from the manager of a big-name group — and I'm talking *really* big. They're thinking about switching agents, and it looks as if I'm in the running. I'll tell you who they are, but this is top secret, understand?"

"Of course."

She leaned so far across the table our noses practically touched. "Three Hams on a Roll."

Three Hams on a Roll?

Christ! Whatever happened to Donnie and Marie?

Chapter 11

"For this Saturday night? Oh, that's terrific." Then, with a trace of suspicion: "Where are the seats?"

I had just arrived at work after my meeting with Lorraine Corwin. And overhearing that short snatch of dialogue when I walked in, I figured it likely that the person Jackie was talking to on the phone was Derwin. Derwin being her on-again off-again guy for a number of years now.

"*Where?*" she shrieked into the receiver. "Listen, Mr. Sport, if you think I'm going to sit in the next-to-the-last-row balcony one more time and try to *imagine* what's happening on that stage . . ."

She was talking to Derwin, all right.

"Don't give me that. A couple of months ago you fed me the same baloney about those being the only two seats available, and the theater was half empty when we got there. You must—" She broke off. "Wait, Dez!" she called after me as I headed for my cubbyhole.

"Hold it, Derwin," she instructed, putting her hand over the mouthpiece while I back-tracked. She waved a pink message slip in my direction and, as she so frequently does, spared me the bother of reading it.

"Ellen just called. She wants you to get in touch with her at work."

"Thanks," I mouthed, as she went back to hanging Derwin out to dry.

"Do you *really* want me to tell you what to do with those tickets?" she put to him just before I was out of earshot.

Ellen's voice crackled with excitement. "They came last night!"

"What did?"

"My shower gifts," she responded, not quite able to conceal her impatience. From her tone, she might just as well have added, "Dummy."

"But you were at the funeral home last night."

"I gave the keys to Ginger."

I couldn't resist. " '. . . who lives in my building,' " I finished for her.

"Huh?" She obviously didn't get it.

"Never mind." But I could feel the grin spreading over my face.

"Anyway, I spoke to this woman from Silver Oaks yesterday, and she asked if it would be okay if somebody dropped off the packages that evening. It was really nice that they were willing to do a thing like that, and I didn't want to make things difficult for whoever was doing the delivering. Also, I could hardly wait to see the gifts. So I said for the man to ring Ginger's bell, and then she let him into my apartment.

"Listen, Aunt Dez, I am *thrilled* with the china. But you've gotta be crazy, springing for anything that expensive with all you must have spent on the shower. My God! That was present enough."

"Yes, especially since it was such a pleasurable experience," I said dryly.

"But that wasn't your fault."

"At any rate, Allison and I — your mother, too," I included with a grimace, "decided it would be nice to start you off with a few place settings."

Now, Ellen had really startled everybody when she selected a dinnerware pattern. I mean, while she's been known to whip up a very decent breakfast, after twelve noon her culinary talents come to a screeching halt. (Don't ask me to explain it, either.) Ellen's idea of preparing dinner is to reheat the Chinese takeout. Well, I suppose even moo goo gai pan seems a little more gourmetish on Limoges.

"What were some of your other presents?" I was foolish enough to inquire.

I expected to hear about the half dozen or so items she was most enthusiastic about. Instead, my niece proceeded to enumerate around fifty, describing some of them in great detail. I probably should have been thankful that a number of the gifts were from more than one guest.

"Barbara and Harriet from your building? They gave us a beautiful crystal vase," she began. "And we got the most *gorgeous* silver tray from my friends at work. It came from Tiffany's," she added, sounding suitably impressed. "Somebody else — I forget who — gave us . . ." And she went on. And on. And on.

". . . Plus, we got three toaster ovens," she finally concluded. But not before relating the specific features of each.

The conversation ended with Ellen's extracting my promise to stop by for a look at her bounty as soon as I had a chance.

Something I was eager to do anyway.

The phone rang as I was reaching to turn on my Mac.

"It's Allison, Desiree. Chief Porchow just telephoned. The autopsy report has come in." Every muscle in my body tensed.

"He'll be over at four to talk to us."

"He didn't give you any idea of the results?"

"None. But I'm feeling very uneasy about this. After all, if Bobbie Jean died of natural causes, why wouldn't he just say that then and there? Why would he want to see us?"

"I'm afraid you're right. You'll let me know as soon as he leaves, won't you." I didn't put it as a question.

Forcing Allison's news from my mind, I spent the next few hours transcribing my notes on this morning's interrogation of Lorraine Corwin. I didn't even break to go out to lunch. This, however, is not to imply that I skipped a meal — which is practically against my religion. In between the struggle to decipher my handwriting and the determination to type at a speed that would not cause your average snail any embarrassment, I managed to consume a BLT (minus the L) and a Coke at my desk.

In spite of my diligence, though, I still wasn't able to finish the job. Because before you could say, "Grace Banner," three thirty had sneaked up on me.

And minutes later the second of my suspects arrived.

Chapter 12

Grace Banner collapsed in the chair.

If anything, she looked even more waiflike than she had on Sunday. Her lightweight cotton dress was suffering the effects of some determined store-to-store shopping, coupled with a temperature that when I last heard — and this was hours ago — was eighty-nine degrees and climbing. The wilted blue-and-yellow print garment clung stubbornly to her thin, boyish frame, broadcasting the absence of even the most minuscule swelling in the chest area. The woman's plain brown hair was in an equally sad state, plastered against her head and hanging in moist clumps to the middle of her neck.

Seated alongside my desk in the only visitor's chair my cigar-box-of-an-office can accommodate, she was soon busily engaged in searching through her purse. She finally pulled out a tissue and hastily wiped her damp forehead. Then she eked out a half-hearted smile. "I'm exhausted. Shopping isn't easy."

"Well, at least you accomplished something." There were three bags at her feet — from Lord & Taylor, Bloomingdale's, and Saks Fifth Avenue.

"I hope so. But once I get home, my family — which includes two very finicky daughters — could decide that they hate everything I've bought, and I'll have to come back and return all of this." Biting her lip, she gestured toward her purchases. "To tell you the truth, I'm already having second thoughts about the cashmere sweater I picked out for Karl — that's my husband. It's apricot, and I'm not sure how he'll feel about apricot." And now, wincing, she inquired shyly, "I hate to ask, but would you mind very much if I slipped off my shoes? I'm . . . well, I'm in agony."

"Please. Be my guest. I've been there myself." (I almost said — unintentionally, I swear — "I've been in your shoes myself." But I bit back the unforgivable pun just in time.)

Grace removed her sensible bone-colored oxfords (which evidently weren't sensible enough) and, bending down, placed them neatly under the chair. She sighed with relief, then fixed me with forthright brown eyes. "You wanted to talk to me about Bobbie Jean."

"I did — that is, I do. But first, would you like me to order up a soda for you? Or how about an iced tea?"

"Nothing, thank you. I had a cold drink a few minutes ago, right before I came up here."

"Well, suppose we get started then. I'd like you to tell me what occurred between you and Bobbie Jean."

"All right." And leaning back in her seat now, Grace cleared her throat. After which she began to lay out the details of her feud with the victim, her voice low and even.

"Karl and I became partners in a restaurant with her."

"When was this?" I asked before she could go on.

"Close to ten years ago. Back then it seemed as if it could turn out to be a lucrative undertaking for all three of us. Bobbie Jean had more money than she knew what to do with, and she was looking to invest in a promising business. And Karl had had a great deal of restaurant experience — he'd managed a number of extremely successful establishments. Also, we were able to find decent space in a good location at a very fair price. And —"

"Had you previously worked in that field, too?"

"No, but I was more than willing to do whatever had to be done to help make a go of the place. And if I have any talent whatsoever, Desiree, it's for following instructions. In other words, I was the ideal fill-in. One day I would act as hostess. The next I might be chopping vegetables or waiting on tables. I even went to bartender school for a few weeks — just in case. You haven't lived until you've tasted one of my piña coladas," she bragged with a little laugh.

"And what was Bobbie Jean's contribution, other than monetary?"

"None. It had been agreed that her participation would be limited to the financing, while Karl and I, who were investing much less, would be responsible for the actual operation of BanJean's — that was the name of the restaurant. It's a combination of Banner and Bobbie Jean. We —"

I jumped in again. "BanJean's was located in Connecticut?"

"Yes, in Greenwich. Just seven blocks from our house." And here Grace paused, apparently anticipating another interruption. But a few seconds of silence convinced her that it was safe to continue. "BanJean's really wasn't doing at all badly. Not when you consider that it had been in existence less than a year. But Bobbie Jean had expected that it would be like an instant magnet for everyone in the area with an American Express card. And when that didn't happen, she took Karl and me to court, claiming that we'd been defrauding her. Or anyway, that was one reason for the law suit."

"What do you mean '*one* reason'?"

Grace flushed. "I should tell you that Bobbie Jean wasn't a very moral person. In fact, she was almost notorious for her, um, sexual doings. And she developed this . . . these *feelings* for Karl." The flush deepened. "I'm not sure exactly when she decided that she had to have him — you know what I mean — but six or seven months after BanJean's opened, she suddenly began stopping in for lunch several days a week. And by herself, too."

"She hadn't done that before?"

"No. She lived on Long Island, and while the restaurant wasn't terribly far from her home, it wasn't right around the corner, either. So previously she would just come in sporadically, mostly for dinner. And always with some gentleman friend."

"What makes you think your husband was the reason for this change in pattern?"

"Because she propositioned him one afternoon when I was out with the flu," Grace said matter-of-factly.

"He told you about this?"

"Oh, not right away. And only under pressure. I noticed that Karl had suddenly begun acting very cool toward Bobbie Jean, even attempting to avoid her. And for her part, after increasing her visits to the restaurant like that, all of a sudden she cut way back on them. Also, she practically ignored Karl when she did show up. I questioned him about it, but he insisted I was imagining things. Eventually, though, I became positive that my imagination had nothing to do with it, and I confronted him. Karl did a lot of hemming and hawing, but like any good wife" — a small smile here — "I nagged the life out of him. And he finally came clean."

Well, I wasn't too surprised to learn that Bobbie Jean's sexual aggressiveness had entered into her falling-out with Grace. The fact is, when Allison had omitted this element from her abbreviated version of the hostilities between the two women, it had crossed my mind that at least this was one feud the deceased had been involved in where she'd kept her panties on. Evidently, however, that had not been from choice.

"Did you ever confront Bobbie Jean about this?"

"Not until she slapped us with that law suit — which was soon afterward. Before then, I was too concerned about what it could do to BanJean's if I brought things out in the open. Anyway, Bobbie Jean denied everything."

"And you think she filed that suit because she was a woman scorned?"

"I certainly think that entered into it," Grace declared. "And I would guess that what she found particularly disturbing about her failure to seduce Karl was that he was *my* husband. Let's face it, I'm no Pamela Anderson.

"Incidentally, Desiree, I happen to be married to a very handsome fellow. Wait." And unclasping the purse in her lap, she extracted a bulky brown wallet and flipped it open to a photograph. Then leaning across the desk, she handed me the wallet. "And by the way, he's a terrific person, as well," she informed me.

The headshot was of a fair-haired man with a dazzling smile and dark, piercing eyes above thick, dark eyebrows. "He *is* good-looking," I agreed, returning the wallet. But the skeptical part of my brain alerted me to the possibility that the photo could be twenty years old or more.

Obviously the possessor of psychic powers,

Grace said, "That was taken last year.

"I recall the first time Karl asked me out," she mused. "I was almost convinced that I'd misunderstood him. But I hadn't. I was the one he wanted when we were in our twenties. And fortunately, I'm still the one he wants. I'm sure a great many people don't understand it, and I don't blame them. Heck, even I don't understand it." At that moment she grinned, a sweet, shy kind of grin. And all at once *I* could understand it. I mean, there was something very vulnerable, very endearing about that expression — and something very appealing about this woman.

Don't go overboard! I quickly cautioned myself. Which was definitely sound advice. After all, there was a one in four chance (or so I persisted in regarding it) that this timid, self-deprecating little lady here had just treated her former partner to a lethal dose of poison.

Grace was now sitting there stock-still, with a faraway look in her eyes, so I prompted, "You were telling me what motivated Bobbie Jean's lawsuit."

"Yes. As I see it, she had been completely traumatized by Karl's rejection. I realize I'm not a psychiatrist, Desiree. I did get to know her fairly well, though, and it's my opinion that Bobbie Jean measured her worth as a human being by her success with men. But anyhow, that suit gave her the opportunity to humiliate my husband — *and* me, for that matter — as she felt she'd been humiliated.

"While it's true that she did have very unrealistic expectations for the restaurant," Grace added, "I don't think she ever believed deep-down that we'd been defrauding her. She *let* herself believe it because she wanted to."

"Precisely what is it you and your husband were supposed to have done?"

"She accused us of falsifying the purchase receipts, which she based on the word of an ex-employee — Ty Gregory — who had a grievance against us. Ty had been a waiter at BanJean's since we opened. He was quite attractive, and for a while there was some talk at the restaurant about him and Bobbie Jean being lovers. From what I gathered, the affair was over before she made that play for Karl, but it's very possible it resumed after Ty was let go — or maybe even before that."

"Why did you get rid of Ty?"

"Karl and I didn't want to, honestly. But we had no choice. From the beginning there were complaints from our customers about his attitude, and we kept warning him that he'd have to be more pleasant to people. But it didn't do the least bit of good. And so about nine months after he started with us, we had to terminate him.

"Well, it wasn't too much later that Ty told Bobbie Jean we were in cahoots with some of our suppliers to deny her her fair share of the profits. The story he gave her was that we purchased inferior meats and produce for the restaurant but that these suppliers were providing us with bills indicating we paid top dollar and bought only the best. Naturally, Ty was also claiming he was fired because we were afraid that he suspected the truth.

"Anyway, the upshot was that Bobbie Jean sued us for fraud. And word of the action got around. Not only did it make the newspapers — which was bad enough — but, in addition to *that,* Bobbie Jean wasn't hesitant about attacking us to anyone who was willing to listen."

And now Grace, looking like she was about to burst into tears, grabbed up a handful of dress fabric and began to twist it. "She eventually lost the suit — luckily, Ty made a terrible witness — but Karl and I lost even more. Our reputations were seriously damaged by Bobbie Jean's taking us to court like that. After BanJean's went under, it was more than a year before my husband could find another position. Even today he's not managing the same class of restaurant or making the same kind of money he once did.

"At any rate, Karl and I made the decision to turn around and sue Bobbie Jean for slander. In hindsight, we both recognize that it was a pretty stupid move on our part. And this would have held true even if we'd won the case — which we didn't. You know, Desiree, I'm amazed at how many people have that 'where there's smoke there's fire' mentality. That suit of ours only served to remind everyone of Bobbie Jean's actions against *us* two years earlier — and raise the old suspicions all over again."

"You seem convinced it was this Ty who manufactured the lie about the suppliers — and not the other way around," I put to Grace. "I mean, isn't it just as likely that it originated with Bobbie Jean and that she induced him — maybe bribed him — to back her up?"

"Well, I can't be a hundred percent certain, of course. But I have to figure it was Ty who dreamed up that little fairy tale. Bobbie Jean had always held creative positions; she knew nothing about the business end of things — particularly when it came to the restaurant industry. It's hard for me to conceive that the idea of suppliers' phonying up receipts would even occur to her. Ty, on the other hand, had to be aware of the existence of practices like that."

I agreed that this made sense. Following which I asked Grace how she and Karl had ever hooked up with Bobbie Jean in the first place.

"Allison and I grew up together. Since grammar school we've been *like that.*" She crossed her middle and index fingers. "And about a dozen years ago we formed a bridge club with some other women. We met once a month on a Saturday afternoon. This was while Bobbie Jean was working for some high-toned fashion magazine in Paris. But soon after the club's inception, she came back home. And, as it happened, one of our members suddenly chose to abandon bridge for golf at that time. So Bobbie Jean — who was an excellent bridge player — asked if she could take Fiona's place. Of course, we were all familiar with her terrible reputation — she'd achieved almost legendary status by that point. But everyone agreed to let her join anyway, primarily because of Allison. Besides, the way we looked at it, we'd just be spending a few hours with her every four weeks over a card table.

"Well, Bobbie Jean and I had only been

casual acquaintances before that — she spent almost half of her adult life living abroad, you know. But as a result of the bridge games we grew pretty chummy. She could be very pleasant, very warm, and nobody else has ever been able to make me laugh the way Bobbie Jean could."

"But didn't the things you'd heard about her give you pause about becoming buddy-buddy with the woman?"

"Initially I kept my distance. But I couldn't help it; eventually I came to really like her. So I chose to think that the stories about her behavior could have been exaggerated or that there might have been extenuating circumstances." Grace smiled ruefully. "You might say I was in denial."

"What she'd done to Lorraine didn't have any effect on you?"

"I knew very little about it. Actually, I hardly knew Lorraine. It wasn't until she'd moved back East and found out that I'd been one of Bobbie Jean's casualties, too, that Lorraine and I became close."

"And how did you feel about Bobbie Jean's having run off with Carla's husband?"

"That didn't even happen until a few years later. I *was* aware that there had been some sort of hostility between Robin —

Carla's mother — and Bobbie Jean. But while Robin seems like a very nice person, it isn't as if we ever palled around together, so I never learned any of the details."

"Nevertheless, in view of everything you'd heard about the dead woman, I'm surprised that you didn't have any qualms about entering into a partnership with her."

"Don't forget," Grace retorted, her tone slightly defensive, "I was determined to close my mind to those stories about her. Besides, Bobbie Jean's sexual escapades were one thing. But, to my knowledge, nobody's ever condemned her business ethics."

"Let me ask you this," I brought up then. "Is there anyone else you're aware of who may have had . . . uh . . . issues with Bobbie Jean?"

Tilting her head back and lifting her eyes, Grace pondered the question for a few seconds before responding. "I'm not really tuned in to the local gossip, but not too long ago there was a rumor making the rounds about this woman's catching her husband and Bobbie Jean in a . . . in a compromising situation — and in the woman's own bed, too. But this person wasn't at Ellen's shower."

I jotted down the name anyway. Just in

case the results of the toxicology report — which Chief Porchow could be revealing to the Lyntons at that very moment — indicated a slow-acting poison, God forbid.

"Did you happen to notice if anything of a suspicious nature occurred on Sunday? And I mean anything at all."

"No, I didn't," Grace answered, appearing genuinely apologetic.

"I think that about covers everything," I said now. "But satisfy my curiosity before you go, okay? With all the animosity you felt toward Bobbie Jean, how could you even consider being around her again?"

"I wanted to find out if the food at Silver Oaks was as sensational as Lorraine claimed it was." And then Grace grinned impishly. "No, seriously, I love Allison and Wes, and I adore Mike, too. *Not* going was never an option."

"Am I correct in assuming that this was the first time you'd been in Bobbie Jean's company since you and Karl sued her?"

"Yes. I'd always avoided her like a case of the measles."

"Well, I give you credit for having the stomach to so much as look at her again."

Another playful grin. "The credit belongs entirely to Xanax. All 0.5 soothing little milligrams of it."

Chapter 13

Just minutes after Grace Banner had squeezed her feet back into the offending oxfords and limped out of my office, I heard from Allison.

"Bobbie Jean was murdered," she informed me in a strained voice. "The poison was in her salad."

So the killer was somebody who was at Silver Oaks that day after all! I said a silent, "Thank you, God," before asking, "Did Chief Porchow give you the name of what was used?"

"It was something called monkshood. Are you familiar with it?"

"No, I'm not."

"I understand from the chief that it's a plant of some kind and that it grows pretty much all over the country, throughout the Northern Temperate Zone, in fact. At any rate, it works very rapidly. It's also extremely lethal — it can even be absorbed by the skin. Although, as I said, in this instance the monkshood went into the salad. Whoever did this awful thing shredded the leaves and then mixed them in with the rest of the greens."

"Porchow bagged Bobbie Jean's salad, I assume."

"On Sunday he collected what remained of it. He told us that initially he wasn't certain that Bobbie Jean had been a crime victim, but he wasn't convinced that she hadn't been, either. And he believes in playing it safe, he said. At any rate, once it was established that she'd been murdered, the contents of the salad were analyzed, and it was found to be the vehicle for the poison."

Now, there are hundreds of toxic substances out there — maybe thousands, for all I know. So it frequently takes weeks, even months, to identify what did the job in any particular instance. That is, if it's ever identified at all. Plus, regardless of its availability, monkshood isn't your everyday poison of choice — not like arsenic, say, or cyanide. "I'm surprised they were able to arrive at this monkshood so quickly," I commented.

"Evidently it was Bobbie Jean herself who steered the toxicologists in the right direction. On the way to the hospital she was trying very hard to communicate with the paramedics, so they removed her oxygen mask for a moment. She brought her finger up to her ear and mumbled what sounded to one of the men like 'ringing,' but he couldn't be positive of this because her speech was so slurred. And then she put her finger just under her eye, and that time she said fairly clearly, 'Green.' The fellow thought she might be hallucinating, however, because Bobbie Jean's eyes were brown. Nevertheless, he spoke to Porchow about what he'd heard, and the chief passed the information on to the medical examiner. Well, it appears that both tinnitus and yellow-green vision can occur with this particular poison."

"So now we know what killed Bobbie Jean."

I had no idea that I'd said this aloud until Allison repeated softly, "Yes, now we know. Incidentally," she went on, "Wes and I weren't sure you'd want us to say anything to the police about our enlisting your help on this, so we kept quiet about it. In order to provide you with as many facts as possible, though, I kept requesting that Chief Porchow elaborate on everything — which, plainly, he did not appreciate — and then I managed to jot down a decent portion of his explanations. I claimed I was taking notes because I'd promised to fill in my son, who couldn't be here today and who had been very close to his aunt."

"Good thinking," I remarked admiringly.

"It wasn't actually a lie, either. I *did* promise Mike I'd call and tell him what the police had learned."

"What else did the chief have to say?"

"He had me go over the list of shower guests, quizzing me on whether there might have been some sort of unpleasantness between Bobbie Jean and any of the women."

"And your response was . . . ?"

"That I wasn't aware of anything like that." Before I could comment, Allison continued in a rush. "I just couldn't bring myself to incriminate my friends, Desiree. Especially since in all likelihood there were others at the affair with a grievance against Bobbie Jean. As I've told you before, my sister-in-law only talked to me about that sort of thing on a 'need to know' basis." Allison paused here (most likely for breath) before adding, "Besides, there's something else to consider."

"What's that?"

"The Silver Oaks staff. I mentioned to you on Tuesday that Bobbie Jean could be very imperious when the mood struck her and that this might have so enraged one of the club's employees that he or she killed her."

While I figured that Allison was grasping at straws here, I didn't feel that anything would be gained by forcing her to face reality. Not yet, anyhow. So I very thoughtfully refrained from pointing out that murder was a pretty extreme response to somebody's demanding that her steak be more well done. But evidently, on reflection, Allison had reached this same conclusion.

"I have since come to recognize what a far-fetched theory that is," she admitted. "But there's another possibility pertaining to Silver Oaks that does make sense. Suppose Bobbie Jean had been having an affair with someone who worked there — something that would hardly be a shock to anyone who knew her. Well, under certain circumstances, this lover might have felt compelled to rid himself of her. For instance, Bobbie Jean could have been threatening to tattle to the man's wife about their liaisons. Of course, that's only one example."

Now, it had been my intention all along to question everyone on the Silver Oaks staff, particularly those who were working at the place on Sunday. But it seemed to me that the management there would be more cooperative if I held off until the official word came down that Bobbie Jean had been murdered.

I'd been hoping to learn two things from a visit to the country club. One was whether anyone had witnessed something untoward that day. The second was whether Bobbie Jean had been engaging in a bit of hanky-panky with any of the Silver Oaks employees.

At that moment, though, it popped into this pea brain of mine that it would also be advisable to question the staff about the victim's relationships with her fellow club members. Listen, who's to say one of them didn't sneak into the dining room that afternoon to put some extra zing in Bobbie Jean's salad?

Still, my primary suspects remained Allison's buddies — at least for the present. I mean, Bobbie Jean had given them such dandy little motives for wanting her dead.

I decided to keep these things to myself, however. "You have a point there," I told Allison. "And I'll be driving out to Silver Oaks as soon as I can set up an appointment."

"I'm glad to hear that." There was relief in her voice.

"But look, Allison," I warned, "from what I've gathered, it's no deep, dark secret that

Bobbie Jean caused those four friends of yours a lot of grief. So I'd be really surprised if sooner or later — and most likely sooner — Chief Porchow didn't find out how much they despised her."

"I was just about to tell you — he's already been apprised of that. When I pleaded ignorance, Wes stepped in and named names, briefly outlining why each of them had such antipathy toward Bobbie Jean. Don't think he was comfortable talking about that, either. But he's absolutely determined that Bobbie Jean's killer be brought to justice." And now Allison tagged on dryly, "Naturally, Wes soft-pedaled her abominable behavior to the extent that this was possible."

"How is he taking the news that she was murdered?"

"He's terribly shaken that somebody hated his little sister enough to poison her. But I've been saying a prayer that once the guilty person is apprehended, it will be easier for Wes to come to terms with what happened."

"Let's hope so," I murmured.

"Chief Porchow also asked if we had any idea who profits from Bobbie Jean's death. Wes told the chief he was familiar with his sister's will and that our son is slated to inherit a fairly substantial sum of money. Aside from that, Bobbie Jean specified a significant portion of her assets to be divided among her three favorite charities. And the balance, which is the bulk of the estate, she bequeathed to Wes."

I was thinking that this gave Allison herself a reason for wanting Bobbie Jean to go bye-bye — apart from having to tolerate the woman all these years, I mean. But while I hadn't examined the Lyntons' bank statements, I didn't imagine that even without that windfall from the deceased they'd be standing on line at a soup kitchen anytime soon.

Right after this it dawned on me that Allison wasn't the only one at that shower who would be benefiting financially from Bobbie Jean's demise. That is, once the "I-do's" had been taken care of. Of course, it was extremely unlikely that Ellen was aware at the time that Bobbie Jean had been so generous with Mike. Besides, the very notion of my nervous Nellie of a niece poisoning anybody was so ludicrous that an abbreviated laugh escaped before I could squelch it.

Allison sounded perplexed. "Has something funny occurred to you?"

"Oh, no. I wasn't laughing. I was . . . umm, trying to clear this frog in my throat."

And to prove it, I treated her to a couple of insincere little coughs.

The conversation ended moments later — but not before Allison brought up the country club again.

"I realize you believe that one of my friends was responsible for Bobbie Jean's death. But you *will* investigate the people at Silver Oaks with an open mind, won't you?"

"Naturally I will."

"After all," she asserted, "you never know."

A statement that, in a way, proved prophetic.

Chapter 14

Practically everything in my refrigerator had gone bad at once: The milk had turned sour. The bread was stale. The peaches were rotten. The onions were squishy. And there were ugly green molds floating around in the applesauce. That wasn't the worst of it, though. My quart of Häagen-Dazs macadamia brittle was now dangerously close to empty. So after slaving over the computer for a good six hours on Friday — and still not managing to transcribe all of my notes — on the way home from work I had to stop in at my neighborhood D'Agostino's to do some replenishing.

I'd just closed the door to the freezer, after uncovering the one remaining container of macadamia brittle in the supermarket, when I turned around to find guess-who standing right behind me. "Hi, Desiree," said Nick Grainger. "I see we have the same taste in flavors." He gave me a buck-toothed (but very attractively so) grin, and as is usual in his presence, my knees became totally untrustworthy.

Why, oh why, hadn't I applied fresh lipstick before leaving the office? "I'm afraid this is the last of the macadamia brittle," I informed him, while simultaneously wishing I could kick myself all the way to the Bronx.

Nick made a face. After which he demanded in mock — or maybe not so mock — despair, "Please say you're joking."

"I wish I were," I responded as I tossed the ice cream into my shopping cart. "Well, I'd better be going. It was nice —"

I was interrupted by my extremely irritated inner voice. *You idiot, you! When opportunity knocks, you suddenly go deaf.*

It — my inner voice — had a point there.

"Look," I told Nick, "I'm willing to share. Why don't you stop down for dessert later?"

Nick's face went crimson. "I have these . . . uh . . . these plans for tonight. But thanks for the invitation. And . . . er, have a good evening." Then he promptly, well, *fled* would be the most accurate description of his leave-taking.

At that moment I came dangerously close to bawling — and in the middle of D'Agostino's, too. The man I'd been having all these stupid daydreams about had just reacted like I was an infectious disease. And I really don't take rejection very well. But then, show me somebody who does, and I'll show you a great big liar.

The telephone was ringing when I walked into the apartment. I quickly snatched up the receiver. Fortunately I was in time to prevent the answering machine from kicking in, something that always makes me crazy. I mean, whenever I hear that recorded voice of mine, I'm in trauma. Listen, you would be, too, if you sounded like Minnie Mouse. (I keep telling myself that some glitch in the equipment is warping the sound. But I suppose it's possible that I'm rationalizing.)

Anyhow, after the usual amenities, my friend the former Pat Martucci, now Mrs. Burton Wizniak, got to the reason for her call. "Have they found out yet what that woman — Bobbie Jean — died of?"

"Monkshood," I told her.

"Monks *what?*"

"Monkshood," I repeated. "It's some sort of poisonous plant. The murderer put the leaves in Bobbie Jean's salad."

"Then she was *poisoned?*"

"That's right."

"Are there any suspects?"

"There are four that I'm concentrating on at present."

"*You're* concentrating on? Don't tell me you're investigating this." And then, not waiting for an answer: "I hope you're at least getting paid for your efforts. *Are* you?" Pat demanded.

I danced around the question. "Why would I work for nothing?"

"Yeah, just as I thought. You're a real sucker, Desiree Shapiro. Do you know that?" I didn't consider this worthy of a response. "And what happens when you can't afford to pay your rent?"

"I'll move in with you and Burton, of course."

"Smart ass," Pat grumbled. "Well, take care of yourself, okay? Just don't pull any heroics."

Which was pretty funny, because I don't *do* heroics.

I was putting away the groceries when I heard from Ellen. "M-Mike just told me. About the monkshood, I m-m-mean. Who do you think could have done a thing like that? Do you think it was one of the ladies who sounded off about her on Sunday?"

"So far they're at the top of my list."

"That p-poor woman," Ellen murmured, starting to choke up.

"Listen, Ellen, I don't approve of murder — you know that. But 'poor woman' hardly describes Bobbie Jean Morton. Your almost-future-aunt was a sexual predator who didn't mind messing up somebody's life in order to get what — or I should say *who* — she wanted."

"I'm aware of that. Still, I kind of liked her those two times I met her. And Mike really cared for her. Maybe she just couldn't help herself." Before I could argue this point, Ellen added, "Anyway, I know you'll be investigating her death, so please promise me you'll be careful. *Very* careful."

"I promise."

And now she shifted gears. "I haven't had any dinner yet, Aunt Dez. Have you?"

Well, I'd been trying to make up my mind between an omelette, a ham-and-Swiss-cheese sandwich, and that onion tart I'd returned to the freezer after Allison's visit. None of which I was especially excited about. And besides, if I stayed home I'd spend my time alternating between cursing Nick Grainger and licking my wounds. And those were a couple of other things that didn't appeal to me much. So I told Ellen that, no, I hadn't eaten yet, either.

"Good. You'll have something here. Mike's at the hospital, and I could use the company. Besides, I'm dying for you to see my gifts."

"Oh, then you're home. I thought you were calling from Macy's."

"I left work early — an upset stomach."

Since dinner at Ellen's invariably means Chinese food, I was taken aback. "You just told me you have an upset stomach."

"*Had.* I'm fine now."

"Still, I think it would be better if you limited yourself to tea and toast tonight. And maybe some Campbell's chicken noodle soup."

"Believe me, Aunt Dez, I'm feeling much, much better. And whether you join me or not, I'm going to be ordering from Mandarin Joy." Mandarin Joy being Ellen's local Chinese restaurant, which would very likely be facing bankruptcy if she ever moved out of the neighborhood.

I allowed myself to be convinced. "Okay," I said, "if you're certain you're up to it."

We settled on the menu over the phone. And after that I hurriedly put on some lipstick — which wound up so far outside my natural lip line that it looked as if I'd gone to the Lorraine Corwin school of mouth extension. Then I practically had a fight to the death with my hair, and as it unfailingly does on humid days, my hair won. Luckily I had a fallback position: a wig that looks exactly like my own glorious hennaed tresses but is far better behaved.

Twenty minutes later I was on my way out the door.

Then I remembered.

I all but ran back to the kitchen and grabbed the macadamia brittle from the freezer. I was going to be sharing it tonight after all.

Eat your heart out, Nick Grainger.

At some point during the thirty-five-minute cab ride from East Eighty-second Street to Ellen's place on West Nineteenth, I thought about the fact that Mike would soon be coming into what his mother had referred to as "a fairly substantial sum of money." And I wondered if I should tell Ellen what I'd learned. I immediately decided against it. It was up to Mike to inform his future bride about a thing like that. Maybe he already had, for all I knew — although this I seriously doubted. I mean, my niece does a lot of things very well. But keeping secrets from her dear old Aunt Dez is not one of them.

Anyway, we had a delicious — and huge

— dinner: dim sum, Chung King spare ribs, shrimp with garlic sauce, and lemon chicken. And if Ellen had even the remnants of an upset stomach, she hid it admirably.

Oncc wc'd cleared away the dishes, we settled down with our ice cream and coffee. (There's no law that says you have to have tea with Chinese food, you know.) Now, I'd intended to stop off for Häagen Dazs Belgian chocolate — Ellen's favorite — before coming here. But the instant I got downstairs it started to rain, and half a dozen people were already jockcying for taxis. Then out of nowhere this beat-up relic with a noisy muffler sputtered to a stop directly in front of me to let out a passenger. And who am I to ignore kismet? Besides, macadamia brittle is Ellen's second favorite flavor. Or so she claims.

At any rate, after gorging ourselves on the ice cream, it was time to look at the shower gifts, which were presently occupying so much of Ellen's small living room that you had to be extra cautious about where you placed your feet. I have to tell you, though, that she'd made quite a haul. Everything from the practical (see "three toaster ovens") to the exotic (how does a mother-of-pearl caviar spoon strike you?).

"Allison offered to let us keep the pres-

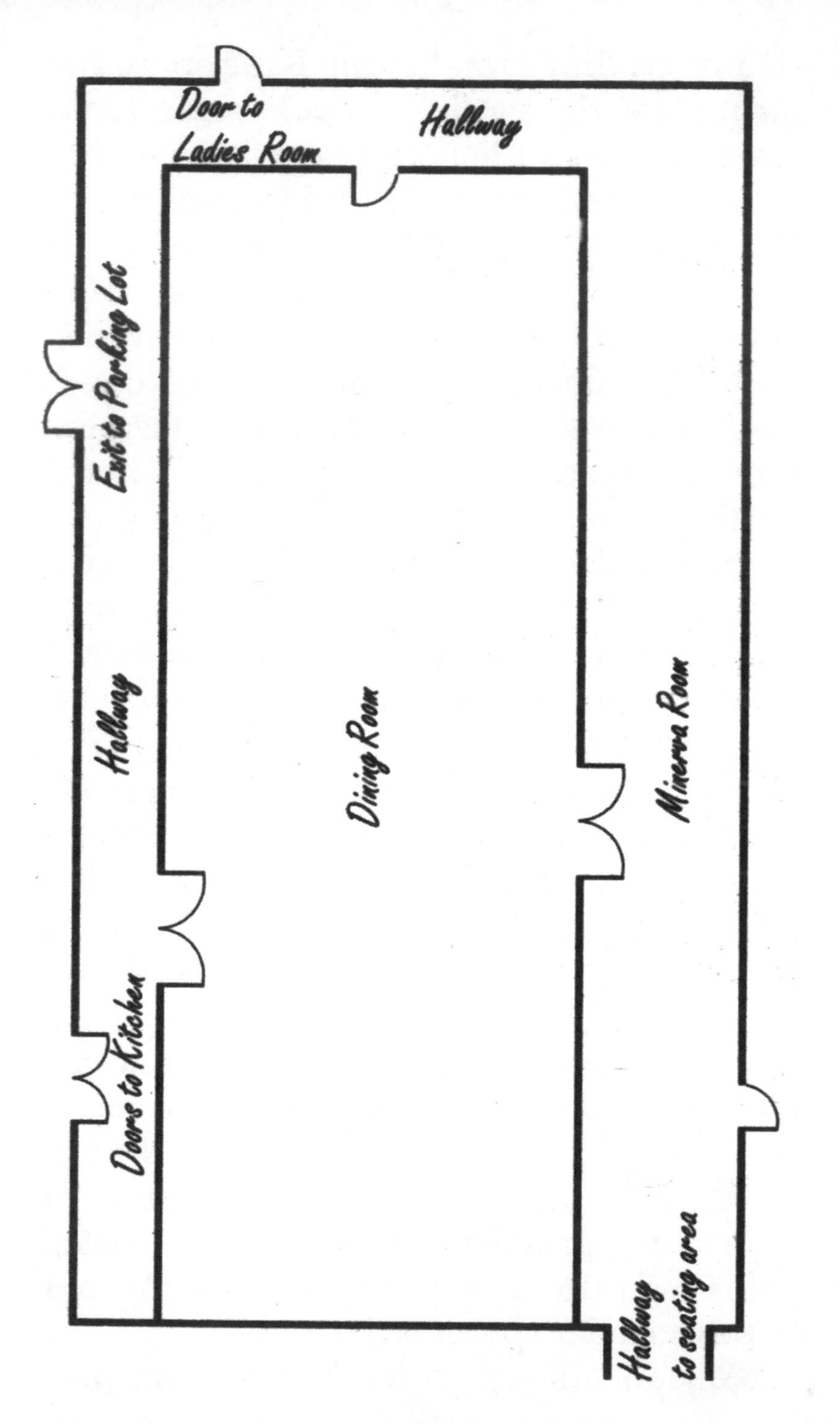
Door to
Ladies Room
Hallway
Exit to Parking Lot
Hallway
Dining Room
Minerva Room
Doors to Kitchen
Hallway
to seating area

ents at her house for a while," Ellen told me once I'd finished oohing and ahhing. "We have to wait until Mike has a chance to drop them off there, though." And then right out of left field: "She must have used the side door."

Well, although I manage to decipher Ellen's non sequiturs at least sixty percent of the time — after all, I've had plenty of practice — just then I was stumped.

"Okay, I give up. Who and what are we talking about?"

My niece looked at me pityingly, as if I was no longer as sharp as I once was. "The killer. Listen, Madam X had to . . . to doctor that salad before we were called in to eat, right? Well, I can't imagine her being able to sneak in and out of the dining room unnoticed if she used the double doors in the front — not with all of us milling around like that. And since the back entrance is almost directly opposite the kitchen, she'd also have run a pretty big risk of being spotted if she tried slipping in that way. So what does that leave?"

This was how I had it figured, too. "The side door," I said, nodding in agreement. It was really the murderer's only sensible choice.

Follow me for a minute.

At one end of the Minerva Room (you know, where we'd had our cocktails and hors d'oeuvres) a left turn brings you to a hallway that provides access to the dining room via a side entrance. Across from this entrance and about six or seven feet beyond it is the ladies' room. So about five minutes (more or less) before lunch was scheduled to be served, Bobbie Jean's killer could — and no doubt did — sashay down that corridor looking to all the world as if she had nothing more sinister in mind than powdering her nose.

I've done a very rough sketch to make it easier for you to visualize the layout. Keep in mind, though, that my skill at drawing fits right in with my talent for the piano and my proficiency at Rollerblading.

I had just gotten to my feet preparatory to leaving when Ellen suddenly turned somber. "Something just occurred to me," she murmured. "If it hadn't been for my shower, maybe she would be here today. What I'm saying is, the shower presented one of the people who hated Bobbie Jean with an opportunity to poison her."

"You could be right, Ellen. It's possible that if not for the shower Bobbie Jean *would* still be with us. But if so, that would almost certainly not hold true for very long. Listen, considering the way that woman lived her life, she practically *asked* to be murdered. And sooner or later, whoever did the job on Sunday would have had another chance to accommodate her."

Ellen appeared to relax a bit.

"Trust me," I assured her, hammering the message home. "The only thing in doubt here is when."

Chapter 15

I'd been advised that, traffic permitting, Saturday's drive to Greenwich, Connecticut, should take slightly under an hour. So just to be sure I'd make that twelve thirty lunch at Robin Fremont's, I'd left my apartment at ten thirty. And no, my math may not be anything to brag about, but it isn't that bad. First, there was that "traffic permitting" business to allow for. And then, my sense of direction being what it is, I had to tack on some additional time for an unintentional detour or two.

Still, I was late. *Extremely* late. If ever you could legitimately lay the blame on an act of God, however, this was it.

I'd no sooner picked up my Chevy at the garage than it started to drizzle. And before long, those gentle little drops morphed into a genuine torrent. Which, I suppose, was nifty for our reservoirs, but it was hell on all of us who were behind the wheel that morning. I mean, I can't even count how often I had to pull onto the shoulder of the parkway because I couldn't see a foot in front of me. *And thank you, WLTW, for that "sunny and 78 degrees with a chance of showers toward evening" weather prediction of yours.*

At noon I called Robin from my cell phone to apprise her of my whereabouts and suggest that she eat without me. But she insisted on waiting until I got there.

"Listen, I love to cook, and I rarely have a chance to fix anything for anyone these days," she told me. "Whenever Carla — my daughter — visits, she's on another silly diet, so she seldom has more than a couple of carrots and a stalk of celery here."

Well, since the woman put it that way. . . .

It was past two before Robin and I finally sat down in her lovely pink-and-white circular dining alcove — and I valiantly attempted to get down a lunch the memory of which still makes my stomach turn over.

Somehow the woman had managed to screw up chicken salad, which I regard as a real challenge. Never before, however, have I tasted so much dressing on so little poultry. I mean, that poor bird's parts were drowning in a sea of wine vinegar. Plus, the chicken chunks, while few in number, were extra-large — and so tough that my teeth started to ache. But it wasn't only the salad that was a minus

10. The accompanying cherry Jell-O mold — and I'm not much for Jell-O molds to begin with — might have been made by Goodyear. The croissants were burned almost to the point of incineration. And dessert was a lumpy custard of some kind that smelled like Shalimar Perfume. (I swear!) But if all this wasn't enough to induce a person to consider fasting, there was the pièce de résistance: a cup of the only coffee I've ever experienced that's on a par with my own. A fitting finale, I suppose, to what had preceded it.

I could now appreciate why Carla was always on "another silly diet."

Anyhow, my hostess and I had agreed to postpone any talk of Bobbie Jean until we were through eating. But once the meal was blessedly over and the table was cleared, we got down to business.

Robin was the one to kick things off. "So Bobbie Jean's salad was poisoned," she said matter-of-factly.

"I see the word has traveled."

"Allison told me. And then yesterday I got a call from that police chief, who also let me know she'd been murdered. What's his name again?"

"Porchow."

"Yes, Porchow. He's paying me a visit this evening. I gather somebody informed him that Bobbie Jean and I weren't on the best of terms."

"Would you mind telling me what happened between the two of you?"

Robin didn't answer at once. And when she did, there was bite in her voice. "My feelings about Bobbie Jean have nothing to do with anything that happened between the two of *us*. They're the result of what she did to Carla. The woman not only wrecked my daughter's marriage but ruined her health in the process." And now Robin focused her attention on the few crumbs remaining on the tablecloth. With the side of her palm, she swept those that were within her reach into a neat little pile in front of her before adding, "Carla and Roy were happy together, too — until Bobbie Jean came along."

I shook my head in commiseration. "How did they meet, Bobbie Jean and your son-in-law?"

"They enrolled in the same class some sort of photography course. She was quite a bit older than Roy, but evidently love closes its eyes to wrinkles. Because it didn't even take a month for Roy Connell to abandon his wife of only two years and move out of their home. Carla, as you might expect, was a physical and emotional wreck after Roy left her. In fact, she was barely functioning.

She stayed with me for eight months, you know. But eventually she got back to herself again, thank God."

"And moved to Manhattan," I contributed.

"That's right. She was determined to make a fresh start. So she took a job there and found a cute little one bedroom not far from her place of employment. She resumed using her maiden name, too. In the meantime, Roy had obtained a quickie divorce, and he and that miserable woman made it legal." A moment later Robin tagged on defiantly, "And I don't care if she *is* dead — she was still a miserable human being."

"I was informed that your former son-in-law died in an automobile accident."

"Yes. Before Roy and Bobbie Jean were even married a year. I understand that not only had he been drinking that night, but that he'd been boozing it up for months because he and Miss Hot Pants weren't getting along that well anymore."

"Tell me something," I said. "Had Carla and the victim ever been friends?" (I asked this not because it was really relevant, but because I'm really nosy.)

"No. Naturally, they were acquainted with each other. Bobbie Jean used to live right next door — with Allison and Wes. And even after she got her own place, she still spent a great deal of time there. But she and Carla were too far apart in age for there to be any sort of friendship."

"Well, I can appreciate why you and your daughter had such bitter feelings toward Bobbie Jean," I commented.

"Listen, there's something I want to make clear. Although neither of us ever forgave Bobbie Jean for what she did, we had nothing to do with her death. It's been seven years since Roy walked out on Carla, and she's been over him for ages. She has a new life now, and there's a new man in it, too. Believe me, if Carla or I had wanted to slip whatever it was into Bobbie Jean's salad, we wouldn't have waited this long to do it."

"Well, the victim did live abroad for quite a while," I pointed out.

"Yes, but on and off. She was back in the States often enough. Even when she made her home in Europe, she'd visit her brother about every six months."

"I'm assuming that Sunday wasn't the first time you were in her company since she ran off with your son-in-law."

"No, it wasn't. Over the years we would occasionally bump into her at various functions."

"When did you see her last? Prior to the shower, I mean."

Robin frowned in concentration. "I think it must have been about two years ago, when Carla and I attended a surprise birthday party for Wes. Bobbie Jean was there with her newest acquisition, that poor Geoffrey Morton. They'd just relocated to this country from some London suburb."

"Her presence must have made it pretty awkward for you — you and Carla, I mean."

"It did. A little, anyhow. But we weren't seated anywhere near Bobbie Jean, so it wasn't too bad."

"This birthday party — were Lorraine Corwin and Grace Banner also there?"

"No. Lorraine was living in California. As for Grace, she sent a very nice gift and her apologies, claiming she'd come down with the flu. But if you ask me, the real reason she didn't attend was that she still wasn't up to any contact with Bobbie Jean. To be honest, I half-expected that she'd be a no-show at Ellen's shower, too."

"Speaking of the shower, it couldn't have been very comfortable there, either, for you and Carla. Particularly since it was held at Bobbie Jean's country club, and, in a way, that made her one of the hostesses."

"We never regarded her as any hostess. Of course, we'd have preferred her being anyplace but. We managed to avoid her, though. Look, it was a shower for Mike's fiancée, and neither Carla nor I would have dreamed of missing it. Besides" — and Robin smiled here — "it was an opportunity to see what Silver Oaks was like."

Now, there was something very sly about that smile — you really had to be there to appreciate what I'm talking about. But at any rate, I got the strong impression that Robin was holding back something of significance. So I gave her an "Oh?" which almost unfailingly produces a response.

Sure enough, she got up and moved her chair closer to mine. Then once she was seated again she cupped her hand to her mouth and spoke in a voice that was barely above a whisper. (I'm surprised the woman didn't check under the table, too, while she was at it.) "Carla's been dating this very nice young man lately. He recently became a member of Silver Oaks — primarily for the golfing facilities. And we . . . umm, wanted to have a look at the place."

Well, considering the nature of that smile Robin had flashed me before, along with this hush-hush attitude of hers, I put two and two together. "Does this mean that Carla and her beau are thinking of getting married at Silver Oaks?"

My hostess seemed to instantly regret

having shared any confidences with me. “I’ve already said too much,” she muttered, looking agitated. “Carla will *kill* me if she ever finds out I mentioned Len to you. The two of them aren’t even close to that stage yet, honestly.”

I clasped her hand for a moment. “I’m glad Carla has somebody she cares about again. And don’t worry. I’ve already forgotten that I ever heard the name Len. Let’s talk about the other guests at the shower for a couple of minutes, okay? Are you aware of anyone else who had it in for Bobbie Jean?”

“I don’t doubt that a pretty sizable portion of the women who were present that day had reasons to despise her.”

“I presume this would include Grace and Lorraine.”

“I guess. But take my word for it, they weren’t the only ones.”

“Can you be more specific?”

“Uh, not really. I wish I could help you out, but I’m just going by what I know of Bobbie Jean.”

“Let me ask you another question. Did you happen to see anyone either entering or leaving the dining room before we were called in to lunch?”

“No, I didn’t.”

“All right, then. Was there *anything* that

struck you as being odd or maybe a bit unusual?"

"Nothing," Robin answered ruefully.

Well, this seemed as good a time as any to find out a bit more about that other matter Allison had touched on last Tuesday. "By the way, didn't you yourself have some kind of quarrel with Bobbie Jean at one point? Apart from this thing with your son-in-law, I mean."

Robin chuckled. "As a matter of fact, I did. I had almost forgotten about that. It wasn't what I'd consider a quarrel, though. I just wouldn't have anything to do with her after what occurred."

"And what *did* occur?"

"One day — and this dates back more than twenty years — I caught Bobbie Jean in our backyard engaging in a little ménage à trois with our fifty-five-year-old gardener and this young kid who was doing some work on our pool."

Now, I didn't want to reveal that this wasn't exactly news to me, so I feigned shock. "Good God!" I exclaimed. I even waited a few seconds (which I figured I'd have needed in order to regain my composure) before saying, "And Bobbie Jean and her playmates carried on like this when you were at home?"

"Actually, I *came* home. Only they had no

idea I'd returned, so they figured the coast was clear. Cliff, my late husband, was in Florida visiting his mother that weekend — this was on a Saturday. And Carla and I had left to catch a train into Manhattan. We were planning to go to the circus. But while we were at the station, Carla complained of nausea. So we turned around and went back to the house. Luckily, we used the front door; otherwise, my preteen daughter would have been treated to the same disgusting spectacle that I witnessed a short while later. And —" Suddenly Robin broke off and glanced at me quizzically. "But how did you find out about this, anyway?"

"I didn't," I stated firmly. "All I heard — and I can't even recall who mentioned it — was that there'd been some unpleasantness between you and Bobbie Jean a long time ago. But you were telling me . . ."

"Yes. Well, I'd just made Carla some tea when it began to rain, and she remembered that she'd left her brand-new sweater on the patio. So I went to get it — and got the shock of my life. There were the three of them, oblivious to the weather, rolling around on the grass in all their natural glory."

"Were they aware that you saw them?"

Robin actually giggled now. "They had to be. I screamed bloody murder."

"Did you ever say anything to Allison and Wes about this?"

"I'd decided not to. Bobbie Jean was responsible for enough friction between them as it was. Oh, I didn't mean —" And now Robin's entire face turned crimson. "There was never any real trouble between Allison and Wes, Desiree," she hastily put in. "They loved each other a great deal — they still do. But Wes has — *had* — a tendency to be overprotective of that sister of his, who, I assure you, was hardly deserving of his loyalty. And every once in a while his attitude got on Allison's nerves. Look, it got on *my* nerves, and I wasn't even living with him.

"At any rate, eventually it was Bobbie Jean herself who forced me to turn snitch. The little witch had gone ahead and related the incident to Allison, just in case the story should get back to Wes. Only she put a slight twist on things. In her version *I* was the female member of the threesome, and *she'd* caught *me* in the act. And listen to this. She also said I'd threatened that if she ever went to her brother or sister-in-law with what she'd seen, I would claim I'd caught *her* in that compromising situation."

"A resourceful soul, wasn't she?" I commented. "What did she say she was doing at your house in the first place?"

"She told Allison that she'd come over to borrow something or other — my turquoise earrings, I think. And when I didn't answer the doorbell, she went around to the rear to see if I was on the patio." Unexpectedly Robin grinned. "But you know what *really* gets me, Desiree? Bobbie Jean was just visiting Allison and Wes that day — she was close to thirty by then and had already taken her own place. So why didn't she carry on in *her* neighbor's backyard?"

I grinned, too. "Good point."

"But seriously, that incident didn't cause any real damage. Allison came to me with Bobbie Jean's story in order to learn the truth about what had gone on that morning. She didn't believe Bobbie Jean's baloney for a second."

"And Wes?"

"As far as I know, he never heard anything about it."

"Well, I think that about covers everything," I announced soon after this. "I really appreciate your cooperation, Robin." I pushed my chair back from the table. "Oh, and thanks for the delicious lunch."

Robin positively beamed at that.

Like I've said many times, truthfulness is not always a virtue.

Chapter 16

Just as I left Robin Fremont's, the rain let up. Still, making it home wasn't the breeze it should have been. The thing is, I got lost twice attempting to find the parkway, and driving around in circles can really eat up the clock.

The prolonged trip did allow me to do plenty of thinking, however. Which, in turn, provided me with the rationale that I was too preoccupied with the investigation to pay attention to where I was going.

I began with a close look at the Fremonts, mother and daughter — although I didn't regard the poisoning as necessarily a joint venture. Now, it had been seven years since Roy ditched Carla for Allison's sexpot sister-in-law. And as Robin pointed out, both she and Carla had had ample opportunity to send Bobbie Jean heavenward or — and this was much more likely — somewhere-elseward way before last Sunday. More important, Carla currently appeared to have a serious romance in her life. So I had some trouble accepting that she and/or her mother would have murdered Bobbie Jean at this juncture. And as far as that nasty little lie the dead woman had told about Robin twenty years earlier, that's exactly what it was: a nasty *little* lie. It didn't amount to diddly when you measured it against all of the heavy-duty unhappiness Bobbie Jean had been generating for so long. In fact, I didn't feel that this incident was even worth taking into account.

Next I examined Lorraine Corwin's status as a suspect. The suffering that the victim had caused this woman was pretty much ancient history by now. I mean, if Lorraine had wanted to do in Bobbie Jean, why hadn't she gotten in her licks ages ago? Yes, I know, until fairly recently Lorraine was living in San Francisco. But she could always have come east for a visit and, armed with a dose of something lethal, gotten herself an invite to some earlier function at which Bobbie Jean had been a guest. Listen, while they say that revenge is a dish that's best served cold, keeping your hostility on ice for thirty-three years is ridiculous. And let's not forget that Lorraine had opened her own company only last year. What I'm saying is that, as with the Fremonts, the timing seemed strange to me. Why would the woman strike out at Bobbie Jean just when she appeared to be really hitting her stride career-wise?

Finally there was Grace Banner to consider. It was a decade since the Banners had entered into that partnership with Bobbie Jean. And less than a year later, she'd accused them of fraud. Well, even allowing for the pokiness of our legal system, Bobbie Jean's civil action against the pair probably went to court within the next two or three years at the outside. And Grace told me that their suit against her was disposed of two years after that. So if Grace Banner *was* the one who tinkered with our girl's salad, then she, too, had been sitting on her hands for a while. (Although, of course, this could hardly compare to her pal Lorraine's putting a thirty-year-plus grievance on hold.) But setting this aside, I went on to examine Robin's suspicion — which was probably valid — that a couple of years back, when Wes was given that surprise party, Grace still couldn't bring herself to come face-to-face with the dead woman. So I put a question to myself. Would a person who wasn't even up to *seeing* her adversary have been capable of killing her? Well, let me say this: I would imagine that to find the courage to commit murder, Grace Banner would have had to swallow a lot more than the 0.5 milligrams of Xanax she claimed she required in order to merely show up at Ellen's shower.

So where did all of my ruminating leave me? Not very satisfied, I'll tell you that. And now I was struck by the unthinkable.

Was it actually possible that all four of these ladies were innocent?

I started to get this queasy feeling that seemed to crop up whenever the possibility of broadening the investigation entered my mind. Then I remembered that I hadn't even spoken to the younger of the Fremonts yet. Maybe Carla would shed some new light on things when we got together on Monday. That was certainly conceivable, wasn't it?

Of course it was. And jutting out my jaw, I elected to remain positive.

At least for another two days.

Chapter 17

There were three messages on the machine when I returned from Greenwich.

The first was from my across-the-hall neighbor, Harriet Gould — one of the shower guests. She'd already phoned twice that week to find out if the autopsy report on Bobbie Jean had come in yet.

"You promised to tell me as soon as you learned anything." *Damn! It had gone completely out of my head!* "But I realize how hectic things can get sometimes, so I didn't think you'd mind if I checked back with you. Anyway, hope everything's okay otherwise. And keep me posted."

The second message was from my right-next-door neighbor, Barbara Gleason — another of the shower guests.

"Anything new on that autopsy report? Call when you have a chance."

And then I listened to the third message.

"Hi," said the male voice, "this is . . . er . . . Nick Grainger." He sounded as if he didn't relish admitting it. "I want to apologize for being so rude to you yesterday, but, well, you kind of caught me off guard. I hope you'll let me make amends — maybe we could have dinner one night. I'll be in touch."

I'm not exactly certain how long I stood there in front of the answering machine. All I know is that I couldn't stop smiling.

When I finally exited my trance, I dialed Harriet's number. She wasn't in. I figured that most likely she and her husband Steve were out to dinner, so I left word. I told her — and now I couldn't seem to keep the smile out of my voice — that I'd *just* been informed of the results of the autopsy and that Bobbie Jean's salad had been poisoned. (Well, "just" could mean different things to different people, couldn't it?)

After this I tried Barbara.

"Hi, Barbara, how are you?" I chirped in response to her "hello."

"Oh, Dez, I'm glad you caught me. Another few seconds and I'd have been out of the apartment — I'm meeting a friend for dinner. Come join us — that is, if you haven't already eaten."

"Thanks anyway, but I've had my supper." Okay, maybe this time I *was* uttering a teeny falsehood. But I was sparing myself some *agita.* Barbara doesn't take too kindly to "No, thank you."

"Say, you sound disgustingly cheerful tonight. Any particular reason?"

"That's simply the way I am."

"Yeah, sure. All right, I'll try and survive without knowing," she mumbled testily. "Has anything happened with regard to that poor woman who died Sunday?"

"As a matter of fact, the autopsy report is in."

"Go on."

"Bobbie Jean was murdered."

"Who? How?"

"Somebody added some poisonous leaves to her salad. As for the 'who,' I believe that the killer was one of four women — all of whom had a strong motive for putting Bobbie Jean out of commission. But I haven't narrowed it down any further than that. Not yet, at any rate."

"Does that mean you're investigating this business?"

"Uh-huh. Mike asked me to."

A restrained "Hmm" was Barbara's only comment.

"Listen, I don't want to keep you . . ."

"Not so fast. What four are we talking about, anyway?"

"It wouldn't be fair to name names. I'm

only speculating at this point."

Now, I expected an argument here. Or at best, a little sample of the petulance Barbara so often employs. But she responded with surprising equanimity. "Okay. But would you care to hear who I think did this?"

"Why not."

"That annoying young thing who went around snapping everyone's picture."

Ginger! She suspected Ginger! It's a tribute to my self-control that I managed to keep from laughing. "What makes you say that?"

"My intuition. But you wait. You'll see that I'm right."

After my conversation with Ms. Nostradamus, I had a quick bite, following which I sat down at the computer and began the never-ending task of typing up my notes. I finally gave up after jerking myself awake for the third time.

It was past ten when I got out of bed on Sunday. I had a leisurely breakfast of Cheerios and an Entenmann's corn muffin (is there any other kind, really?), along with the coffee of the damned. And then I phoned the Silver Oaks Country Club. I asked to be connected with the manager.

It was a fairly lengthy wait before a woman got on the line. "Mr. Novak isn't in today. This is Janice Kramer, the assistant manager." *Ahh, the strawberry blonde.* "Perhaps I can help you."

"My name is Desiree Shapiro, Ms. Kramer. We've met a couple of times — I was one of the hostesses at last Sunday's disastrous bridal shower."

"Oh . . . of course. I remember you, Ms. Shapiro." But the tentative note in her voice contradicted the words. The way I saw it, though, it was nice of her to make the effort. "All of us at Silver Oaks are very shaken by this terrible thing," she said quietly. "Ms. Morton was well liked here, you know. And not only by the other guests, but by our entire staff, as well."

I can only hope that when I die people spout the same sort of lies about me. "I also happen to be a private detective, Ms. Kramer, and I've been hired by the family to look into Mrs. Morton's death. I'd appreciate it if you could arrange for me to have a brief talk with your employees."

"The police have already questioned everyone who works here."

"I'm aware of that. But Mrs. Morton's family is anxious that I conduct a separate investigation."

Ms. Kramer appeared to hesitate.

"I can have Dr. Lynton — Mrs. Morton's

brother — call you to confirm this."

Two or three additional seconds of hesitation. "That won't be necessary. I believe almost all of last Sunday's staff is in today. I imagine those are the people you'd be most interested in speaking to, so it might be worthwhile for you to come out to Silver Oaks this afternoon, if you can make it."

"I'll be there."

"Fine. I'll see you then." I was about to say good-bye when she added, "Umm, Ms. Shapiro? I hope you don't think that anyone in our employ would —"

"No, I don't. Somebody there may have some important information without recognizing its significance, though." And now my brain caught up with my hearing. "But didn't you just tell me that *almost* all of last Sunday's staff would be at the club today?"

"That's right. One of our people — a waiter — went on vacation this past Monday. I think he's due back the Monday after next. I'll check the schedule and let you know when you get here."

Seeing that majestic mansion again, that sweeping, picture-perfect front lawn, I felt a baseball-size lump in my throat. Could it have been only one week ago that this lovely setting had served as a venue for murder?

A slim, gray-haired woman with a very pretty face occupied a small office to the right of the entrance. She looked up at the sound of my footsteps.

"My name is Desiree Shapiro," I informed her, stopping at her door. "I'd —"

"I'm Kathy Marin." Jumping to her feet, she approached me with a fixed smile and an outstretched hand. "Ms. Kramer had a minor emergency to attend to," she apprised me as I shook the hand. "She should be back shortly, but in the meantime she asked me to assist you. She said that you'd probably prefer to interview everyone individually."

"Yes, I would."

"Then follow me, won't you? And I'll get you settled."

I was shown to a tiny room that, I swear, wasn't an inch larger than the cubbyhole I occupy at Gilbert and Sullivan. Somehow, however, somebody had managed to squeeze a desk and *three chairs* into these microscopic quarters. I was still marveling at this accomplishment when Kathy invited me to make myself comfortable. She indicated the chair behind the desk, and I plopped down on the hard, thinly cushioned seat. *Make myself comfortable? She had to be kidding!*

"May I get you something?" she offered. "Some coffee? Or a soft drink, perhaps?"

"No, thanks, I'm fine."

"Shall I begin sending people in now?"

"Uh, maybe you wouldn't mind answering a few questions for me before you do."

Kathy Marin was plainly flustered. "No, no, of course not. But I'm afraid I don't know anything that would be helpful to you. I wasn't even in last Sunday."

"That's okay. As long as I'm here, I may as well speak to *all* the employees — any who are around today, I mean. This will only take a couple of minutes. I promise."

Never having met me before, the woman appeared to accept that as gospel. And in this case, it actually turned out to be true. "All right," she agreed, gracefully — if reluctantly — placing her trim little posterior on one of the chairs on the other side of the desk.

"What is it you do here, Ms. Marin?"

"I'm Ms. Kramer's assistant. And do call me Kathy."

"And I'm Desiree. Were you acquainted with Mrs. Morton, Kathy?"

"Not really. Just to say hello to."

"Did you ever hear any gossip pertaining to her?"

"Gossip?"

"For example, possibly a staff member had some sort of trouble with her."

"Uh-uh. Not to my knowledge, anyway."

"Or maybe there was a problem between Mrs. Morton and one of her fellow club members."

"I'm not aware of anything like that."

"Well, then, what about an affair?"

Plainly puzzled now, Kathy lifted two nicely shaped eyebrows. "I beg your pardon?"

"I'm sorry. I didn't put that too clearly. I want to know if there was ever any talk about Mrs. Morton's being romantically involved with either another club member or someone on your staff."

"If she was, I never heard about it."

"Well, thank you very much, Kathy."

"That's it?"

"That's it. I told you it would only take a few minutes." I had to smile at her obvious relief.

"Why don't I have the first person come in, then," she said, rising. "And just call me — I'm on extension six — whenever you're ready to see the next member of our staff."

I might as well have stayed home.

For close to three hours I interviewed waiters and busboys and chefs. I interrogated the tennis instructor, the golf pro, a couple of restroom attendants — and I can't even recall who else. But if the victim had been feuding with anyone at Silver Oaks, both she and the party of the second part had managed to keep it pretty damn quiet. Plus, if Bobbie Jean had added another notch to her belt — to commemorate a recent lover, I mean — you couldn't prove it by these people.

The truth is, though, this didn't disturb me that much. Remember, I was still clinging to my original assumption that it was one of Allison's four buddies who'd given her sister-in-law's salad that little something extra. What *did* disappoint me — in spite of my resolve beforehand *not* to be disappointed — was that nobody who'd been working the shower last Sunday had spotted any of the women entering or leaving the dining room before lunch was served. Actually, not one of them saw or heard anything at all that could add to the pathetically little I already knew.

I stopped at Kathy Marin's office to thank her for her assistance before I left.

"Any luck?" she asked.

"None."

"Well, there's always Dominick." But

she didn't look that encouraged herself.

"Dominick?"

"Dominick Gallo, one of our waiters. Janice — Ms. Kramer — said that if by any chance she didn't return by the time you were finished, I was to give you his name and home telephone number. Dominick's the only employee who was in last Sunday who isn't here today. Oh, and Janice said to tell you that she was right; he's expected back at work a week from Monday."

Well, having scored a big zero with my questioning, I no longer held out any real hope for tomorrow's interview with Carla Fremont, either. I'll tell you how discouraged I was at that moment: so discouraged that even the fact of Nick's phone call failed to buoy my spirits. I took the slip of paper Kathy extended to me and stuffed it into the jacket pocket of my yellow linen suit. *A fat lot of help Dominick'll turn out to be,* I groused to myself.

If I had a tail it would have been between my legs when I left the Silver Oaks Country Club that day.

Chapter 18

And don't think my mood was any better Sunday evening. I was depressed with a capital D. By now I was actually dreading tomorrow's meeting with Carla Fremont, certain it would be another total washout. I'll tell you something. If it were somehow possible to leave myself behind me, I'd have been out of that apartment in a flash.

Anyhow, at a few minutes to eight, I was curled up on the sofa trying to decide which awful TV show was a little less awful than the rest of them, when the phone rang.

My heart jumped into my throat. *Nick!*

Wrong.

"Is this Desiree Shapiro?" a man inquired. He had a perfectly nice voice, but since it wasn't Nick Grainger's voice, my heart resumed its proper place in my anatomy.

"Yes, it is."

"This is Chief Porchow over in Forsythe, Ms. Shapiro. We've gotten the autopsy results on Ms. Morton." His tone became almost confidential. "She was poisoned. But maybe you've already heard."

"As a matter of fact, I did hear. Mrs. Morton's sister-in-law — Allison Lynton — told me."

"I'd like to check out a couple of points with you, if you don't mind. According to the information you provided to Officer Smilowitz, you barely knew the deceased."

"That's right."

"Could you elaborate a little on the 'barely'?"

"Well, Mrs. Lynton and I were the ones who gave that bridal shower; it was for my niece, who's engaged to Mrs. Lynton's son. Bobbie Jean — Mrs. Morton — was a member at Silver Oaks, and she arranged for the affair to be held there. She met us up at the club twice to help us organize things."

"And those were the only times you were in her company?"

"Yes."

"So I don't suppose you could have had much of a motive for wanting her dead."

"None at all," I said flatly.

"Would you have any idea who might have had ill feelings toward the victim?"

Well, since Wes had already fingered Allison's four buddies for the chief, I figured there was no reason for a lie here. (Which is something I only resort to out of absolute necessity — or, on occasion, compassion.) "Actually, from what I've gathered, there was an unpleasant history of some sort between Mrs. Morton and some of Allison Lynton's close friends."

"And who would those friends be?"

I ticked off the names.

"Anyone else, Ms. Shapiro?"

"No one I'm aware of."

"I have just one more question for you." *Now, where have I heard that before?* "Did you see anyone going in or out of the dining room prior to lunch being served?" *God, it felt strange listening to my own words coming out of someone else's mouth.*

"No, no one."

"Then let me ask you this. Did you notice anything at all of a suspicious nature that day?"

This made it two questions, but I should talk. I really felt for the man at having to give him another no, but what could I do? "Umm, no," I admitted sheepishly.

He seemed to take this in stride. Obviously, it was a response he'd become pretty much accustomed to with this case. And, boy, could I empathize with that!

The brief interrogation concluded with

Chief Porchow's extracting my promise to contact him if anything pertinent should occur to me.

I'd fallen asleep watching television (that's how stimulating a show it was) when the telephone jarred me awake.

Nick! I thought, ever hopeful.

It was Ellen.

"I just got a call from the Forsythe chief of police," she said anxiously.

"I'm certain he's getting in touch with everyone who was at the shower," I assured her.

"Honestly?"

"Honestly." I wasn't positive, but I imagined I heard a sigh of relief. "You weren't concerned that he might consider you a suspect, were you?"

"Of course not." But my niece isn't nearly as accomplished a liar as I am.

"He phoned me this evening, too," I informed her.

"Oh." And this time I knew I heard a sigh of relief. "Did you mention that you've been investigating the murder on your own?"

"Uh-uh. I didn't see any point in it. Besides, I hated to ruin what was left of the man's day. So I decided to keep my mouth shut — for the present, at least."

"You think he would object to your looking into things?"

"What do *you* think?" I countered.

"I think he wouldn't have been overjoyed by the news." And she giggled. Well, Ellen's infectious little giggle hadn't punctuated a conversation of ours since Bobbie Jean's death. And I was inordinately pleased that it was making its return.

"How's Mike?" I asked then.

"Pretty good — considering."

"And his parents?"

"Allison's okay, but Wes is still very depressed. He's going in to the office tomorrow, though. He says if he doesn't get back to work he'll drive himself *and* Allison crazy."

He was probably right, too.

Soon after Ellen and I finished talking, the phone rang for the third time that evening. It was past ten by now, and having been wrong twice already, I wouldn't even let the name "Nick" enter my head. So I wasn't that disappointed to find my friend Pat on the other end of the line.

She and Burton had come home from the movies a couple of minutes ago, she reported, and there was a message from the Forsythe Police Department on her machine. She was asked to contact Chief Porchow in the morning. "I was wondering what it could be about. Any ideas?"

"They simply want to verify the information you gave Officer Smilowitz. For instance, they'll probably ask you again how well you knew the victim. And now that it's been established that a murder was committed, they'll naturally want to find out if you spotted anything out of the ordinary that day. That kind of thing."

"Just what I figured," Pat declared, although I'd definitely detected a hint of uneasiness in her voice. And believe me, Pat Wizniak's nerves are a whole lot steadier than Ellen's.

But it's a funny thing. It seems that even when people are innocent and have nothing whatever to hide, getting questioned by the police is liable to make them squirm a little. I probably shouldn't admit this, being a PI and all, but under other circumstances that call from Chief Porchow might have made me the slightest bit jumpy, too.

As it was, though, I was too depressed to let it affect me.

Chapter 19

When I woke up on Monday I immediately convinced myself to wait until after tonight's seven P.M. meeting with Carla Fremont before sticking my head in the gas oven. And once again I began looking to this last of my suspects to provide some encouraging input.

Listen, I was trying really hard for optimism.

Anyhow, in the meantime I had a one-third-decent day. The decent part being that I was unusually productive, transcribing a large portion of my notes. As for the two-thirds that weren't so decent, first, Jackie and I had lunch at a new Italian restaurant that really showed some promise — until a damn fly did a damn swan dive into my minestrone. Then, when we were walking back to the office, I succumbed to a silk scarf that seemed to wink at me from the window of this little boutique. Even on sale — a *nonrefundable* sale — that scarf was ridiculously expensive. But I was a hundred percent positive it would be perfect with my light blue suit — only to discover later that it did not go with the suit at all. Or with anything else in my closet, for that matter.

But about that get-together with Carla . . .

On the way home from work I did some shopping in preparation for her visit. Remembering Robin's remark about her daughter's penchant for celery and carrots, I marched right past the cheese store in favor of the greengrocer's, where I painstakingly selected the freshest and most appetizing assortment of vegetables.

When I got upstairs I made some dip — and then suddenly my poor excuse for a brain actually started to function. I mean, hadn't I speculated on Saturday that Carla's rejection of her mother's cooking might not have been attributable to a diet at all — but to an innate desire for self-preservation? I hastily took the onion tart out of the freezer — you know, that same onion tart that had so obviously failed to impress Allison last week.

I'd just removed it from the oven when the doorbell sounded. It was seven o'clock on the button.

As soon as she walked in, Carla Fremont reinforced what I'd concluded at the shower: She was definitely no slave to fashion. The faded navy sweatshirt she wore was at least two sizes too large for her skin-and-bones figure. (Compared to Carla, my niece Ellen was a candidate for Weight Watchers.) Also, the girl's tan chinos were frayed at the bottom, and there was a large spot in the middle of the left leg. They did fit okay, though, being only slightly baggy. (In my book, slightly baggy is definitely preferable to slacks so tight you don't have to wonder about what type of panties a person has on underneath — assuming a person is even wearing panties, that is.)

Carla obviously didn't patronize the cosmetics counters any too often, either. Her only makeup was a touch of lipstick — although skin as pasty as Carla's practically cries out for some camouflage. And it pained me to think of what a little long-lash mascara could have done for those short, next-to-invisible eyelashes.

However, Carla's biggest mistake — looks-wise, I'm talking about — was her hair. Kind of greasy, and a nondescript shade of brown, it just hung there, completely limp. Trust me, this wasn't the best style for *anyone*. Even Heather Locklear might have had trouble pulling off a hairdo like that. But what made it such a disaster for Carla was how it accentuated her too-thin face — and the somewhat prominent nose in the middle of it.

And then there were those yellow teeth of hers.

Now, all this may sound pretty catty to you. But seeing her again, I realized that Carla's neglect in the appearance department might have facilitated Bobbie Jean's getting her hooks into Roy Connell. And I found myself disturbed by the possibility that Carla's new guy — this Len that Robin had mentioned — could someday be faced with the same sort of temptation her ex was. And could prove to be every bit as shallow.

Anyhow, as soon as my visitor had made herself comfortable on the sofa, I asked what I could get her to drink, and she said she'd love some red wine if I had it. I did.

After pouring two glasses of Beaujolais, I took a chair opposite her and waved at the food on the coffee table. "Help yourself," I invited. And Carla did. Totally ignoring the platter displaying those lovely vegetables I'd so carefully picked over at the greengrocer's, she cut herself a slice of onion tart. And shortly after this, another.

The zeal with which Carla was attacking that tart led me to conclude that if there was even a shred of hope there'd be any of it left over for my supper, I'd better restrict myself to the crudités. Which have never been my hors d'oeuvre of choice.

At any rate, after we'd spent about ten minutes sipping and chewing and engaging in a fair amount of polite conversation, I figured it was time to get down to business.

"Tell me about your relationship with Bobbie Jean, Ms. Fremont," I began.

"We didn't *have* a relationship. And the name's Carla, Desiree."

I nodded. "I understand she married your former husband."

"That's right. She worked him pretty good, you know — this, in case nobody told you, was while Roy and I were still husband and wife. And then all of a sudden, before I was aware of what was happening, we weren't anything to each other anymore." Carla brushed something — very likely a tear — from just below her left eye before going on. "Bobbie Jean was so much older than Roy, too," she grumbled. "She was past forty, for crying out loud. What could he possibly have seen in a woman that age?" I winced. (I have a tendency to take comments of this nature personally.) "And why would *she* have wanted *him*, for that matter? He wasn't rich. He wasn't really what you'd call good-looking. And to be honest, he wasn't even that bright."

"Umm, you and Roy had been happy together before Bobbie Jean entered the picture?"

"Yes, we were." She sounded as if she was daring me to challenge this.

"I heard that less than a year after Roy and Bobbie Jean were married, he died in an automobile accident."

"That's right. And I hold Bobbie Jean responsible."

"Why is that?"

"He had started to drink — quite a bit, too. Which should give you some idea of how blissful he was with his new little wifey. Roy seldom had more than one glass of beer when he was living with me. Anyhow, from what everyone said, Bobbie Jean did nothing whatsoever to persuade him to cut down."

"Maybe everyone was mistaken," I ventured. "Maybe she tried, but she wasn't successful."

Carla glared at me. "She actually encouraged his drinking."

"Are you saying Bobbie Jean wanted him to get into an accident?"

"I wouldn't go that far. But she enjoyed getting crocked herself on occasion — ask Allison — and she liked having Roy join her. The thing is, though, Bobbie Jean was able to control the habit while Roy apparently wasn't. And she just didn't care enough about him to see to it he went on the wagon — or, at the very least, to make sure that he didn't drive when he had a snootful."

"You're certain she didn't make the attempt?"

Carla snapped out the next words. "Has anyone bothered to fill you in on what happened that night — the night he died?"

"All I was told is that your former husband was in a fatal car crash."

"Then allow me to enlighten you. My ex and his dear wife had been out to dinner with another couple, and both Roy and Bobbie Jean had tossed back quite a few. Well, when it came time to leave, Bobbie Jean informed Roy that he wasn't in any condition to get behind the wheel and that she'd have Bill and Maureen O'Grady — the other couple — drop her off."

"So she did try to talk him out of driving."

Carla's voice rose. "Aren't you paying attention? She made a *statement* — that was all. According to the O'Gradys, she didn't even *suggest* to Roy that he go with them, too."

"Didn't they — the O'Gradys — speak to Roy about letting them take him home?"

"Of course. But he wouldn't listen. And before they could stop him, he just sped away. He might have listened to his wife, though — if she'd taken the trouble to reason with him." Carla didn't say anything more for a while, and I was about to break the silence when she blurted out, "Look, if not for that ho he left me for, Roy Connell would be alive today. I don't have the slightest doubt of that."

"You sound like you still have a great deal of bitterness toward Bobbie Jean."

"You'd better believe I do! And the fact that she's gone doesn't make me loathe the woman any less, either. She not only wrecked my marriage, she was also responsible for Roy's death. And, God help me, I really loved the man. But that all happened a long time ago. Too long ago, I should point out, for me to suddenly decide to take my revenge at your niece's shower. Besides, I'd been very involved with someone else until recently — until this past weekend, to be precise."

I was genuinely saddened by this revelation. Considering all she'd been through courtesy of the victim, the girl certainly deserved some happiness in her life. Unless, of course, she'd had a hand in Bobbie Jean's demise. (As I've said before, I don't condone murder — no matter what.) But anyway, I didn't quite know how to respond — after all, I had no clue as to how Carla herself felt about the breakup. So out came the old standby. "Oh," I murmured.

My visitor smiled crookedly. "Yeah, 'Oh.' I wanted him to commit, and he wanted a little time to think it over — three or four years' worth. But why am I going into this?"

"Maybe it will still work out," I suggested timidly.

"I don't even care anymore," she stated with an unconvincing display of bravado. "There's only one thing that concerns me now."

"What's that?"

"How do I tell my mother?"

"She likes this man?"

"My mother, Desiree, would like Count Dracula if there were any possibility of his becoming her son-in-law. She used to fall all over Roy, too, when I started bringing him around."

"She must have been pretty devastated by what Roy . . . when Roy became involved with Bobbie Jean."

"She was. Particularly because she was so worried about me — I was inconsolable for a while." And now Carla eyed me suspiciously. "But don't you dare get it into your head that my mother was the one who poisoned that bitch." And unexpectedly, she grinned. "My mother wouldn't have the *patience* to bide her time for seven years — not for *anything*."

Carla took a sip of wine now, then very purposefully set the glass on the coffee table. "And speaking of the poisoning, I understand that Bobbie Jean's *terribly* unfortunate passing was caused by something in her salad."

"Yes, whoever did this included the leaves of an extremely toxic plant — it's called monkshood — with the rest of the salad greens."

"I only regret that she didn't have a long, agonizing death. That would have been a fitting end for Bobbie Jean Morton."

Merely considering this alternative brought a smile to Carla's lips and a sparkle to her brown eyes. I half anticipated that any minute now she'd start to rub her hands together with glee. But she confined herself to celebrating the thought with another generous piece of onion tart.

"Do you have any idea who might have killed Bobbie Jean?" I brought up at this point.

"No. Believe me, there wasn't one person

at the club that day with the *cojones* to murder somebody."

"Well, forget about who murdered her, then. Let's talk about who would have liked to. Naturally, I'm only referring to the women who attended the shower."

"Well, I can name two ladies who no doubt would have been happy to see Bobbie Jean dead and buried, but it's hard to picture either of them actually *doing* anything to speed up the process. Anyhow, there's Grace Banner, for one. Grace and her husband were stupid enough to go partners in a restaurant with good ole Bobbie Jean, and it seems that she gave the Banners a pretty rotten time of it, suing them for theft or fraud or something. Then there's Allison's ex-roommate, Lorraine . . . Lorraine . . ."

"Corwin," I supplied.

"Yeah, her. Bobbie Jean stole her fiancé. But that goes back thirty years, if not longer. Still, they say Lorraine never got over it. She never did marry."

"Anyone else?" I asked automatically.

Carla hesitated long enough to allow me to hope. Could it be that she was going to hand me another, more promising suspect? "Carla?" I prompted.

"She would never have killed her,

though." And then with emphasis: "Absolutely not."

"Who's that?"

Once again the girl hesitated, avoiding my eyes now. "Listen, there's no way she'd have poisoned her husband's sister."

"Allison? You're talking about *Allison?"* My voice had shot up so high that my throat ached.

Carla scowled. "I just *said* that I was positive she didn't do it." A moment later she reflected quietly, "I can't imagine what it must have been like for Allison, though, having to put up with that woman all these years. Some of them with the bitch living under her own roof, too. And it had to be doubly tough on her in view of the fact that Wes thought Bobbie Jean practically sprouted wings."

Not quite accurate, of course. I mean, Wes actually had a pretty good fix on his sibling's character; he simply chose to dump all the blame for her flaws on the poor thing's having had such an unfulfilled childhood. Carla's assessment hardly merited a correction, however.

"But you're still certain Allison didn't do it," I put to her. It was half statement, half question.

"That's right. The Lyntons have always

had a great marriage — in spite of Bobbie Jean. And I can't conceive of Allison's murdering the sister Wes was misguided enough to be crazy about. She would never have hurt him like that."

"Then we agree."

I was about to pose another question, but Carla preempted me. "And don't ask me to come up with anyone else who might have wanted Bobbie Jean in her grave, because I can't. I've shot my load."

Well, that ended that.

I did bring up a couple of other matters, though. Had the girl seen anyone entering or leaving the dining room before lunch that day? Well, had she noticed *anything* that was at all suspicious?

As expected, the inquiries produced a "no," followed by a second "no."

After which Carla got to her feet.

"Would you like to hear what I have to look forward to tonight?" she said as we began walking to the door.

"What's that?"

"Informing my mother that a new son-in-law is not in her immediate future. She will positively wallow in self-pity. She'll probably keep me on the phone for hours, too. And are you interested in hearing what I can look forward to tomorrow night?" This time

I had no chance to respond. "Meeting with the Forsythe chief of police and answering the same damn questions I just answered for you."

Standing in the open doorway, I told Carla how much I appreciated her cooperation. And then we said good night. The girl already had one foot in the hall when she spun around to impart a few words of inspiration.

"Life is crap," she muttered.

Then she turned on her heel and was gone.

Chapter 20

There wasn't a speck of onion pie left over — in spite of my denying myself so much as a sliver. But I can't say that I really minded having to rethink my supper menu; I regarded Carla's gluttony as a testimonial to my culinary skills.

Anyway, after considerable deliberation, I decided to stir-fry some of the vegetables sitting on the cocktail table. Which, with the addition of soy sauce and chopped garlic — along with a little of this and a dash of that — turned out to be a pretty tasty dish.

I had no sooner plugged in the coffee when the doorbell rang. It was Harriet from across the hall, and there was a cake box in her hand.

"Steve's in Florida," she announced. "He flew down this morning. It seems Pop's seriously considering remarrying."

"That's great!" I blurted out, a reaction that was completely in my own self-interest. Pop (a.k.a. Gus, a.k.a. "the ball-buster") being Harriet's eighty-plus father-in-law and my sometime suitor — whether I liked it or not. And I didn't like it one bit. "Come in and tell me all about it." I pulled her into the room, practically yanking her arm out in my excitement.

"She's a divorcée," Harriet informed me as soon as she was seated at the kitchen table. "Oh, I almost forgot," she said, handing me the box in front of her. "This was supposed to be Steve's dessert tonight. It's cherry cheese cake. I thought maybe you'd like some."

"I certainly would. Thanks."

I cut us a couple of slices of the cake, then quickly poured two cups of coffee and joined her at the table. "You were saying?"

"Steve's worried sick about his father, Dez. This woman — the divorcée — is more than thirty years younger than he is."

"What, in heaven's name, could she want with Pop?"

Harriet took a sip of the coffee and grimaced. Which didn't hurt my feelings at all, since almost everyone reacts to my coffee that way. And after that she had a couple of bites of the cheese cake, no doubt to erase the taste of the vile brew. "Money," she responded at last.

"Pop has money?"

"No, but Steve thinks that maybe *she* — her name's Gladys — is under the impression that he does. Anyhow, Steve wants to meet the woman and find out what's what."

"That's probably a good idea," I granted grudgingly, concerned that this could lead to Steve's throwing a monkey wrench into this blessed union. And Harriet must have had the same fear. I mean, if the world's most annoying old man became the world's most annoying old *married* man, there was a good possibility that he'd cut down on those frequent — and often prolonged — New York visits of his. Which, I assure you, Harriet didn't look forward to any more than I did.

"Oh, incidentally, I heard from that Forsythe police chief this morning," she said then. "He asked me a million questions." *Probably more like four or five.* "But Steve claims that's pretty much routine. Anyhow, I told the chief I'd never even met the poor woman before. And he seemed to believe me."

"I'm sure he did."

"Have you any idea yet who killed her?"

"Well, I had it narrowed down to four suspects, but now I'm not certain I'm on the right track."

"Would you like my opinion?"

"Sure," I told her, anticipating that Harriet's nomination for perpetrator would be as off the wall as my other neighbor's. Barbara, if you'll recall, had somehow divined that it was Ellen's friend Ginger who'd sent the victim on to her reward.

But Harriet's idea was a little more general — and a lot more apt to be true. "I wouldn't be shocked if it turned out that this Bobbie Jean had been playing around with the wrong woman's husband or lover or something. After all, she was a very sexy-type person, and I imagine men must have found her extremely attractive."

"Apparently they did — at least for a while. None of her three marriages lasted, you know."

"But to have that sort of a hold on men, even if it's only temporary . . ." Harriet smiled wistfully.

I can't say that I didn't share her sentiment. The truth is, though, I found the victim's effect on the male sex somewhat puzzling.

Okay. I was willing to concede that she was fairly good-looking. And that her slim figure included a couple of really outstanding protuberances, which — from what I saw at Ellen's shower — she wasn't too modest to advertise. (Although why men are so obsessed with breasts totally escapes me.) Nevertheless, I really had to marvel at the woman's success with the opposite gender. Listen, there are ladies of my acquaintance with equally impressive fronts — along with a whole bunch of qualities Bobbie Jean evidently lacked — who don't score particularly well with men.

"She certainly was the quintessential femme fatale, wasn't she?" Harriet murmured.

"Let's just say that if she'd ever been able to bottle whatever it was she had, she could have made Bill Gates look like a pauper."

Once Harriet was back across the hall I began to rehash my meeting with Carla Fremont. And I had to concede that as far as advancing the investigation, it had been a complete washout. I tried to give myself a pep talk. Could be that Carla *had* provided an important clue, one that I'd somehow missed. And it could also be that I'd pick up on it when I went over my notes. However, considering that I intended to transcribe the notes tomorrow and study them on Wednesday, at the latest, this was a little hard to buy into. I mean, what were the odds I'd suddenly get smarter by then?

Right after this I began thinking about

how Carla had again been kicked in the head by a man she cared about. The girl was right. Life *was* crap — or, at any rate, what she'd sampled of it so far. But after all, there was —

The telephone interrupted my ruminations. It was close to eleven. Could Nick possibly be calling at this hour?

He couldn't. Or, anyway, he wasn't.

"I hope I didn't wake you," Harriet told me, "but I know you never go to sleep until one." (A slight exaggeration — there have been times when I've made it to bed before midnight, although not that often, I admit.) "Good news. I just heard from Steve, and he said that before he even got down to Florida, Pop had changed his mind about remarrying. In fact, it appears as if my father-in-law and his lady friend might have come to a parting of the ways."

I shivered. And not from the cold, either. "And you consider this *good* news?"

"Don't you? Pop's in circulation again. Not only that, Steve told me he asked about you. He wanted to know if you were still available." Before I could respond, Harriet giggled. "Just kidding, Dez," she assured me, continuing to giggle.

As far as I was concerned, though, this was no subject for levity. (Listen, if — as the result of being cajoled, browbeaten, and emotionally blackmailed by my friend Harriet here — you'd spent as many agonizing hours with her pain-in-the-butt father-in-law as I had, you wouldn't exactly be laughing your head off, either.) In fact, I failed to see what she could find so amusing. I mean, the woman was positively giddy. Then it occurred to me that after entertaining the possibility — however briefly — that Pop would no longer be foisting himself on her all that often, Harriet must have been shaken to the core by Steve's bulletin. In fact, it may have sent her straight to the cooking sherry.

And you know something? Between my lack of progress in solving the murder of Bobbie Jean Morton and the prospect of the dreaded Pop's return to New York, all of a sudden that cooking sherry didn't sound half bad.

Chapter 21

I admit it. I'm as big a busybody as the next one. (Okay, bigger.) Still, being privy to one of Jackie and Derwin's little squabbles is something I'd just as soon avoid.

With my luck the way it was lately, though, when I got to work on Tuesday Jackie was on the phone, lacing into that significant other of hers. I wondered — but only for an instant, maybe — what Derwin's transgression had been *this* week. Well, whatever it was, to put himself in jeopardy so soon after being on the receiving end of that last tongue-lashing I'd overheard, the guy had to be either the bravest or dimmest soul God ever created. Listen, you'd think that he'd have been walking on eggs — at least for a while — wouldn't you?

But maybe he was emboldened because of the way things eventually turned out that other time.

I mean, remember those cheapo theater tickets he'd acquired for that past Saturday night? Well, Jackie had finally agreed to go to the show with him, all the while bitching like crazy that they'd be sitting at least a mile away from the stage. That, however, was nothing compared to the bitching she did once the performance was over. According to Jackie — and she'd really ranted on about it at lunch yesterday — this was one of the worst musicals ever produced on Broadway. It was such a stinker, in fact, that she actually appreciated being so far removed from it. And what did those newspaper critics have for brains, anyhow, giving garbage like that such rave reviews?

At any rate, feeling as she did about the show, she'd let up on Derwin regarding the seats he'd bought. But apparently the man wasn't averse to pushing his luck. Because right now Jackie was screeching — and before I met Jackie I never knew that it was possible to screech in a near-whisper — into the mouthpiece. "What do you mean your dark blue suit? It's a formal wedding, Derwin. *Formal!* And every other man at the affair will be in a tuxedo."

There was a pause, during which Jackie rolled her eyes heavenward. Acknowledging her with a wave, I intended to head for my cubbyhole. But she held up one hand, signifying that I was to wait.

"Listen," she said to Derwin a moment later, "I will not — repeat *not* — be embarrassed in front of all my friends. And that's that." She stopped laying down the law at this point to allow for his rebuttal, after which her voice suddenly took on a deceptively reasonable tone. "You're right, Derwin. I suppose that if you're not comfortable spending the money to rent a tux, it isn't fair of me to try and force you to do it. Besides, even though I'd love for you to come with me, there's no reason I can't go by myself. Charlotte mentioned that they were expecting quite a few unattached people."

And now Jackie leaned back in her chair and let Derwin entangle himself in the net, a smile spreading slowly over her face.

She looked over at me, mouthed "one minute," and then, enormously pleased with herself, went on to wrap up things with Derwin. "Believe me, Derwin, I'm not angry. I told you I — What was that? No, I really wouldn't feel right about it, honestly. I wouldn't want you to — We-ll, if you insist . . . but only if you're sure," she was magnanimous enough to finally agree. "I'll meet you at that rental place on Fifth at twelve thirty, okay?"

Once she and Derwin had said their goodbyes, Jackie remarked tersely, "Men can be such a trial." (Unfortunately, I had no up-to-date information on this subject.) "I just wanted to tell you that your dentist's office called. There was a cancellation, and they can see you on Thursday at four. They asked that you get in touch with them by noon today if you can make it. Want the number?"

"I have it."

"You're not going to call, are you?" she accused.

"No. I can't make it Thursday."

"*Can't* — or won't?"

Well, if Jackie thought she was dealing with another Derwin here, I was about to set her straight. "You decide, why don't you?" I suggested snippily as I flounced down the hall.

The instant my bottom made contact with the desk chair, I rummaged around in my shoulder bag for this crumpled slip of paper I'd dumped in there that morning. Then, after checking the phone number written on it, I lifted the receiver.

But I suppose I'd better backtrack a bit . . .

I had gone to bed at around one A.M. yesterday, thoroughly exhausted. But did this mean I'd been able to sleep? Ha! I kept agonizing over the investigation — and my growing lack of confidence with regard to the outcome. I was engaged in acting out my frustration by pounding the living daylights out of my pillow when it came to me: "Vincent What's-his-name!" The recollection propelled me to a sitting position, and I switched on the light. Getting out of bed, I hurried over to the closet and removed my yellow linen suit, fishing in the pocket for the paper Kathy Marin at Silver Oaks had given me.

I opened it up. DOMINICK GALLO, it read. (Okay, so I'd screwed up a little on the name.) Right below that was the waiter's home telephone number. I smoothed out the paper and laid it on the bureau before returning to bed, where I soon proceeded to inflict another round of abuse on my pillow.

Anyhow, I was presently listening irritably to a recorded telephone message at the Gallo home. "We're away right now," a young female voice was saying. *Must be the man's daughter,* I speculated. "We'll be back on Sunday, August thirty-first. Uh, that's Labor Day weekend," she added for the caller's edification.

Well, it's not that I really *expected* that Dominick Gallo would be spending his free time at home. But then again, not everybody takes off for Pago Pago on their vacation, right? Or even for Coney Island, for that matter. Don't get me wrong, though. While I didn't figure Gallo would prove to be any more of an asset to the case than anyone else at Silver Oaks had been, I couldn't afford *not* to talk to him, particularly with the way things seemed to be shaping up. Which is why I was so ticked off that he wasn't available here and now. Patience, I concede, has never been one of my long suits.

And by the way, I lectured silently — and to no one at all — as I hung up the phone, *that family should be aware that it's not overly clever to announce to the world how long you intend to be gone. I mean, the Gallos were liable to come back to find that somebody had given them a housecleaning they didn't appreciate.*

I spent the rest of the day transcribing my notes. But my output wasn't anywhere near as impressive as it had been on Monday, when my stubby little fingers had moved at a rate of speed that was probably a first for them — and most likely a last, as well. I have a feeling, though, that I'd subconsciously slowed down today. The reason being that I was far from eager to review yesterday's get-together with Carla Fremont.

The thing is, I had little hope that I'd learn anything from a study of that meeting. And having already pretty much dismissed this Dominick Gallo from my mind — he was not only currently out of town, but he was a long shot to begin with — I would then be forced to ask myself the question I most dread having to deal with in an investigation:

Where do I go from here?

Chapter 22

I was not in the best of moods when I got home from the office. And I had no intention of going within five feet of either the refrigerator or the stove that night. So borrowing from Ellen's at-least-three-times-weekly game plan, I called our local Chinese takeout. Unfortunately, Little Dragon is known more for the quantity than for the quality of its food. However, their stuff isn't that bad if you're really hungry — which I was. Anyhow, it was a couple of minutes before seven thirty, and I was just polishing off a humongous combination plate when the phone rang.

"Hello," I said. Or at any rate, that's what I wanted to say, only my mouth was full of fried rice so I don't think it came out that way.

"Er, Desiree?"

I hastily gulped down the rice. "Yes, this is Desiree."

"This is Nick Grainger," the voice informed me unnecessarily. "Uh, I hope I'm not interrupting your supper or anything."

Now, I was all set to tell him that I'd already finished eating. But then something — I later decided it was the Fates — made me bite back the words. "Oh, no," I substituted for the truth, "as a matter of fact, I just got in."

"Listen, I know this is last-minute notice — and I apologize — but until about two minutes ago, when my brother canceled on me, I didn't expect to be free tonight. Since I am, though, I was wondering if there was any possibility of your having dinner with me later."

I hesitated for a split second. After all, as much as I enjoy food — and contrary to what you may have assumed — my stomach is not really expandable. But Nick put his own interpretation on this fleeting moment of indecision.

"Please say you've forgiven me for D'Agostino's, Desiree. I can't believe I behaved so stupidly. I was hoping for the opportunity to prove to you that I'm not as big a jerk as I gave you reason to believe I am."

"All right, I'm willing to reassess you," I responded with this inane little titter.

"Great. I'm still at work — I have a florist shop about six blocks from our mutual apartment building — but I'll be closing in half an hour. I can pick you up in around forty minutes, if that's okay."

"Can you give me an hour?" Then I realized that my apartment could betray me — the place smelled like Eau de Chinese Takeout. "And it's really not necessary that you call for me. Why don't I meet you somewhere?"

"Sure, if you'd rather do that. What kind of food do you prefer?"

Now, the thing is, I didn't see where this made much difference. How was I going to be able to find room for anything anyway? So I foolishly answered, "All kinds. You choose."

"Do you like Chinese?"

Oh, shit! "Yes, I do." I never got a chance to add the "but." Which is probably just as well, because what could I possibly have told the man? "I've had enough Chinese food for one night, thank you very much. However, for the pleasure of your company I'm willing to eat a second supper of another ethnic origin — and stuff myself to the point of explosion." Listen, no matter how I phrased it, that's what it would have boiled down to. And talk about a lease-breaker! I mean, it was enough to induce a guy to relocate to the wilds of New Jersey. At any rate, before I was able to put my foot in it,

Nick named a rather elegant Chinese restaurant about a ten-minute cab ride from my apartment.

"See you in an hour," he confirmed.

"Could we make that an hour and ten minutes?" I said, tacking on the travel time.

"Sure," Nick agreed with a laugh. "Whatever you say."

I don't know how I ever managed to get myself ready that evening. Between my nervousness at finally going on this long-hoped-for date and the fear that I'd gag the instant I looked at anything edible, I was a wreck.

I was so discombobulated that I tripped getting out of the shower, and only a last-minute grab for the towel rack prevented me from flying head first across the bathroom. Plus, my hand was so unsteady that I had to redo my eye makeup twice. But it was either that or show up resembling a cross between an owl and a chipmunk. Even my wig gave me grief that night. And who did it think it was, anyway — my real hair?

I arrived at the restaurant fifteen minutes late — which actually wasn't too bad, all things considered.

The maitre d' ushered me to the booth

where Nick was seated sipping a glass of white wine. And let me tell you, a skinny little fellow with a buck-toothed grin can have the impact of a Mel Gibson on certain members of the female gender. Namely me.

He got to his feet immediately, and I noticed the impeccable fit of his light blue sports jacket. The man was like something out of *GQ*, I thought appreciatively.

He gave me a brief hug. And then, as I slid into the booth: "I hope you're hungry."

"Umm, to be honest, I had a very late lunch." (This being as close to honest as I intended to get.)

"I'm sorry to hear that. The food's really good. But could be you already know that. Have you been here before?"

"No, but I've heard some very really nice things about this place."

"Well, why don't we relax over drinks for a while. Maybe you'll work up an appetite."

I was cringing inside. But I forced a smile. "Maybe," I said.

Chapter 23

Moments after my merlot had been served — Nick was still working on a glass of chardonnay — he said quietly, "I'd like to tell you why I was . . . well, the way I was at D'Agostino's the other night."

"Please," I protested, "that isn't necessary."

"Maybe not for you, but it is for me. I was pretty upset when I ran into you, Desiree. Of course," he put in quickly, "that still didn't give me license to act like such a fool, but I want you to know that I don't normally behave like that — honestly. Less than an hour earlier, though, there was . . . uh . . . I'd had a confrontation with my ex-wife." He reddened. Despite his insistence on going into this, I could see that Nick wasn't any too comfortable discussing his personal life with a virtual stranger.

Nevertheless, I got the idea that he felt compelled to explain further, so I all but tripped over my words in an attempt to cut him off. “I can understand why you might not have been in a very sociable mood.”

He was determined to continue, however, although with obvious reluctance. “It wasn’t the fact of my arguing with Tiffany — our fights are practically legendary.” *What did the man expect from a woman named Tiffany, anyhow?* (And in case you’re thinking what I imagine you might be, there’s a big difference between a Desiree and a Tiffany.) “But this had to do with my son — he’s nine years old,” Nick was saying. “I’d gone to her apartment to pick him up — and for the second week in a row she gave me some cockamamie excuse about why I couldn’t have Derek for the weekend. I was really worried about this being the start of some sort of pattern — you can never be certain with Tiffany. So believe me, Desiree, I wasn’t fit company for anyone that evening.” His smile was forced. “Not even for myself.”

I was groping for something encouraging to say, but at the same time, I was leery of coming across as too Pollyanna-ish. I finally settled for, “Let’s hope you’re wrong — about that being a pattern.”

“Apparently I am — or was. Tiffany called the next day to assure me there would be no problem this weekend.”

“Well, that’s good.”

"Seems that way. But we'll see." And then, anxious now to move off the topic, Nick said hastily, "Tell me about you, though. Somebody mentioned that you're a private detective."

"Word certainly gets around in our building, doesn't it?"

He chuckled. "Don't knock it. Gossip's an important learning tool. Anyhow, what sort of private detecting do you do?"

"You mean do I have a specialty?"

"Yes, *do* you?"

"Uh-uh. I've investigated everything from a missing boa constrictor to murder. Although lately murder has taken a big lead over my boa constrictor-type cases."

"Are you conducting a murder investigation now?"

"As a matter of fact, I am."

"I'd like to hear about it."

Well, since he appeared to be genuinely interested, I went into a very sketchy recitation about Bobbie Jean and the four shower attendees who utterly despised her.

"So?" Nick put to me when I'd finished.

I looked at him, puzzled.

"So which of them do you believe poisoned her?"

"I'm beginning to think that none of them did."

At this point the headwaiter stopped at the table to ask if we were ready to see the menu yet.

Nick left it to me. "Desiree?"

"Sure," I said valiantly. I mean, sooner or later I had to bite the bullet, right?

The wine helped. Only not enough. Probably because, as usual, I was limiting myself to just one glass. Anything more than that and there was a good possibility I'd wind up sliding under the table. Actually, I'm exaggerating. But after that first glass of wine I have a tendency to slur my words a bit — something I wasn't too keen on demonstrating this evening.

Still, by the time my shrimp with black bean sauce arrived (I'd begged off any appetizers), I was able to look straight at the little buggers without blanching. And almost immediately I resorted to this strategy I have for dealing with situations like this. (A strategy, incidentally, that I rarely find the need to press into service.) Here's how it works. First I start moving my food around the plate with such apparent zest that nobody seems to notice how few trips the fork makes to my mouth. Then later, at the appropriate moment, I casually drop my napkin over the plate, concealing what remains of the dinner. Which tonight would consist of practically the entire meal — everything but two or three mushroom slices, a couple of chunks of green pepper, and a single shrimp.

At any rate, over our entrees, Nick informed me that he'd been the sole owner of his Lexington Avenue florist shop for close to eleven years, having bought out his former partner: his father.

"That has to be the best profession — working with flowers all day long."

"I have to admit that I'm kinda partial to it," he affirmed.

I asked what the shop was called.

"Oh, don't worry, my dad and I came up with something extremely creative: Grainger's."

"That does have a ring to it. Tell me, what's your favorite flower?" I put to him.

This gave Nick pause. "You know, Desiree, I can't even remember the last time anyone asked me that. And the truth is, I don't really have an answer for you. Naturally, it would be practically un-American not to love roses, and they *are* among my favorites, particularly tea roses. But I'm partial to camellias, as well. Also irises — I love irises. And in the fall, I always feel that chrysanthemums lend a kind of exuberance to the season. And there's —"

I held up my hand. "Stop!" I said laughing. "I suppose it would have been a lot easier on you if I'd asked for your *least* favorite flower."

"No doubt. How about you, Desiree, any special preferences?"

Now, I wanted to avoid being specific. After all, with Nick a florist, whatever I said could be taken as a hint. Of course, this was just plain silly. I mean, I wasn't *volunteering* the information; I'd been *asked.* Nevertheless, I responded, "I suppose I'm like you; my taste is pretty eclectic."

We got into a discussion about movies during dessert — and by that point I was actually up to handling my chocolate-and-vanilla ice cream, mixed (which I very diligently mushed up the way I like it). Later on we covered our hobbies, our childhood traumas, and our least-liked celebrities.

I don't know how long we sat there talking after the dishes had been removed from the table, but eventually I developed this feeling that the headwaiter was giving us the fish-eye. And I shared this impression with Nick.

"Harold always looks that way," he assured me.

Nevertheless, we headed for home within minutes.

* * *

Nick got off at my floor to see me to my apartment. And standing there in the hall, we told each other what a lovely evening we'd had. Then he gave me a slightly more prolonged hug than he had when he'd greeted me, said he'd call soon, and headed for the elevator.

Once inside, I leaned against the door and smiled — insipidly, I'm sure. Nick Grainger had turned out to be every bit as nice as I'd hoped he'd be. I mean, forget his appearance. It was possible I'd respond to the man even if he were good-looking.

Anyway, I finally abandoned my reverie and walked into the living room. The red light on the answering machine was flickering.

Nonchalantly, I pressed the button.

Then, with a mixture of incredulity and fear, I listened to the message that would catapult my investigation into a crisis mode.

Chapter 24

"The police paid me a surprise visit this afternoon," Allison stated in a flat, unemotional voice. "And I'd like to talk to you about it. Please don't call me back. I wouldn't want Wes to learn anything about this. I'll phone you again in the morning." And then, almost as an afterthought: "It seems that I've become the favorite in the 'Who Killed Bobbie Jean?' sweepstakes."

Allison Lynton a murderer? I had to play the message again; I just couldn't believe I'd heard what I heard.

It's funny. When I'm really upset about something I either throw myself all over the bed — often until dawn — or I conk out at once. This latter reaction, I suppose, being a handy little escape mechanism my subconscious keeps in reserve. Anyhow, in this instance I made one of my express trips to dreamland. I mean, I fell asleep so quickly I don't even remember laying my head on the pillow.

It was just before seven thirty when I awoke on Wednesday. In anticipation of Allison's call, I made a beeline for the kitchen and put on the coffee to ensure that I'd be fully conscious when we spoke. She phoned at twenty to eight. "Ohh, Desiree. I'm so relieved to find you in. I was concerned that you might already have left for work." *At this hour? Fat chance!* I thought, while almost simultaneously noting that Allison sounded a whole lot more animated than she had last night. In fact, I could detect a note of anxiety in her tone.

"What's happened, Allison?"

"Chief Porchow and that other officer — Sergeant Block — were here yesterday. The police . . . uh . . . discovered something that leads them to look upon me as a very viable suspect in my sister-in-law's poisoning."

Discovered something? My mouth went so dry that I could barely get the words out. "What was that?"

"I believe it would be better if we discussed this face-to-face."

"I agree. I'll drive up to Greenwich this morning, if that's okay with you."

"I'd just as soon come to New York. I could be at your office by ten, ten thirty. All right?"

"Fine."

Now, consider that I'd grown genuinely fond of Allison Lynton. Then factor in that I am by nature extremely inquisitive — nosy, if you insist. And you can understand why the two-plus hours that followed were among the longest I'd ever spent.

Allison was wearing a cotton sheath in a shade of green that was almost identical to the color of her eyes. Her silver hair was pulled back into an elegant French twist, as it had been on the few previous occasions I'd spent in her company. And, as usual, she had applied her makeup both sparingly and effectively. The cool, confident appearance she presented, however, was precisely that: an *appearance.*

The instant she sat down on the other side of my desk, she began to fidget, distractedly drumming her fingers on her right thigh.

"How about some coffee?" I suggested.

"Thanks, but I've already had three cups today. If you don't mind, I'd really like to get started."

"Whatever you say."

But regardless of her intention, Allison sat there for I don't know how long without uttering a word. I had pretty much made up my mind that a bit of prompting might be in order when she ended the silence.

"You're aware of Wes's devotion to Bobbie Jean, so I'm certain you can appreciate that she would have been a fairly constant source of friction between us. In fact, our squabbles with regard to my sister-in-law date all the way back to our engagement days. Even when she was living abroad, some point of dissension involving Bobbie Jean always seemed to crop up. In spite of this, however, my husband and I managed to keep our conflicting opinions about her from causing any serious damage to our marriage. Which, when you consider it, has to be viewed as something of a miracle.

"This past winter, though, something occurred that I was just unable to deal with. Call it the straw that broke Allison Lynton's back." She eked out a short laugh. "I believe I mentioned to you that Bobbie Jean and Geoffrey — her last husband — were in the midst of a trial separation when he had his fatal heart attack?" She was looking to me for confirmation.

"Yes, you did."

"Well, the truth is, Bobbie Jean was hardly lonely being apart from her husband. Although she supposedly hoped to reconcile with him, she kept herself from becoming too despondent over the estrangement by taking up with other men, one of whom was a neighbor of ours — a *married* neighbor.

"Before long, news of the affair got back to Wes and me. And predictably, as disturbed as he was by Bobbie Jean's latest . . . lapse, Wes invented a rationale for it. This time the culprit was the trial separation. According to her devoted brother, Bobbie Jean was searching for proof that men continued to find her irresistible — ergo, Geoff still cared for her." Allison made a face. "In other words, Wes's reasoning had it that she was sleeping with Harry — our neighbor — to convince herself that Geoffrey would soon be eagerly returning to her. *Please!*"

"I'm assuming that she was in love with the man — her husband, I mean."

"I couldn't say. My personal opinion is that she was not, that she never had been, actually. I'm not at all convinced that she was even that keen to have him move back in with her. Knowing Bobbie Jean as I did, I believe she just wanted Geoff to want her again."

Allison placed her hands in her lap now and moistened her lower lip with her tongue. "At any rate, with that episode I'd simply reached my limit. Sister or not, I couldn't bear listening to Wes explain away that woman's abhorrent behavior even one more time. I told him so, too — and none too gently, either. The result was that a definite rift developed between us."

She took a deep breath before going on. "Shortly after this, I ran into a friend who mentioned that Justin, an old high school beau of mine, had lost his wife eight months earlier. Justin and I had kept in sporadic touch over the years — although I hadn't heard anything from him in quite a while. Well, I sent him a note telling him that I'd only recently learned of his wife's death and extending my condolences. He called to thank me for writing, and we had a long talk. Nothing of a very personal nature — primarily we just did some catching up. And then Justin proposed that we have lunch one day. Naturally, this wasn't wise, the state of my relationship with Wes being what it was. But the state of the relationship was also the very reason I agreed to meet with Justin — if this makes any sense to you."

"It makes perfect sense," I told her.

Allison spoke slowly now, and with obvious pain. "Regardless of my vulnerable emotional condition, however, I never intended that our reunion would go beyond that one lunch, Desiree. But it did. There were more lunches, and eventually —" She broke off, unable to continue.

I pressed her. "Eventually?"

"We . . . we . . ." She reached in her purse for a tissue and dabbed at her eyes.

"Eventually you became intimate?" I provided gently.

"Yes, but only once," Allison acknowledged in a tremulous voice. "Of course, even once was too often. And it's not as if I were in love with Justin — I don't even find him particularly attractive. I can't understand how I could have betrayed Wes like that. And for what? For being a loyal brother?"

Okay, go ahead; call me a self-righteous prig. But I don't happen to be a big fan of adultery. What's more, as far as I know, it's never proved a cure-all for a troubled marriage. Nevertheless, I could conceive of how Allison might have gotten involved with her former sweetheart in an effort to escape from her marital problems — even if only temporarily. Besides, the woman hardly needed a lecture on morals from me, especially then. "Don't be too tough on yourself, Allison," I said in my most sympathetic tone. "With the sort of tension you were under, it's not too difficult to imagine how something like that might occur."

"Thank you, Desiree, but you don't have to make excuses for me. No one is more aware than I that there *is* no excuse. And the saddest part of all this is that I absolutely adore my husband. And I always have."

I was puzzled as to where this was heading. So after a minute or so, I put to her, "And your relationship with Justin somehow resulted in the police calling on you yesterday?"

"I was about to explain. I have no idea how, but Bobbie Jean discovered that Justin and I had been . . . uh . . . together. Or at least this is what I believed at the time. In retrospect I realize there's a strong likelihood that she was merely fishing. Someone might have spotted the two of us having lunch and mentioned it to her. I certainly wouldn't put it past my sister-in-law to pretend to know more than she actually did in order to trick me into an admission." Allison shook her head ruefully. "If so, she succeeded."

"She confronted you, I gather."

"Yes, two or three weeks after I'd broken it off with Justin. Wes and I were more or less back to normal by then — or, considering what I'd done, as normal as we can ever be again. I pleaded with Bobbie Jean not to say anything to him, if not for my sake then because of the pain it would cause him if he were to learn that I'd been with another man."

"What was Bobbie Jean's response?"

"At first she wouldn't give me any indication as to whether or not she planned on going to Wes with what she'd found out. She just asked how it felt to have *her* sit in judgment of *me*, for a change. She appeared to consider this reversal of positions some sort of divine retribution. Then she said that she'd have to devote some thought to her intentions. She was leaving for Hawaii the next morning and would be gone for two weeks. She'd let me know her decision when she came home, she said.

"Well, unfortunately — *very* unfortunately, as it has turned out — I wouldn't allow myself to simply sit around and wait. I wrote Bobbie Jean a letter to the effect that I'd never been unfaithful to Wes before and, more important, that I never would be again. I also made another attempt to impress upon her that telling him about Justin and me was the surest way to break his heart.

"At any rate, when she returned from her trip, Bobbie Jean announced that she'd reached the conclusion that it was best to let the matter drop. And until yesterday, I was under the impression that that was the end of it. Apparently, however, she'd kept my letter in the event she changed her mind. Or perhaps to hold over me the next time my attitude was what she might regard as holier-than-thou. There's even an outside possibility that she forgot its existence, since it was very soon after Bobbie Jean's Hawaiian vacation that Geoffrey died."

I gulped. "And the police got their hands on that letter?"

"Yes. They were at Bobbie Jean's, looking through her things to see if there might be something there that could shed some light on her murder." And then, dryly: "Apparently they feel that the search was worthwhile."

"Just what did they say to you?"

"Chief Porchow told me that it was obvious Bobbie Jean had been threatening to acquaint her brother with what he referred to as my "indiscretion.' And I informed him that she'd agreed to keep my secret months ago. He said that this was probably true. But then he very pointedly asked why I supposed she'd been holding on to the letter like that."

"And?"

"I insisted that I hadn't a clue, that I was astonished it had still been in her possession. But Porchow appeared to be extremely skeptical. He has this misguided theory that I'd been fearful Bobbie Jean would renege on her promise to me, even suggesting that

I'd had some advance knowledge that she was planning to go back on her word." Allison tried hard to paste a smile on her lips, but she wasn't quite able to pull it off. "I guess things don't look too good for me, do they?"

"I wouldn't say that. All the police have on you is a *possible* motive. And trust me, that's hardly something they can take into court."

"I can only pray that you're right," she responded quietly. "Do you have any idea yet who *did* kill Bobbie Jean?"

"No, not yet."

"Oh."

You can't imagine the amount of dejection that was packed into this one little word. And it shot through my mind that Allison was either totally convinced that the poisoner was someone other than one of her four buddies or that, given her present circumstances, she didn't much care *who* it was at this point.

"Listen, I'll just have to light a fire under myself and solve this thing in a hurry, won't I?" I said, hoping that I at least *sounded* optimistic. "Tell me, how did your session with the police end?"

"The chief informed me that they'd be in touch."

"And Wes knows nothing about the visit?"

"He was at the office when the police showed up at the house. But perhaps I ought to talk to him about . . . about all of this before somebody else does. Do you think I should, Desiree?" Allison looked as though the last thing in the world she wanted from me was a yes.

Nevertheless, she'd asked for my opinion. "Umm, I guess that might be wise."

"The problem is, I'm not at all certain that I have the courage to tell Wes that I betrayed him. It took hours before I was even able to force myself to contact you about . . . the situation." She managed a crooked grin. "And there's not even any danger of your asking for a divorce."

After this, for what seemed like a long while — but was probably not much more than a minute or two — neither of us said anything. Then Allison murmured, her eyes filling up, "God, Desiree, what will I do if I lose him?"

And now Ellen's almost-mother-in-law put her hands over her face and wept.

Chapter 25

What a mess!

Once my visitor left, I kept myself occupied for the longest while by staring unseeingly into space and, in the process, managed to furnish myself with a queen-size headache.

In spite of all my attempts at reassurance — reiterated even when she was halfway out of the door — I hadn't succeeded in totally convincing Allison Lynton that she had nothing to fear from the police.

I didn't blame her, either. The truth is, I hadn't been able to convince myself.

Not that I considered for a single second the possibility that Porchow and company might be on the right track. (Although why I was so sure that Allison didn't dispose of her sister-in-law I couldn't tell you. Maybe it was because she was Mike's mother, and any mother of the man who was going to marry my niece just wouldn't do a thing like that.)

However, there *was* reason to be concerned.

I had to concede that the fact that she was being viewed as the prime suspect in Bobbie Jean's death wasn't completely without merit. After all, to my knowledge, Allison was the only one present that Sunday with an alleged motive for the murder that didn't date back a hundred years. And while this alone was hardly enough to get the woman dragged off to jail in handcuffs, there was always the chance that something unexpected could crop up to incriminate her further.

For instance, suppose that someone should suddenly (and mistakenly) remember spotting her sneaking into the dining room at the crucial time. The thing is, while Allison and I had been practically joined at the hip that afternoon, she did make a short trip to the ladies' room ten or fifteen minutes before lunch was served. It was even conceivable that another someone had noticed her walking down that hall — which, if you'll recall, also led to the dining room's side entrance.

Obviously, as certain as I was that Allison had as much to do with poisoning Bobbie Jean as I did, I couldn't afford to simply ignore the brand-new status the police had bestowed upon her. Listen — and the thought of this practically made my head explode — it wouldn't be the first time an innocent person had been brought to trial — and even convicted.

Clearly I'd have to work a lot harder — and pray for a sudden infusion of smarts — to ensure that this didn't happen.

It required two Extra-Strength Tylenols — and about fifteen minutes to allow them to take effect — before I was in any condition to transcribe the remainder of my notes on Carla Fremont. And then an hour and a quick sandwich at my desk after this, I began to review Monday night's interview with her.

But in spite of my resolve, I didn't make much headway. Concerns about the Lynton marriage wormed their way into my head — which they had absolutely no business doing. I mean, I should have been concentrating on the murder, not the couple's relationship. Still, I debated with myself as to whether Allison would summon the courage to tell Wes about that brief fling of hers — before he heard it from someone else.

I'd no sooner pushed this topic from my mind, than all these questions about Nick replaced it: (*1*) *How long had he and this Tiffany person been married?* (2) *Why had they split up? (3) Was Nick as devoted a father as he appeared to be? (4) Was his son a nice little boy? (5) Forget (1) through (4). Could I count on Nick's calling me again?*

My concentration being what it was that day, at just past four thirty I threw in the towel and shoved the Bobbie Jean Morton file in my attaché case. Not much more than a half hour later I was home — listening to another unsettling message on the answering machine.

"This is Chief Porchow. Please give me a call as soon as possible."

Before I had time to fret about his purpose in contacting me, I picked up the receiver and dialed the number he'd left.

"Ah, Ms. Shapiro, I appreciate your getting back to me so promptly," he said. "There are one or two matters I neglected to go over with you when we spoke the other evening, and I wonder if I might stop by to see you tonight."

Uh-oh. I was 99.9 percent positive of the reason he wanted to interrogate me, and I wasn't all that anxious to supply him with any answers. "I guess so," I agreed none too cordially. "That is, if you don't think we can do this on the phone." I already knew how he'd respond, but what the hell, it was worth a try.

Porchow's voice was firm. "It would be preferable if we could sit down and talk."

Well, like I said, it was worth a try.

It had been arranged that Chief Porchow would be at my apartment around eight. But it was a few minutes after nine when he finally put in an appearance, his dour sidekick, Sergeant Block, two paces behind him.

"Sorry, Ms. Shapiro," the chief told me, "we had a crisis of sorts this evening."

"No problem," I assured him. Actually, though, there *was* a problem. Before cutting out of the office, I'd solemnly vowed to study my notes tonight. But now it looked as if I'd have to break my word to myself. I mean, the later these men left, the less alert I'd be. And Lord knows, whatever meager faculties I possess were going to have to be in top working order if there was the slightest hope of my making progress with this case.

At any rate, the two policemen seated themselves like bookends at opposite ends of the sofa. "Can I get you something to drink? A cup of coffee, maybe?" I inquired. (True, my brew is rarely well received, but recently a number of people — well, one, anyway — told me it wasn't really that terrible.)

"I'd love some coffee," the chief said, immediately following which he held up his palm. "On second thought, I'd better not. I've already had five cups today." The gods must have been smiling down on that guy is all I can say.

"Likewise," the sergeant grunted, the gods evidently, extending their largess to him.

I plopped down on one of the club chairs facing them, steeling myself for the worst. Still, as he was flipping open his notebook, I noticed again how attractive Porchow was. He had such strong, even features. And from this close range I was able to appreciate his eyes, which were a beautiful blue-green. Aside from his physical attributes, though, from my limited experience with the man, I'd formed the impression that he hadn't been short-changed when it came to gray matter, either. *You know,* I apprised myself, *he'd be nice for Barbara.* (As in Barbara who lives in the next apartment.)

Looking over at his left hand, I checked out that all-important finger. Naked. *Hey, this shows promise.*

It was at that moment that Chief Porchow began his questioning, forcing me out of my matchmaking mode. "Tell me, Ms. Shapiro, how well do you know Ms. Lynton — the victim's sister-in-law?"

"Not very. But enough to recognize what a lovely person she is."

Ignoring the testimonial, he glanced down at his notebook and traced some of the data with his finger. "Her son is engaged to your niece."

"Yes, that's how we came to meet."

"You weren't acquainted prior to that — not even casually?" he asked.

"Nope. I'd never even set eyes on her until Ellen and Mike became serious."

"Still, I assume you've been in her company on a number of occasions since then."

"A few."

"I was told that Ms. Lynton and the deceased didn't get along."

"I don't believe they were very close, if that's what you mean," I responded evasively.

"I imagine that with the sisters-in-law having a less than friendly relationship, there must have been some sort of negative rub-off on the Lynton marriage."

"I couldn't say."

And now the seconds seemed to drag by slowly, almost interminably. And in spite of the admirable performance of my brand-new air conditioner, I became conscious of the perspiration that had been building up on the back of my neck and behind my knees. Finally, his tone somewhat hesitant, the chief declared, "Er, there's a possibility that the murdered woman had been threatening Ms. Lynton."

"Threatening her?"

"I won't go into any of the specifics, but we have it on fairly reliable authority that Ms. Morton may have been about to reveal something that Ms. Lynton preferred remain a private matter. Are you aware of anything like that?" Well, I'd say this for him: He was certainly being circumspect about Allison's affair. (Barbara could be getting herself a real gem here.)

"I don't know a thing about any threat." Then, for good measure, I elaborated with, "Or anything Mrs. Lynton might have been threatened *about*." I mean, while I do try to avoid telling an out-and-out lie, I wasn't going to help the police build a case against an innocent person. Besides, it wasn't as if I were under oath or anything.

Porchow frowned. "Let me ask you something else, then. We're trying to determine, as accurately as possible under the circumstances, the movements of all the shower guests before the group went in to lunch." (They were trying to determine the movements of *all* the guests, my patootie.) "Ms. Lynton claims the two of you were together from the time you arrived at Silver Oaks until you both entered the dining room. Is that correct?"

Again, I felt that I had no choice. "Yes." I made it a pretty loud "yes," too, to give it more weight.

"Ms. Lynton wasn't out of your sight even for a few minutes?"

"No, she wasn't."

"Neither of you went to the powder room?" he persisted.

"No."

Looking none too pleased at having come up empty (a feeling I am all too familiar with), the chief smoothed out a nonexistent wrinkle in his pants. "I see," he muttered. "Well, at any rate, thanks for your time." He handed me his card. "In the event you think of anything you want to share with us."

And now he and that chatterbox Block rose simultaneously.

Showing them to the door, I slipped on my matchmaking hat again. First I made a mini production out of checking my watch. Then, as we stood on the threshold, I commented nonchalantly to Porchow, "These hours of yours must get your wife crazy. My late husband was on the force for a while, so I can empathize."

"That's one problem I don't have."

Which told me zilch. "Does this mean that your wife is really understanding — or that you're single and available?" My hand flew to my mouth. I couldn't even believe what had just come out of it!

Apparently that made two of us. Porchow's jaw seemed to go slack, and he was slow to formulate his response. "Uh, you're a very charming lady, Ms. Shapiro," he said, turning a deep shade of pink. "But I'm engaged to be married in October."

Chapter 26

The next morning the phone rang at a few minutes past nine thirty, just as I was securing the door behind me.

Leaving my keys dangling from the lock, I rushed back into the apartment, grabbing the receiver on the third ring.

"This is Wesley Lynton." It took a moment before I translated the "Wesley" into "Wes." Which I admit wasn't terribly swift of me. "I telephoned your office, and your secretary suggested that I might still be able to reach you at home." There was a sense of urgency in his voice.

"Is everything all right?"

Wes's laugh was heavy with irony. "I suppose that depends on what you mean by 'all right.' Listen, Desiree, it's extremely important that I see you. Would it be possible for you to meet with me today? I could be at your office at noon, provided, of course, that you have nothing else on your calendar for then." And smack on the heels of this, evidently feeling that some amplification might be in order, he added, "I'll arrange for one of my partners to see whatever patients I'm not able to reschedule."

To his obvious relief, I told him I'd be available whenever he could make it in to the city.

"That's good, very good. Thank you," he mumbled. "Uh, just one more thing. I would appreciate it if you didn't mention my call — or the matters we'll be discussing this afternoon — to anyone. I don't even want Allison or Mike to know about this. Agreed?"

Well, I wasn't anxious to commit myself like that. I mean, what if it turned out that Allison and/or Mike *should* be aware of what he had to say? But the man sounded so distressed that I didn't feel I had any option. "Agreed."

As I'd feared, I was too tired after Porchow and Block left the apartment last night to tackle Bobbie Jean's folder. But I figured I'd be able to put in some study time before Wes arrived. What I hadn't figured was that Jackie would have other plans for me.

She waylaid me as soon as I got to work. "You have to do me a favor."

"What's that?"

"You know that wedding Derwin and I are attending in a couple of weeks? Well, as soon as I received the invitation I went out and bought a gown — it's a formal affair. But then last night I tried it on for my neighbor Rochelle. She kept assuring me that she liked the dress, but I could tell by her face that she was just trying to be nice. And to be honest, Dez, all of a sudden I wasn't too crazy about it, either."

"Maybe you just —"

Jackie's scowl made it clear that she resented the interruption. "Anyhow, Rochelle told me that if I was unhappy with the gown, she'd be glad to lend me one of hers. Also, I have something else of my own that I could wear. It's old, but nobody has to know that, right? I'd really like you to see all three of them on me and give me your opinion."

"Be glad to. You can model them for me after work."

"You don't understand. We have to do this before lunch. If you don't absolutely *love* any of them, I'm going up to Bloomie's at noon and see if I can find a dress there."

"Gee, I —"

"Please, Dezee dear?"

"Dezee dear?" That was a new one on me. And it made me want to gag, too.

"The ladies' room in five minutes?" Even Jackie's eyes were pleading with me now.

"Make it ten," I said resignedly.

When we reconvened in the powder room, Jackie had already slipped into one of the gowns in contention — a navy silk sheath with spaghetti straps — and was frowning at herself in the full-length mirror.

"So what's the verdict?" she demanded.

"Is that the dress you bought recently?" I was stalling for time while I tried to come up with a tactful way of offering my critique.

"No, this is Rochelle's." She screwed up her face. "I look pretty awful in it, don't I?"

Well, Jackie is fairly large-boned. And as I recalled from the couple of occasions when she'd had both Rochelle and me up to her apartment, there was a bit more of her than there was of this neighbor lady. Which would account for the gown's pulling across Jackie's stomach and straining at her ample hips. (I won't even talk about how it cupped her tush.) At any rate, I finally came out with, "I wouldn't say that" — although it was certainly the truth — "but I think you should be able to do better."

She was already wriggling out of the thing and heading for one of the stalls as I spoke.

She emerged in a two-piece peach number

— also silk — that I recognized instantly, having been with her when she bought it at Lord & Taylor several years back. I'd loved it on her then, and I still did. It was a perfect fit. Plus, the color did really nice things for her complexion and blondish-brown hair.

"You look sensational in this," I enthused. "Why would you have even bothered to shop for anything else?"

Jackie wasn't persuaded. "Do you really think so?"

"Absolutely."

"Why don't I try on the new dress anyway, so we can compare." She was back in the stall before I could respond.

The third gown was a lavender moiré that just sort of hung on her. "I'm crazy about the color, aren't you?" At the mirror now, Jackie's head was at an almost impossible angle as she struggled to catch a rear view of herself.

"It's a lovely shade," I conceded.

"But — ? I can tell there's a 'but.' "

"But peach is every bit as becoming to you, Jackie, and the style's so much more flattering."

"I suppose you're right." But she still sounded doubtful.

I checked my watch: eleven thirty. "If you don't wear the peach, you're out of your mind," I proclaimed, before scooting out of there.

After all, I had a homicide to wrestle with. And I could probably still get in a half hour of work if I was lucky.

As it happened, I wasn't — lucky, I mean. Not in that regard, at least. I returned to my cubbyhole to learn that Wes was already in the reception area, impatient to supply me with the kind of information that would, once again, lead me to view this case in an entirely new light.

Chapter 27

Wes, I decided, looked even worse than he'd sounded. Worse, in fact, than when I'd seen him at the funeral home. There was a tic in his left cheek that I didn't remember being there before. His eyes, which appeared to have sunk further into his head, were watery and bloodshot. And the aristocratic face was only one shade removed from chalk white.

He was seated across the desk from me now, and I'd just apologized for keeping him waiting. "Something came up, something that required my immediate attention." (I omitted, of course, that this "something" was a fashion consultation.) "And I didn't expect you until noon," I reminded him.

"Yes, I realize that, and it's perfectly all right. I'm just thankful you're able to meet with me today."

"What's the matter, Wes?"

"I won't beat around the bush. It's Allison. I've become aware that not too long ago she'd . . . she'd been seeing another man."

"Oh," I said, striving to register at least mild surprise.

"You don't have to pretend to know nothing about this. Allison told me she was here yesterday and that she'd confided in you about . . . everything."

I could feel my face getting warm; I was probably turning red now. God, I hate that! "And she, uh, talked to you about the . . . uh . . . the situation?"

"She did. Although I'm not certain she would have if I hadn't confronted her. Since Tuesday evening, however, she'd been acting very unlike her usual self: agitated, jumpy — I even had the impression that she was frightened of something. But when I originally tried to find out what was upsetting her — this was on Tuesday — I wasn't successful. She attributed her state of mind to some sort of reaction to my sister's murder, maintaining that the longer we remained in the dark as to the identity of Bobbie Jean's killer, the more unnerved she seemed to get. Things came to a head last night, however, when I returned from the office and found her in our bedroom, crying her eyes out.

"Well, to keep this narrative from being any longer than it has to be, I urged Allison to tell me what was *really* troubling her. And she finally did."

My heart went out to Wes. But I didn't have the slightest idea how to respond to this, so I just sat there like an idiot, waiting for him to go on.

"I won't insult your intelligence, Desiree, by claiming that my wife's involvement with somebody else is easy for me to accept."

I opened my mouth to protest that Allison had never been *involved* with the man. Not in the true sense of the word. But then I thought better of it.

"It's not that I absolve myself of any responsibility," Wes continued thoughtfully. "My sister was very dear to me, and I had a tendency to try to find a modicum of justification for her actions, although at times it's quite probable that none existed. Well, Allison often took exception to this. And understandably so, too," he was quick to add. "At any rate, the friction between us over my persistent defense of Bobbie Jean's behavior finally escalated to the point where Allison could no longer tolerate the situation. And this led to . . . well, you already know what it led to. I'll tell you something, Desiree. When she admitted to being intimate with this fellow Justin, I had an almost uncontrollable desire to put my fist through the wall. I still do. But I love my wife — that hasn't changed. And I'm hoping we can work our way through our problems." Evidently recognizing now that he'd revealed more of his feelings than he'd intended to, Wes pressed his lips together and shook his head. "I'm digressing," he muttered. "What brought me here to see you is this ridiculous theory the police have evidently latched onto: that Allison is culpable in Bobbie Jean's death."

He fastened his gaze on me. "I'm quite sure I already know the answer, but why do you think my wife's . . . indiscretion . . . along with the letter she wrote, of course, suddenly caused her to emerge as suspect number one?"

"It appears to be because her seeming motive for doing away with Bobbie Jean is of recent origin."

"That's how I have it figured, too. But what would you say if I told you that she isn't the only one whose motive doesn't date way back?"

"I'd say that I'm anxious to hear the rest of this."

"And you're about to. Let's start with the Fremonts, Desiree. I understand they're alleging that Carla and her boyfriend called it quits only this past weekend. Not true. The breakup was two weeks *prior* to the shower. And why would they lie?" It was obviously a rhetorical question, because Wes hurried on. "So it would appear that at the time of the murder everything was rosy between Carla and this beau of hers."

"And if that *had been* the case," I summed up, "it would be highly improbable that either Carla or Robin would have been in a homicidal frame of mind that day."

"Precisely. According to Allison, Carla never got over Roy — not completely. But she finally did find someone else, and things seemed to be going well for her at last. Allison and I were very happy about that, and Robin was almost delirious. Now that they've split up, however, it wouldn't surprise me if Carla — and by the same token, her mother — reverted to blaming Bobbie Jean for the girl's not having a man that she cared about in her life."

I wanted to say that Bobbie Jean deserved the blame — or anyhow a good portion of it. I mean, if she hadn't taken up with Roy in the first place, Carla wouldn't have had any need to replace him — and been in a position to have her heart trampled on all over again. But with a little effort I managed to keep my mouth shut. Wes had suffered quite enough lately without my sticking it to him like that.

"So you see," he said, a new intensity in his voice, "the Fremonts had what could be regarded as a *very* recent motive for killing my sister. And they're not the only ones. It wasn't that far in the past that Lorraine Corwin had a wrenching disappointment to deal with, for which it's likely she also holds Bobbie Jean responsible."

"I assume that this had nothing to do with losing her fiancé to Bobbie Jean."

"I suppose I'd have to say that the two matters are interconnected. You see, what the fiancé never learned was that Lorraine was pregnant when he left her for Bobbie Jean — Lorraine herself wasn't aware of it at that point. At any rate, she went ahead and had the baby, subsequently giving him up for adoption. Well, a number of years later she attempted to contact the boy. But apparently the adoptive family had moved out of state somewhere or perhaps out of the country — I'm not certain of the details — and she was unable to locate him. Then about three years back she became positively obsessed with this desire to see her son again. I'm not a psychiatrist, Desiree, but Lorraine had just entered menopause, and I believe the realization that this was the end of her capacity to bear children might have contributed to her obsession. To continue, though . . . It took quite some time, but a private detective she hired eventually found the son living in Idaho — he's a young man now, of course, and he has children of his own. Sadly, however, the fellow absolutely refused to see her. It put Lorraine into a deep state of depression — even causing her to leave her job."

"And then a year and a half ago, she pulled up stakes and came back east," I remarked.

"That's right. Ostensibly to make a new start."

" 'Ostensibly?' " I echoed.

"I don't consider it too far-fetched to speculate that this failure to initiate any sort of meeting with her only child might have revitalized Lorraine's old hatred for Bobbie Jean. After all, if she and her fiancé had remained together, they would have raised the boy themselves. I think we'd be remiss in not considering the possibility that Lorraine either moved here specifically to murder my sister or took advantage of the opportunity when it arose."

"You're right," I agreed.

"And recently little Grace Banner, too, had something additional to lay on my sister's doorstep. I assume you've been advised of her husband's failure to land a position equal to the one he held before entering into that partnership with Bobbie Jean."

"Yes, Grace told me about all of that. She said that Karl's employment difficulties were a result of Bobbie Jean's charging them with fraud."

"I suppose that's true enough," Wes conceded unhappily. "I'd venture to say, however, that there was something Grace didn't tell you. This winter Karl was found to have developed cardiac arrhythmia, although fortunately not too serious a case — not as yet, anyhow. His doctors feel that his condition is very likely stress-related. Now, I don't deny that this stress *might* be attributed, at least in part, to the reversals in the fellow's professional life — I understand that he views his present job in particular as well beneath his talents. But I'll wager Grace hasn't the slightest doubt that her husband's illness stems directly from that unfortunate partnership of a decade ago."

"Tell me something. Do *you* believe the Banners were guilty of fraud?"

"No, I don't. But I believe Bobbie Jean honestly thought they were. Not that this excuses her — she should have made sure of her facts before leveling that sort of an accusation. But her actions were prompted by extremely poor judgment, Desiree — and not by malice, as many people seem to think."

"I'm confused," I declared then. "Allison had to be aware of her friends' latest troubles. I mean, I'm taking it for granted that she's the one who kept you informed. Am I right?"

"You are — with one exception. But I'll explain about that in a moment. The only thing she didn't mention to me was the extent to which those women held my sister responsible."

"She didn't say a word about any of this when she came to see me yesterday, though. And obviously she wasn't any more inclined to enlighten Chief Porchow."

"No, she wasn't. I've been knocking myself out trying to persuade her to tell the man what she knows, but she won't hear of it. My wife can be pretty stubborn when she wants to be." And now Wes smiled for the first time since he'd walked into my office. It was a faint, but unmistakably indulgent smile. "Allison maintains that if this Porchow could erroneously target *her* for Bobbie Jean's murder, he might do the same to one of the others. And she says that she couldn't bear to have that on her conscience. Also, she insists that the police will eventually recognize her innocence on their own. Naturally, she made me swear that I wouldn't contact the authorities, either." Another smile. "So I contacted you instead."

"You realize that the time may come when I'll have to go to the police myself."

"It's certainly occurred to me. But I'm confident that you won't supply them with the source of your information unless you have no other option. At any rate, I still feel that I've done the right thing in filling you in on all of this. At least I've provided you with new areas to pursue in your investigation. And Desiree? I'm counting on your promise not to reveal to Allison or Mike that we've had this meeting."

"I'll do everything I can to keep this between the two of us."

Wes looked at me gratefully. "Thank you."

"I have a question, Wes. Allison told me that you were the one who let Chief Porchow in on the grievances the women had against your sister. So why didn't you yourself bring up Lorraine's son at *that* point? And Carla Fremont's busted romance? And Karl Banner's heart condition?"

"I only found out last weekend that Carla and this Len had ended their relationship prior to Ellen's shower. It was the first Allison had heard about it, as well — that was the exception I just spoke about. Allison and I were doing some food shopping on Sunday, and we ran into the woman who'd introduced the two — she's the fellow's cousin and a former neighbor of ours. Greta — our former neighbor — was in town visiting her brother. She lives in Chicago at present. At any rate, we stopped to chat, and during the conversation she said how terrible she felt when Len phoned her a few weeks back and told her that he and Carla were no longer together."

"So Robin hadn't confided this to Allison," I mused. "Were you surprised?"

"Very. As a rule, there's virtually nothing Robin doesn't talk to her about. But Allison was genuinely stunned. Now, let's assume for a moment that neither of these ladies is culpable in Bobbie Jean's death. Robin might initially have been hoping this parting was a temporary one, so she decided to keep that unfortunate development to herself for a while. Or else Carla prevailed upon her not to say anything. In any case, though, after Bobbie Jean was poisoned, their purpose in altering the timing of the split was as you and I agreed a few minutes earlier."

"No motive at the time of the murder."

"Exactly. And of course, if one or both of these women had had it in mind to kill my sister, it would have been all the more reason to hold off disclosing the breakup and then lie about when it occurred.

"Now, as for Karl Banner, it didn't enter my mind to mention his ailment to the Forsythe police, especially since we can't be certain the condition is even indirectly related to those old accusations of my sister's. Nevertheless, I can appreciate that it was a stupid oversight on my part not to call this matter to the attention of Chief Porchow. Until this business with Allison, however, I had no idea that a current motive would have any greater significance for the police than one that had been festering for years. I never thought about it, I guess. Just plain stupid, as I said," he muttered.

"And Lorraine Corwin — the same reasoning holds true there?"

"Pretty much. But, in addition, there was the fact that some thirty-odd years ago Allison had sworn me to secrecy about Lorraine's pregnancy. And if I was to be true to my word, I had to continue to remain silent about the son she'd given birth to."

And now, for what must have been a full minute or two, Wes stared down at his hands, his forehead pleated up like an accordion, the deep furrows on either side of his nose becoming deeper still. At last he told me, "Who am I kidding, though? If I'm being honest with myself, I have to admit that there's another reason I didn't bring up

Lorraine's grief with Porchow. Or Karl's heart condition, either."

"What's that?"

"Look, I'm not claiming that Bobbie Jean didn't make her share of terribly wrong decisions. *More* than her share, most probably. But I believe one should take into consideration — although I'll spare you the particulars — that my sister's childhood left her with some deep emotional scars. And incidentally, despite what you may have heard, she wasn't without admirable qualities, a great many of them, actually. I couldn't have asked for a more devoted sister — or a better friend.

"I imagine it's a case of wanting to have it both ways, Desiree," an obviously embarrassed Wes confessed. "Because as anxious as I am to see her killer brought to justice — and God knows it's on my mind every waking minute of every day — that's how much I wanted to ensure that the police didn't come away with the wrong impression of my sister."

The wrong impression?

"I grant you that her conduct as it pertained to those ladies was hardly commendable. But this *was* in the past. And you have to admit that she couldn't possibly have foreseen that her actions would cause the repercussions they did. More importantly, however, I did feel that I'd provided the authorities with all the facts they would require. So . . . well . . . I just couldn't bring myself to include what I regarded as some extraneous information. The sort that might lead them to determine that she was . . . that might make it sound as if . . . as if Bobbie Jean weren't a nice person."

Chapter 28

Only minutes after Wes left, I picked up — probably for the hundredth time — the file labeled BOBBIE JEAN MORTON. Today, however, I was fired up. Maybe, thanks to Wes's information, I would look at this file with entirely new eyes.

Still, I didn't immediately open the folder. Instead, I pondered for a bit over some of the things that had passed quickly through my mind during the meeting with Wes.

When he had talked about Carla Fremont, I'd been puzzled by her decision to postdate the breakup. I mean, hadn't she been at all concerned that the police would learn the real facts from her rat ex-boyfriend? Now, however, I reasoned that there'd been little chance the authorities would interrogate him. Besides, if he did put a lie to her story, Carla could always maintain she was fearful that the truth might have been regarded as a motive for eradicating Bobbie Jean.

As for Carla's devoted mother — ditto. In

spite of the serious nature of my ruminations, I had to smile at this point. Meryl Streep had nothing on Robin Fremont. Listen, you should have witnessed the performance she gave that day I drove out to talk to her. Carla would practically have her life, Robin got me to believe, if the girl ever found out that she'd confided in me about this Len. And all the while, of course, the couple was already history. I speculated that Robin might even have been the one to come up with the idea of playing a little loose with the date of the split. Which brought me to another matter. If Robin had poisoned Bobbie Jean, did she do it *with* her daughter — or *because* of her?

Good question, right?

I moved on to Grace Banner. As soon as Wes mentioned her name, I'd once again silently speculated as to whether the timid Grace had it in her to commit murder. At this moment, however, I concluded that the state of her husband's health could very well have provided Grace with sufficient incentive to rise to the task.

Of course, I had no such reservations about Lorraine Corwin. When Wes was discussing the most recent consequence of his sister's appropriation of her fiancé, I'd conjured up a fleeting picture of Lorraine sneaking into the dining room in order to ensure that Bobbie Jean's next meal would be her final one. And in this vision of mine there was a diabolical smile on the woman's face.

Well, I still hadn't a clue as to which of these ladies had actually messed with the victim's salad. But one thing was for sure: By acquainting me with the additional motives all four had been attempting to conceal, Wes Lynton had infused my investigation with a new vitality.

I opened the folder all but convinced that any page now I'd be identifying a murderer.

Right after supper I was back to poring over my notes. It was a slow, painful process, since I was positively paranoid about overlooking something. I was so immersed in my work that it took me a while to realize that the phone was ringing. I grabbed it just as the answering machine was about to kick in.

In response to my "hello," a male voice inquired tentatively, "Jo?"

Already in a snit at having been interrupted, I retorted testily, "Do I *sound* like my name is Joe?"

"Don't take out your PMS on me, lady. I was trying to call my girl. Her name is Jo.

J-O. Jo." And he slammed the phone down in my ear.

I got very little satisfaction out of muttering, "Creep," into the dead receiver.

I wrestled with my notes for another half hour before the telephone butted in again.

"Aunt Dez?" Ellen said. "I *had* to call you. Ginger — you know, who lives in my building — just stopped in with the pictures."

"What pictures?"

"The ones she took at the shower. With all that happened there she forgot to have them developed until the other day. I feel kind of guilty, everything considered, about getting so excited about some photographs. But they came out really well, and I *would* like for you to see them." And as a little incentive: "There are a couple of really great shots of you."

Now, these *were* mementos of Ellen's shower, so despite the tragedy that had occurred only a short time later that afternoon, I'd normally have been anxious for a look at them. But there were other matters on my mind just then — namely, uncovering a killer. So I wasn't exactly straining at the leash to sit down with a bunch of pictures. Add to this that I was beginning to get just the tiniest bit discouraged. I mean, I'd already made a sizable dent in the folder, and so far nothing had jumped out at me. But I told myself there was still an ample amount of ground to cover. Regardless, though, Ellen was eager to show me those photos, and I couldn't just slough her off. "When can we get together so you can check them out?" she was asking.

I realized that in a day or two I'd probably be grateful for a break — particularly if things didn't go as well as I'd been hoping they would. "Are you and Mike available to have dinner here Saturday night?"

"That would be great. I have Saturday off, and Mike should be home by late afternoon, so we can make it whenever you say."

We settled on eight o'clock before I returned to my labors.

I only got to study two-and-a-quarter more pages before the phone rang for the third time that evening.

How am I supposed to make any progress here anyway?

I was about ready to chew a few nails when I lifted the receiver. My "hello" came out more like a grunt than a word.

But the "Hi, Dez, it's Nick" that greeted me made a remarkable difference in my mood.

"Oh, hi, Nick," cooed Little Miss Sweetness herself. "How are you?"

"Fine, just fine. Listen, you sounded a little harried for a moment there. Am I catching you at a bad time?"

"No, no. I was slightly out of breath, that's all. I was, umm, running the bathwater, and I didn't hear the phone at first."

"Oh. Anyway, how are you?"

"Also fine."

"Good. I just called to touch base," Nick informed me. "I thought I'd better try you tonight in case you're heading out of town tomorrow."

"Heading out of town?"

"For a long weekend." He chuckled. "You do know this Monday's Labor Day, don't you?"

"Of course," I responded more firmly than was necessary, since it had completely slipped my mind. "But I'll probably have to spend most of the time right here in my apartment — working."

"That's too bad. They're predicting great weather."

"What about you? Are you doing anything special?"

"I have my son, Derek, for the entire weekend, and we'll be going to the Jersey shore. My sister has a summer home there. Uh, listen, Dez, how does a week from Saturday sound?"

"A week from Saturday?" (I really do have to try to break myself of this dumb habit of repeating what somebody else says.)

"I guess I'm not making myself very clear," Nick admitted. "If you're free then, I thought we might have dinner."

"I'd like that."

We agreed that Nick would call for me at eight thirty. Then I said that I wished Derek and him a happy Labor Day, following which he wished me a productive one.

I was positively euphoric about Nick's asking me out over a week in advance. I mean, could things get more encouraging than that? It was necessary to remind myself that it wasn't as if the man had proposed, for heaven's sake. (And anyhow, it was far too early in the relationship to decide whether this was even to be wished for.)

I finally persuaded myself to settle down to business again, but I wasn't able to accomplish much of anything. I don't deny that I was acting like a sixteen-year-old. Unfortunately, however, I couldn't induce my emotions to catch up with my age.

Besides, how could I possibly be expected to concentrate on my notes — now that Nick Grainger's face was superimposed on every page?

Chapter 29

On Friday I was at the office by an ungodly nine fifteen.

Jackie's eyes opened wide enough to practically touch her eyebrows when I showed up. "What happened, Dez?" she inquired with what looked suspiciously like a smirk. "You having the apartment painted or something?"

Well, I can't tell you how often Jackie has made this same crack when I've put in an appearance before nine thirty. And it didn't strike me as being particularly funny the first time she said it. So ignoring this pitiable attempt at humor, I started down the hall.

"Dez?"

I turned back.

"Thanks for letting me try on everything for you like that yesterday. I realize how busy you were. Oh, and I decided you were right, too — I'll be wearing the peach."

It doesn't take much to bring me around.

In other words, I'm easy. "That's okay, Jackie. I was glad to do it. And I'm really happy it's going to be the peach."

Seated at my desk a few minutes later, I was filled with self-disgust. My behavior last night seemed more sophomoric than ever now that I was looking at it in the uncompromising light of day. Here I was, grappling with what was literally a matter of life and death, and I'd allowed some guy I barely knew to totally short-circuit my thought processes. I removed Bobbie Jean's file from my attaché case, determined to make up for my lapse.

It was just after two when I finished going over the last page in the manila folder.

Reviewing my notes with Wes's revelations in mind hadn't advanced the investigation one little bit. Something that was particularly hard to accept thanks to those foolish expectations of mine.

Thoroughly deflated, I went out for a sandwich and a sorely needed break. I returned within a half hour to find the office decibels greatly reduced.

"Almost everyone's already left," Jackie informed me. "The holiday," she added, in the event I needed reminding.

"I know," I retorted huffily, "Labor Day."

"You going away at all?"

"Uh-uh. How about you?"

"Nope. Derwin and I will probably take in a couple of movies. And I've already notified him that I expect us to have dinner at at least one decent restaurant over the weekend — someplace where you don't have to carry your own tray. Then another night I may cook us a nice meal myself — that is, if I decide he deserves it. You made any plans?"

"Well, Ellen and Mike are coming over tomorrow night. She just got the pictures her friend Ginger took at the shower, and she's anxious to have me see them. Other than that, I'll probably be doing the same thing I've been doing for close to two weeks now: trying to find out who poisoned Bobbie Jean."

"Was Mike's father able to shed any light on the case?"

"Wes? Actually, he had some surprising things to tell me. But I'm not that sure any of it will turn out to be very significant."

I refused to let the fact that I would have registered a dark gray on the mood-swing scale deter me from getting down to business again. So as soon as I was back in my cubbyhole, I began typing up my notes on the meeting with Wes. After all, I couldn't swear that I'd absorbed every little thing he had to say. At least, that's what I told myself. But I wasn't very convincing.

Nevertheless, I kept at it until I'd transcribed every last word and then run off the hard copy. It was five o'clock before I was ready to exit my office, by which hour some young law clerk and I were the only living creatures on the premises. (That is, if you didn't count the big, fat roach I'd spotted in the ladies' room ten minutes ago.)

Leaving the young law clerk — and the roach — to hold the fort, I headed home, resolved to studying these latest additions to the Bobbie Jean Morton file immediately after supper.

I'd just kicked off my shoes and set the omelet fixings on the counter (these fixings consisting of virtually every mold-free item in the refrigerator) when the phone rang.

"What are you doing?" It was my neighbor Barbara.

"You mean this minute? I was about to take something to eat."

She adopted her most imperious tone. "Forget it. I'm treating you to dinner."

"Why would you do a thing like that?"

"Because I won a raffle." Her attempt to conceal it notwithstanding, a hint of excitement managed to sneak into her voice when she added, "First thing I ever won in my life, too. Anyhow, the raffle entitles me to dinner for two at the Reel Thing, this new seafood place on Seventy-ninth."

"Lucky you! And I thank you for thinking of me, Barbara. I'd love to go, but I have an awful lot of work to do tonight, and —"

"The work won't run away. It'll be there when you get home. I promise."

"Gee, I don't know. I —"

"I'll make you another promise, too: I won't even mention calories."

Now, Barbara has this habit of counting calories. Only not hers — mine. And let me tell you, it's pretty tough to enjoy your meal when somebody — particularly somebody who's no thicker than a matchstick — is sitting there, scrutinizing every morsel that winds up behind your lips. "We-ll . . ." I was weakening, but I still hadn't been completely won over.

Barbara, however, sensing victory, closed in for the kill. "I understand they have wonderful scampi."

Sold.

The food turned out to be very good — better than very good, really. Barbara had the grilled tuna, which, while not exactly my cup of tea, she pronounced "exquisite." I ordered the scampi, and it was, as Barbara had indicated in her pitch to me, "wonderful." It wasn't until dessert (fresh fruit salad for her, crème brûlée for me) that my devious host confessed the truth: Actually, she'd never heard a thing about the scampi here.

At any rate, we talked pretty much nonstop throughout the meal.

Barbara, who's a grade school teacher, told me how much she was looking forward to the start of the new semester — solid proof of that old adage about absence making the heart grow fonder. I mean, almost every time I see her during the school year, she's carping about her little charges or their parents or the administration. And sometimes she takes aim at all three at once.

After this she reported on her matchmaking Aunt Theresa's latest offering. This one was the stockbroker nephew of Aunt Theresa's new neighbor. It seems that Aunt Theresa had met the nephew by chance, just as he was leaving Mrs. Murray's apartment — she's the new neighbor. And Staten Island's version of Dolly Levi had, naturally, managed to wheedle a few crucial statistics out of the fellow's relative. According to Mrs. Murray (who, it goes without saying, was completely unbiased), Barbara's prospective soulmate was intelligent, kind, generous, personable, and the earner of large bucks. Aunt Theresa's contribution was that he was also extremely handsome. "As handsome as Tyrone Power, even," she'd declared to Barbara. (This comparison to the long-dead movie star in lieu of someone slightly more contemporary we attributed to Aunt Theresa's being close to ninety.) She did have to admit, however, that there *was* a slight impediment to the coupling — actually, two. The man was almost certainly past sixty. Plus, it had somehow slipped her mind to establish whether he was married or single. "Well, after all, I am going on ninety," she'd reminded Barbara in defense of the oversight.

"Just minor details," I put in at this point, laughing.

"So your advice would be to wait a while before I start shopping for my trousseau?" Barbara inquired, straight-faced.

"*I* would." Suddenly I could feel my cheeks burning, as my own clumsy attempt at playing cupid for my friend here came to mind. And, the thing is, I should have realized that it was a lousy idea to begin with. I mean, Barbara's not what I'd consider a snob — honestly. But in some areas — like men, for instance — she does have champagne tastes. What I'm getting at is that she'd no doubt prefer a stockbroker (or a doctor or a lawyer) to a policeman. Even if he was Forsythe's *chief* policeman.

"So how's the Bobbie Jean thing going?" she asked then.

"Don't ask."

"I assume this is the work that's awaiting you tonight."

"Yup."

"No luck yet, huh?"

"I'm afraid not."

"You haven't forgotten what I told you, have you?"

"Uh, what was it again?"

"Shame on you, Desiree Shapiro! Quite obviously you don't place much stock in my opinion. Which, if you'll recall, is that it was that annoying little camera freak who poisoned the woman."

Once again I managed to avoid bursting into laughter at this ludicrous suggestion.

"Listen, I'm very intuitive," Barbara said, intense now. "And I get this creepy feeling at the back of my neck just thinking about that girl."

Her neck? Really! This time I wasn't quite able to keep the beginnings of a grin from putting in a brief appearance on my face.

"Go ahead, laugh if you want to," she muttered irritably. "If you had any sense, though, you wouldn't dismiss the possibility out of hand like that."

I made what I considered a very reasonable observation. "But Ginger had never laid eyes on Bobbie Jean until the shower."

"You know this for an absolute fact? Besides, even if you're right, how can you be sure she didn't commit the murder to avenge somebody? — her mother, for example. Or someone else she was close to whom the dead woman might have wronged."

It seemed prudent to tell Barbara I'd look into it. So that's what I told her.

I'm not sure she believed me, but she left it at that. "By the way," she brought up right after this, "I received a call from the Forsythe police last weekend. This detective — or whatever he was — asked if I'd ever met the victim before, if I'd noticed anything of a suspicious nature that Sunday — the usual."

And now I permitted myself a full-wattage smile. " 'The *usual?*' You make it sound as if you're grilled by the police on a regular basis."

"Yeah. I head up the list of *America's Most Wanted.*" But she smiled back at me.

* * *

About an hour later we were standing in the hall of our mutual building, only a few feet away from our respective apartments. I thanked Barbara for the lovely dinner and the thoroughly enjoyable evening.

"Anytime," she said. "Any time I win another raffle, that is. And look, be sure you question that pesky little girl with the camera."

We said good night and I was already at my door when I heard: "And remember whose neck it was that helped you solve this case."

Chapter 30

I didn't have a prayer of doing any work that night.

Mostly I think this was due to that bottle of pinot grigio — my contribution to the meal. The waiter had poured with such a generous hand that I'd exceeded my one-glass limit — although only by a fraction, really. Still, it was enough to induce me to head for my comfortable bed instead of that ubiquitous manila folder.

I didn't go near my notes the next day, either, since I was completely occupied with getting ready for my company that evening. I was, however, fully committed to devoting all of Sunday to studying Wes's information — a commitment that, as things turned out, would soon evaporate.

Anyhow, by ten thirty on Saturday morning I was at the greengrocer's. From there I headed over to the cheese store for some Brie and a chunk of Port-Salut. Then came the bakery and following this, our local

Häagen-Dazs. My final stop was the supermarket, where I picked up the rest of the ingredients for my dinner with Ellen and Mike.

Since I hadn't allowed myself any time for advance preparation, the menu had to be simple — and, believe me, it was. In fact, the entrée was such a cinch to make that years ago a friend of mine had labeled it "Moron's Chicken." At any rate, after I finished shopping, which was the most time-consuming element I had to contend with, I mixed up this tangy sweet-and-sour sauce and poured it over the chicken parts. Then as soon as the chicken was sitting in the refrigerator awaiting its stint in the oven, I fixed the salad and cooked up some wild rice with mushrooms and onions. The hors d'oeuvres were no problem at all. In addition to the cheeses, there were, fortunately, some wild mushroom croustades in the freezer. (You might say I have a thing for mushrooms.) Dessert was equally effortless: store-bought cookies and Häagen-Dazs.

The kitchen chores tended to, I permitted myself a lunch break. After which I straightened the apartment a little and set up the folding table in the living room.

And now I could relax for a while — in a nice, fragrant bubble bath.

I'd gotten as far as sticking one big toe in the tub when the phone rang. I made a grab for the towel — and it ended up in the bath-water. Swearing in a totally unladylike manner, I hurried into the kitchen au naturel and snatched up the receiver.

I was greeted with "Hi, Jo baby."

"You again," I seethed.

"Rotten bitch!" the caller retorted.

I won't even repeat what *I* had to say to *him* — but only after he was no longer on the line.

Ellen and Mike arrived about five minutes early. Mike was looking fit and attractive in slim olive chinos. And Ellen might have sashayed down the runway in her beautifully tailored rust pants outfit.

They had obviously put the recent tragedy aside, at least for the moment. I mean, it didn't take any eagle eye to see how happy they were. Ellen's cheeks were flushed, her eyes were shining, and her smile could have blinded you. Mike had to bend practically in half — which he did in order to kiss me — before I was able to make out that his cheeks, eyes, and smile were likewise. (Ellen's intended is about eight feet tall. Or so it seems from down here.)

Now, it's a real imposition on my Lilliputian kitchen to expect it to accommodate more than one person at a time. So when Mike went in there to open the wine they'd brought, I stayed in the living room with Ellen. My niece didn't waste a second before plopping down on the sofa, directly in front of the mushroom croustades. "It would have been kind of gauche to reach," she explained with one of her infectious giggles as she helped herself to an hors d'oeuvre.

"Mbe we shd wt ntil ltr before lkn thr ta pctrs," she told me with puffed-out cheeks. After which she held up an index finger and swallowed. She flashed me a guilty little grin. "Sorry. But I just love these. Anyhow, I was suggesting —"

"I know what you were trying to say: that maybe we should wait until later before looking through the pictures." (There are instances when I think I must be a truly amazing woman.) "I was about to suggest that myself."

Dinner was relaxed and pleasant.

If Mike had any idea of his mother's current difficulties with the police, you couldn't tell from his mood. And since the man had employed me — in a manner of speaking, that is — to probe the murder of his aunt, I was quite certain that if he *were* in possession of such a troubling piece of information, he'd have deemed it relevant to pass this on to me. What did surprise me a little, though, was his not bringing up the investigation at all. But then I decided he probably figured that if there'd been any new developments, I'd have gotten in touch with him. Mike's lighthearted demeanor also gave me the feeling that he was unaware of the state of his parents' marriage. Which would make sense. I mean, I couldn't see either Allison or Wes being anxious to confide something like that to their loving son.

At any rate, once we'd finished dessert and cleared the table — I'd turned down both my guests' offers to help with the dishes — we vacated the dining room and moved on to the living room. Which was not much of a move, being that in my apartment these are one and the same.

The instant she sat down on the sofa, Ellen reached into her handbag and whipped out three of those familiar yellow Kodak envelopes.

"My, Ginger did shoot a bunch of pictures, didn't she?" I remarked, taking a seat next to her.

"Yes, didn't she?" Mike agreed, smiling. He was sprawled in one of the club chairs opposite us, those long legs of his extending so far they were only about an inch short of my toes.

"There's one of you that I'm just crazy about," Ellen told me, riffling through the snapshots. "Wait'll you see it."

"Don't bother, Ellen. I'll come across it eventually."

She passed me the contents of the envelopes and then, as I began going through them, leaned over me, studying every single picture as if she'd never set eyes on it before.

Anyway, about those photos . . . I should probably mention that Ginger didn't give Annie Liebowitz any reason to start peeking over her shoulder. Of course, to be fair, Ginger's equipment — one of those little point-and-shoot things — wasn't exactly state-of-the-art. In any case, many of the photographs were blurred, some to the extent that initially I didn't even recognize the subjects. Still, there were a few beautiful shots of Allison, whose near-perfect features, I imagine, don't present a photographer with much of a challenge. And there were I-don't-know-how-many pictures of Bobbie Jean, most of them so clear as to belie the fact that it was Ginger behind the camera. In these, the victim alternately smiled, mugged, scowled, and in one pose — complete with hands on hips — conveyed total exasperation. I found myself pretty much zipping through all the prints of Bobbie Jean. It was hard for me to see her so full of life on film without being affected by the realization that this life was soon to be stolen from her.

I did go fairly slowly with the rest of the batch, however, making an effort to say something complimentary whenever this didn't stretch credibility too far. At one point Ellen grabbed my arm to induce me to linger over one of the prints even longer. It was a really nondescript likeness of me talking to a couple of women whose backs enabled me to identify them as Barbara Gleason and Harriet Gould. "Was I right?" my niece exclaimed. "Didn't I tell you there were some terrific pictures of you?"

Well, I had no idea what she was seeing that I wasn't. The best you could say for that picture was that it wasn't completely out of focus. But, lucky for me, I was able to avoid coming up with a response by a loud, jolting sound. And I'm talking *loud*. I mean, I damn near bolted out of my seat.

A glance at Mike — who was now fast asleep — marked him as the source of this eruption. "Mike snores sometimes," Ellen advised me, stating the very obvious.

Anyway, the next print was of the Fremont ladies, who were evidently whispering to each other, much as when I'd first seen them at the shower. Now, though, their heads actually appeared to be touching. They were a real study in contrasts, those two, Robin's fashionable attire only serving to accentuate Carla's slipshod grooming habits. Later I came across mother and daughter again. Here, they were standing with Allison and me, undeniably false smiles pasted on both faces. (The camera, apparently, had been a lot more perceptive than I had.) A third photo, which was about as unflattering as you can get, captured Carla for all time — stuffing a stuffed mushroom into her mouth.

There were also three snapshots of Lorraine Corwin. In the first, taken from much too close up, her entire top half was cut off. But the long white gloves and that obscenely large ring left no doubt that this was Lorraine. She fared slightly better in the second picture — her head had been spared, and there was even a glass of champagne pressed to her lips. In the final shot Lorraine was gesturing expansively to Grace Banner.

It struck me how similar Grace's expression was in that photograph to another one in which she was all by herself, leaning against the wall, and to yet another showing her engaged in conversation with an extremely large female with a beehive hairdo. Grace Banner had the identical frown on her face in all three photographs.

"Very nice," I said to Ellen when I'd looked through all of the prints. I attempted to return them to her, but she shook her head.

"Oh, no. This is your set. Mike and I have our own. And we're making up two more besides, one for his parents and one for mine. But listen, Aunt Dez, let's get the dinner dishes out of the way now."

I firmly refused the assistance. Ellen had just begun to protest when Mike awoke with a start.

"Geez, I must have dozed off," he mumbled, rubbing his eyes. "Fine company I've been, huh, Dez? I'm so sorry about this."

"Don't be silly. It's understandable, considering the hours you put in at the hospital."

"How'd you like the photos?" he inquired.

I repeated what I'd told Ellen. "Very nice."

Mike's grin was almost conspiratorial. "Yeah, I know. Ginger's not too talented with a camera, but she loves taking pictures. And Ellen's really thrilled to have these."

* * *

About ten minutes later Ellen and Mike left for home. Very slowly I made for the kitchen, shuddering at the thought of what awaited me there. I can't say there were *that* many dirty dishes to deal with (although, from my point of view, there were certainly enough). The big problem, though, was that by then I was in imminent danger of falling asleep standing up. And the thing is, I must be one of the only people in Manhattan — or maybe the entire country — who doesn't own a dishwasher. But there just isn't room in that cramped little area for both a dishwasher and an additional cabinet, and I'd opted for the extra storage space.

Tonight I thoroughly regretted that choice.

But not for long.

Chapter 31

Standing at the sink (and yawning), up to my elbows in soapy water, I thought about those shower pictures. Probably because it beat thinking about all the crud-encrusted dishes still stacked up on the counter.

It occurred to me then how nifty it would have been if Ginger's snapshots had given me a clue to Bobbie Jean's killer. Not that I'd expected anything of the sort, you understand. Which was just as well. Because all they showed me was that Carla and Robin Fremont had false smiles, that Lorraine Corwin wore long white gloves (a real revelation), and that Grace Banner was not at all happy to be present that day.

Tomorrow I would *definitely* — I mean no matter what — study my notes on that conversation with Wes. Although I certainly wasn't counting on any dazzling insights there, either.

And now it struck me that my handling of this case might have been torpedoed by my own myopia. I'd spent most of these past couple of weeks examining motive. And while I grant you that the *why* had to be a crucial factor, the truth is, I'd never moved very far beyond it. Other than questioning some of the Silver Oaks staff members — which should have been merely a first step — I hadn't so much as *attempted* to learn who was where between the time the salads were placed on the tables and the moment when we were called in to lunch. Inexcusable, really. After all, I've been in this business long enough to recognize that opportunity is often the key to the solution of a crime. And what about checking into the possibility that one of my suspects was familiar with poisons? Frequently possession of some specific knowledge is —

Possession of some specific knowledge!

Suddenly I was wide-awake, every nerve in my body quivering like crazy. Grabbing a dishtowel and drying my dripping hands along the way, I made a beeline for the living room — and the file in my desk.

Hurriedly, I skimmed through my notes until I located all of the verification I was searching for.

Restricting my focus to a single individual at this point, I began to examine the facts in my head. And as a result of the information

I had just uncovered, what followed was a rapid — and almost inevitable — progression. I mean, I was practically forced to recognize the vital piece of evidence that until now my cluttered little brain had failed to absorb.

I don't know why, maybe because it afforded me a certain satisfaction, but immediately after this I went through that batch of photographs of Ginger's. Then taking a good, long look at one of them, I nodded.

Chief Porchow could expect a call from me in the morning.

Chapter 32

Sunday or no Sunday I was up at seven. After all, these were very special circumstances.

I was so wired last night that I did something I've never *ever* even considered doing before. I left the dirty dishes strewn all over the kitchen — some of them in the sink, the rest on the counter — and went into the living room to watch TV, hoping to unwind a little.

I was pleased to find a favorite movie of mine, *All About Eve*, on one of the cable channels. It didn't matter that the film was already close to halfway over. I'd seen it enough times (dozens, easily) to have no trouble filling myself in on what had transpired earlier. I must have conked out almost at once, though. The last thing I remember is Margo Channing (Bette Davis) warning everyone to fasten their seat belts because it was going to be a bumpy night.

When I opened my eyes again there was an infomercial on the screen. Some young pitchgirl (she looked to be barely out of her teens, so I refuse to call her a pitchwoman) was selling this miracle cream that was guaranteed to protect me from wrinkles for the rest of my days — or my money back.

I dragged myself off to bed.

And now I wasn't able to sleep. It must have been about six in the morning before I finally dropped off — only to waken an hour later.

The funny thing is, though, I wasn't tired at all. In fact, I'd rarely felt so completely energized. I had finally fingered Bobbie Jean's killer!

I just had to convince the police that I knew what I was talking about.

It required muscles I didn't know I owned to remove all that nasty crud from yesterday's dinner dishes. But finally, at ten after eight, the last little plate was squeaky clean and back on the shelf with the rest of its ilk.

Then I put in a call to Chief Porchow.

The chief wasn't in today, the man on the other end of the line advised. Well, I'd been afraid of that. I crossed my fingers that Porchow wouldn't be unavailable this entire Labor Day Weekend.

"Is there any way he can be reached?" I pressed.

"I'm not certain. It's his day off. Who am I speaking to, please?"

"My name is Desiree Shapiro, and this is in reference to the murder of Bobbie Jean Morton. I have some critical information for Chief Porchow."

"I'll try to contact him for you, Ms. Shapiro. Let me have your phone number, and I'll get back to you."

Less than five minutes later I heard from Porchow himself.

"What is it you have to tell me, Ms. Shapiro?" he inquired politely — although with a certain degree of skepticism.

"It's sort of complicated to discuss on the phone."

"And this can't wait until tomorrow?"

"I suppose it can, but I figured you'd be anxious to hear what I've discovered."

My response must have hit him straight in his duty-bound psyche, because he said — but not without some reluctance — "I have a few things to see to this morning. I could be in Manhattan in the early afternoon, though. Suppose we make it your apartment at around two o'clock — all right?"

"Sure. But if it would be any easier for you, I'd be happy to drive out there," I offered.

"I'd really appreciate that, if it wouldn't be too much trouble for you."

I assured him that it wouldn't be any trouble at all, following which Chief Porchow provided me with very detailed instructions to the Forsythe Police Station.

On the way out to Long Island I began to rehash my last little get-together with the chief. I mean, talk about embarrassing!

That evening, immediately after questioning his marital status, I'd tried to explain to the man that my only reason for becoming so personal was that I thought he might be interested in meeting a friend of mine. One look at his face, however, and I could tell that he wasn't having any of this "friend" business. In fact, I knew exactly what was going through his mind: *A friend? Now, where have I heard that one before?*

But as awkward as I felt about seeing the guy again, what I had to convey to him today was far too important to permit my discomfort to interfere.

Chief Porchow's directions had been so precise that I only made one unwitting detour before arriving at the station house, which occupied a small Colonial-style building that, from the outside, could have fooled you into assuming it was a private home.

The place was hardly a hub of activity this afternoon. Milling around the large main room were only three officers — two male and one female. A second woman, a middle-aged lady in street clothes who'd doused herself with an almost lethal dose of Obsession, was seated at a desk off to the side. She was occupied at present with polishing her nails and cracking her gum. (Isn't it reassuring that these can be done simultaneously?) She raised her head at the sound of my footsteps.

"C'n I help you?" she called out, punctuating the question with a snap of the chewing gum.

I walked over to her. "My name is Desiree Shapiro. Chief Porchow is expecting me."

"Yeah, he told me. Follow me."

The chief occupied a fairly spacious office, attractively if rather sparsely furnished in teak and brass.

He rose and leaned across his desk to shake my hand perfunctorily. "Have a seat, please, Ms. Shapiro," he invited, gesturing to the chair facing him. Then, once I was seated: "Now, what is it you're so eager to pass on to me?"

"Uh, I think . . . rather, I *know* who killed Mrs. Morton."

"And how did you happen to come into possession of this information?"

"Well, I've, uh, been investigating her murder, too."

"I don't quite understand. According to your own statement, you hadn't even met the deceased until recently."

"That's true. But . . . umm . . . her nephew requested that I check into things."

"Her nephew?"

"Yes, Allison Lynton's son — the fellow who's engaged to marry my niece."

"He was concerned that we might have come to regard his mother as a suspect — is that it?"

"Actually, he doesn't have the slightest idea about that. Mike spoke to me about looking into Mrs. Morton's death as soon as it happened."

"I gather he doesn't regard the Forsythe Police Department as capable of apprehending his aunt's killer," Porchow commented wryly.

"Oh, it's not that. It's just that with a private investigator who's practically in the family, Mike thought —"

"Whoa! Back up! Are you telling me you're a *PI?*" From his tone and the extremely unfriendly expression that accompanied it, Porchow must have had difficulty restraining himself from adding a *yecch.*

I smiled weakly. "Guilty."

He muttered something to himself that sounded like, "Just what I needed." After which, he addressed me directly. "May I ask why you didn't mention this before?"

I hunched my shoulders, gave him another weak smile, and mumbled, "It never came up."

"Right," he said none too pleasantly. "Well, let's just get on with this. You're claiming that you've identified the person who poisoned Ms. Morton."

"Yes."

"Okay. Let's hear it, then."

"I'd better begin by filling you in on how I came to the conclusion that I did. Last night I suddenly realized that the killer had to have some *specific knowledge* in order to commit this crime. Keep in mind that she brought monkshood with her that Sunday. Not arsenic, not cyanide — monkshood. A *plant.* Which is a pretty decent sign that all along the perpetrator's intention was to poison the salad. I mean, it would be kind of obvious to have those little leaves floating around in the champagne, for instance, right?"

"So you're saying that whoever did Bobbie Jean was familiar with this particular poison."

"That's certainly true, of course. But what I'm getting at is that she also had to be aware that (a) it's customary at Silver Oaks for the salad to be placed on the table *before* the guests go in for lunch and (b) the dining room is accessible by a door other than the main entrance. Both of which would indicate that the perp was someone who'd been to the country club prior to that Sunday."

"Don't you think this same thing occurred to us, Ms. Shapiro?" Chief Porchow growled. (As you may have noticed, this was not a particularly cordial meeting.) He reached for a pencil now and began idly tapping it on his desk, which I found terribly distracting. "Those women we viewed as possible suspects were all questioned regarding a previous visit. None of them, however, admitted to having set foot in the place before."

Now, I won't pretend that I wasn't jolted by Porchow's having picked up on this important clue before I had. But I took consolation from the fact that *I* was about to tell *him* who murdered Bobbie Jean — and not vice versa.

"Naturally," he continued, "I'm excluding Ms. Lynton when I say this, considering that she couldn't very well deny having been at the club prior to that Sunday.

The problem is," he said meaningfully, "Ms. Lynton has an alibi, at least at the present time. Someone who claims to have never left her side that day. Not for one single moment." I started to squirm. "As for the others, I haven't been able to confirm the truthfulness of their responses."

"Well, *I* can confirm *positively* that one of those ladies wasn't leveling with you, Chief Porchow."

"Proves nothing, I'm afraid. Nothing at all." Porchow tapped the pencil more forcefully now, as if for emphasis. "If this alleged poisoner of yours did lie, she may merely have been attempting to remove herself from suspicion."

"Do you really believe that an innocent person would realize the implications involved in a prior knowledge of the place? And by the way, my information came from two separate sources — both of them very good friends of the killer's — who casually mentioned it to me in conversation."

"Explain something, Ms. Shapiro, will you? Why would the guilty party say anything to *anyone* about having been to that club before?"

"I suppose it's because she had no idea this would wind up being relevant. Either she hadn't decided to kill Bobbie Jean — Mrs.

Morton — at that point, or she hadn't figured out yet how she'd be going about it."

"That may very well be the explanation. Still, lying about her familiarity with the crime scene is hardly proof that the woman you have in mind did the murder."

"There's more. Please, just hear me out. You see, that familiarity is merely what led me to put up my antennae. After this, I was able to appreciate the significance of another factor."

"Listen," an exasperated Chief Porchow muttered, snapping that lousy pencil in half, "don't you think it's time you ended this little game of yours? Just who is it you've damned as Mrs. Morton's poisoner?"

"I'll show you."

I opened my handbag and began rummaging around for one of Ellen's yellow photo envelopes, which had apparently made its way to the bottom of the bag. *I mean, wouldn't you know it?*

As I was frantically searching for the thing, Porchow drummed his fingers on the desk. Causing me to appreciate the pencil. "I'm *wai*-ting, Ms. Shapiro."

At last I laid hands on the envelope. I placed it in front of him with a flourish.

"Meet the killer of Bobbie Jean Morton," I said triumphantly.

Chapter 33

Dramatic as it was, this proclamation did not exactly inspire Chief Porchow to jump up and down. Emptying the envelope of the three prints it contained, he spread the photographs in front of him. "Lorraine Corwin," he said matter-of-factly.

"That's right."

He inclined his head to one side as he looked to me for an explanation.

Stretching across his desk, I gestured toward the snapshot of the headless Lorraine Corwin — the shot that most clearly illustrated my point. "Don't you see?" I all but shouted, rapping my knuckle on one of Lorraine's long white gloves.

It was obvious that he didn't.

I settled into my chair again. "Let me explain, okay? According to what you told the Lyntons, monkshood is a highly toxic substance that can be absorbed by the skin. This means that whoever stirred in those leaves would have been an idiot not to wear gloves. In fact, it's more than likely she had on a pair of plastic gloves underneath the cotton ones, to be doubly certain of avoiding contamination."

Porchow countered with, "Sounds reasonable. But who's to say one of the other suspects didn't have a pair or two stashed in her pocketbook that she utilized at the appropriate moment?"

"And wasted all that time pulling them on and taking them off? Listen, the perpetrator had to have had serious concerns about being discovered; it was essential to her that she get in and out of that dining room in a great big hurry. Actually, I have a theory with respect to the exact way the killer — Miss Corwin — added the poison to the salad."

"All right. Let's hear it," Porchow instructed, his curiosity apparently causing his irritation with me to dissipate — or at least go on hiatus.

"I believe she mixed in the poison with her finger."

"Her *finger?* But why? Why not use a spoon?"

"Because a gloved finger is more efficient. If she performed that little chore with a utensil of some kind, she'd first have had to get it out of her handbag. And then, when she was through, it would have been necessary to deposit whatever it was in a bag or container of some sort before returning it to her purse. I realize I'm talking a matter of seconds here. But I don't think it's an exaggeration to say that every second was precious to the murderer."

"True," Porchow murmured thoughtfully. "But if the woman used her finger, the same thing would apply insofar as timing — at any rate, once she'd finished doctoring the salad. She'd then have had to do something about the gloves, correct?"

"Sure, but that's the beauty part. She could sneak out of the dining room and go across the hall to the ladies' room *while still wearing them.* There, of course, she could remove them where no one would catch her at it: in one of the stalls."

"And once this was accomplished?"

"You mean what do I believe happened to the gloves?"

He nodded.

"Well, I can't picture her stowing them away somewhere and risking that they'd eventually be found. No, I think Miss Corwin must have stuffed them into a plastic bag and carried them around in her purse for the rest of the afternoon. It's doubtful she'd have regarded this as much of a gamble, either. After all, she had to be aware that it wouldn't immediately be established that a homicide had even been committed. So what were the odds of anyone's checking out the personal belongings of the guests? And if one of the other ladies should happen to ask about the gloves, she could simply claim that she'd removed them in order to eat her lunch. Which is exactly what I figured when I saw her later on."

"I don't know . . ." the chief mused, idly picking up one of the prints and examining it. "Wait a minute," he said sharply. "If Ms. Corwin had it in mind to do what you're accusing her of, what about this ring of hers? Taking off the gloves would have necessitated that she first slip off the ring. Then once the gloves were off, she'd have had to put it back on again, this time on her bare finger — I'm assuming she wore the ring for the remainder of the afternoon." His raised eyebrows indicated that he was expecting validation.

"Yes, of course she did. But, really —"

"You're going to tell me that it was no big deal. That the ring could come off and on in a hurry. Still, the woman would have wanted to return to the other guests as soon as possible. So if she was planning to commit a quickie little murder that day, why saddle herself with an extra piece of business to contend with — no matter how minor? Wouldn't it have been more expedient to leave the ring home?"

I laughed. "Consider who we're talking about here. I don't believe Lorraine Corwin would have regarded that as an option. She would have felt naked if she hadn't dressed up those plain white gloves with a flashy piece of jewelry. Listen, you've no doubt paid Miss Corwin a visit. Was she or wasn't she wearing a few tons of jewelry at the time?"

Porchow couldn't suppress a grin. "Well, she *was* pretty weighted down."

And now, tilting back in his chair, the chief cleared his throat. "I have to admit that you've presented me with a very interesting theory today, Ms. Shapiro." His tone, which bordered on apologetic, tipped me off as to what would follow. But even though I'd been forewarned, the next words utterly destroyed me. (Okay, maybe I'm exaggerating the least little bit, but this is exactly how I felt at that instant.) "The problem is, though, that you haven't provided me with a shred of proof.

"Let's begin with the first point you made — I'm referring to a familiarity with Silver

Oaks. I won't even dispute that your niece's party wasn't Ms. Corwin's introduction to the club. But the fact remains that this might hold true for one or more of the other suspects, as well." It would have been too much to expect him not to throw Allison at my head again. Which, of course, he did. "We *know,* for example, that Ms. Lynton had been there before that Sunday."

I decided that a reminder was in order. "But we can actually *prove* Lorraine Corwin *lied* about this. And I still maintain that nobody but the perpetrator would be aware of the significance of having some familiarity with the place."

Now, I suppose I should interject here that it was a vague recollection of something Allison had told me that sent me scurrying to my file last night. It didn't take long, either, to confirm that Lorraine had mentioned to her friend how much she'd enjoyed the food on a visit to Silver Oaks the previous year.

Checking further, I'd located another pertinent conversation, one that had pretty much slipped my mind. Grace Banner had also talked about Lorraine's praising the food there. In fact, Grace had even joked that this was what had motivated her to attend the shower. This exchange between the two women not only verified that Lorraine was already acquainted with the country club, but simultaneously implied that Grace was not.

My notes with regard to the questioning of Robin Fremont added even more substance to the growing suspicion that Bobbie Jean's killer had been uncovered at last. Robin had said plainly that she and her daughter wanted to see what the club was like, hinting that it could be the site for the girl's maybe future wedding.

Well, I'd learned since then that this insinuation about a wedding site had been just plain baloney. Nevertheless, there was nothing in my file to dispute that the occasion of Ellen's shower marked the first time Robin (and Carla, as well) had been to Silver Oaks. Ditto Grace Banner. And my opinion of the truthfulness of both ladies was reinforced about a thousandfold once I was struck by the very serviceable nature of Lorraine Corwin's gloves.

But back to Porchow . . .

Shaking his head, he was now asserting almost pityingly, "If lying amounted to evidence of murder, most of the people I know would be behind bars. And I'm afraid I'd have to join them."

"But the gloves," I protested.

"I'm getting to that. Look, I agree that already having the gloves on would have saved valuable time. But I can also make the argument that the *real* perpetrator might not have been clever enough to consider something like that."

"I still don't —"

"I'm not saying you're wrong about any of this, Ms. Shapiro. But I'm not persuaded that you're right, either. Listen, I appreciate your wanting to help. But I have to stress that if Ms. Morton's killer is to be apprehended, it's crucial that the police department be allowed to do its job without outside interference. I can't — and won't — tolerate anything that might compromise our investigation. Understood?"

"Understood," I answered meekly.

Now, having recently managed to convince the chief that I had designs on him — and in light of the degree of panic this appeared to generate in the man, I had to assume that he hadn't yet entirely disabused himself of this notion — Porchow did a surprising thing just then. Getting up from his desk, he walked over to me and gently placed a hand on my shoulder. I can only surmise that this had been prompted by my expression, which must have led him to conclude that the possibility of my suicide could not be disregarded.

There was a note of genuine kindness in his voice when he said, "But if anything substantial should occur to you based on what you've *already* observed, give me a call, and I promise you I'll look into it."

Which didn't make me feel the least bit better.

Based on what I'd already observed? Was I supposed to experience an epiphany, for heaven's sake?

And what in hell did he mean by "substantial," anyway?

Chapter 34

Driving back to Manhattan, I succeeded admirably in driving myself crazy. (Pun intended.)

I admit that, emotionally speaking, I'd had my ups and downs — mostly downs — during the course of this damn investigation. But until now I hadn't felt good enough about my progress to be this miserable on learning that I hadn't really made any headway. If you know what I mean. This afternoon, however, I'd have had to climb up to reach rock bottom.

It wasn't just depression I was wrestling with, though. Almost as soon as I got behind the wheel I began to saddle myself with self-doubt, as well.

Was I positively, one hundred percent certain that Lorraine Corwin had murdered Bobbie Jean?

For a few seconds there, I actually wavered. Chief Porchow didn't consider that lie about Silver Oaks, coupled, of course, with what I continued to regard as the all-important gloves, to be sufficient proof of the woman's culpability. Well, maybe I shouldn't be that satisfied with the conclusion I'd arrived at, either.

But, no. The police had to be concerned with what would stand up in a court of law, while my sole interest was the truth. And I still maintained that only the guilty person would have recognized the significance of a previous visit to the club. Plus, Lorraine was the one suspect who didn't have to waste precious seconds in the dining room pulling on a pair (probably *two* pairs) of gloves. As for Porchow's argument that the "real" perp might not have been smart enough to figure out the advantage of wearing gloves to Ellen's shower, well, with speed so crucial to the lady's getting away with murder, how could that have failed to occur to her?

This thought led me to the chief's observation about the ring, and I couldn't help but smile. Even with the key element of speed in mind, the flamboyant Lorraine's very nature seemed to dictate that she couldn't *not* wear a ring of some kind to spiff up her attire.

After this I must have concentrated entirely on the road for all of about two or three minutes before I was back to taxing my poor, put-upon brain. I suddenly recalled that it was Lorraine who'd first introduced the possibility of Bobbie Jean's death having been a homicide. It was on the day of the shower, in fact — just before the woman left for home. I wondered briefly whether she would have brought up a thing like that if she herself had committed the crime.

Why not, though? Lorraine wasn't delivering this opinion to the authorities. But then again, suppose she *had* mouthed off to the police. What harm would there have been in that — even if they later discovered there'd been foul play? If anything, with Lorraine's being the one to broach the subject, she'd probably have been viewed as a rather unlikely assassin. I decided that if Mrs. Corwin had given birth to any stupid children, none of them was named Lorraine.

By the time I got home I'd managed to work my way through all the sticking points. Which left me with one small question: What next?

Chief Porchow had requested — no, *mandated* — that I desist from checking into Bobbie Jean's murder. But while I didn't have the slightest idea where I could go with my investigation at this stage, I had every intention of going *somewhere* with it. And it isn't that I was so sure the Forsythe police wouldn't eventually arrive at the truth — they might very well. I just couldn't afford to chance it. Listen, if I left it to them, any day now I might be baking Allison a cake with a file in it.

It was when I was standing in front of the door to my apartment, turning the key in the lock, that I determined what my next move had to be.

Right after supper I dialed Dominick Gallo's home number. Last week his answering machine had notified me that the vacationing Silver Oaks waiter was due home today. And I didn't care if he hadn't even had a chance to unpack yet; I'd waited long enough to talk to him. The truth is, while I didn't expect to learn anything from Gallo, I considered him a loose end. And I hate loose ends.

"Hello," said a rich baritone voice.

"I'd like to speak to Mr. Gallo, please."

"You already are," the man responded. I could actually hear the smile.

I gave my name and explained that I was a private investigator looking into the death on Sunday, August seventeenth, of Mrs.

Bobbie Jean Morton. "The autopsy report shows that Mrs. Morton was poisoned," I apprised him.

"I heard."

"You *did?*" I mean, Gallo had gone away somewhere the day after the murder — when the cause of death had yet to be established. "Didn't you just return from vacation?"

"Yup, a few hours ago. But a couple of the people I work with at Silver Oaks got in touch with me while I was up in the Poconos — they filled me in on what happened. And then about an hour before you called, I spoke to the Forsythe Chief of Police — he'd left a message on my machine last week. I told him I didn't know anything."

"It's always possible that you know more than you think you do, Mr. Gallo. That's why I'd appreciate it if we could talk in person for a few minutes. How about tomorrow? — at any place that's convenient for you. I could drive out to Silver Oaks or we could meet somewhere or we could do this at my office or in your home." The words tumbled out on top of each other before the man had an opportunity to interrupt.

The second I concluded my pitch, however, I had doubts about the necessity for a meeting. I imagine I'd requested it out of habit — I've discovered that it normally pays to interrogate somebody face-to-face. Besides giving you a much better chance of wearing down your subject, other factors come into play, as well. You'd be surprised at what you can learn from a twitching upper lip or a pulsating vein. In this instance, though, it was extremely improbable that there was anything *to* learn. The dismal results of that afternoon I'd spent seeking information from the other Silver Oaks employees had to be regarded as an indication of what I could look forward to with Gallo.

I was actually relieved when he nixed the idea of a get-together. "Driving out to Long Island to see me would be a waste of your time, Ms. Shapiro. Believe me."

"Well, okay," I agreed readily enough. "But there are a couple of matters I would like to cover with you. We could do it now, though, on the phone." I threw in, "I promise that it won't take long," as an incentive.

"All right."

I proceeded to ask Dominick Gallo pretty much what I'd asked his coworkers. At this juncture, however, it was mostly to establish some sort of rapport with him before posing the only question that really mattered anymore.

At any rate, going through the motions, I established that Gallo knew the victim only by sight. Also, that he had no knowledge — or so he claimed — of any romantic entanglement and/or feud she might have had with either a Silver Oaks employee or one of her fellow country club members. In fact, he assured me he'd never heard anybody mention her name.

And then I put the big one to him: "Did anything take place that Sunday that struck you as being at all unusual?"

Gallo hesitated before replying. It was only a split-second pause. And I probably wouldn't have been aware of it if I hadn't been so anxious for a positive response — my low expectations notwithstanding. "No, nothing."

"Listen, if there *was* something, please tell me."

"But —"

Before he could reiterate his denial, however, I went to work on the man. "Look, Mr. Gallo, I find it extremely difficult to accept the possibility of any murderer's not being apprehended. But that the killer of Bobbie Jean Morton might never be brought to justice is something I refuse to let myself so much as consider. Please. Let me tell you a little about this woman."

And then, with no compunction whatsoever, I proceeded to lie my glorious hennaed head off. "She was very special — a warm-hearted, generous, and much-loved human being. Nobody I've come into contact with has had anything but praise for that lady." (I almost gagged here, recalling how — whenever they spoke of the dead woman — the suspects all sounded as if their tongues had been dipped in venom.) "Bobbie Jean Morton donated untold sums to charitable causes. She did volunteer work at the hospital. And she delivered meals to home-bound AIDS patients. Not only that, but she made every effort to keep her good works a secret. I think you should know this, too. Mrs. Morton recently lost a husband she was very much in love with. And almost simultaneously she had to grapple with some additional personal problems, problems that required a great deal of courage for her to overcome. That's not all, either. . . ." I went on in the same vein for a short while longer. And when I was through I'd almost convinced myself that Mother Teresa wasn't worthy to so much as touch the hem of Bobbie Jean's skirt.

"I wish I could help you, Ms. Shapiro. It sounds as if Ms. Morton was a wonderful person. But, honestly, *I* didn't notice anything out of the ordinary going on that day."

Now, I could have sworn he'd given that "I" just the least bit of emphasis. "Who did, then?"

"I don't understand what you mean."

"*You* didn't notice anything suspicious. But somebody else saw or heard something and told you about it. Am I right?"

Seconds ticked off before Gallo politely declared, "No, you're not."

"Look, I hope you'll do whatever you can to persuade this individual to come forward." I was almost pleading with the man. "I realize that a lot of people want to avoid getting involved in anything like this. But you have to wonder — don't you? — how these same people would feel if someone close to them were harmed and all the witnesses shut *their* eyes to what had occurred."

"I take your point, Ms. Shapiro. But you've got this wrong. Nobody mentioned spotting anything peculiar. Not to me, anyway."

My sigh came all the way from my toes. "All right. Let me give you my phone number, though — just in case."

I recited the number, and then we said good-bye. But just before we hung up, Dominick Gallo murmured so softly that the words were all but inaudible, "I really am sorry."

Chapter 35

Postponing dinner for a while, I sat down at the kitchen table with a cup of coffee. (I figured if that God-awful stuff didn't shoo the cobwebs from my head, nothing would.) It took only five or six sips before I deemed myself fit to analyze my conversation with Gallo.

Predictably, I began by challenging myself.

When I'd asked the man whether he was aware of anything unusual transpiring that Sunday, had I *really* picked up on a telltale bit of hesitation? And later, with regard to this same topic, had he *really* emphasized the "I"? (As in "*I* didn't notice anything out of the ordinary going on that day"?)

After all, how likely was it that the very last employee of Silver Oaks that I questioned was the individual who could help me nail the killer? I reminded myself that if I'd actually heard what I thought I had, Gallo wasn't the one who could wrap up this case for me. It was some nameless, shadowy friend of his, someone I'd probably interrogated earlier.

Of course, I still had to concede the possibility that my imagination had been on overdrive, being that I was so desperate to get Lorraine Corwin into one of those fashionable prison jumpsuits I've always admired on TV.

Well, one thing was definite, anyway. I'd done everything I could to induce Gallo to put a little pressure on his buddy — assuming, that is, there even was such a buddy. I mean, by the time I was through painting that laudatory word picture of Bobbie Jean, I wanted the amoral witch for my very best friend, for heaven's sake!

Nevertheless, I made up my mind that if Dominick Gallo didn't contact me in the next few days, I'd take another stab at him.

And now I switched to the problem of the moment: figuring out how to move the investigation in the meantime.

But before I had a chance to give this any serious consideration, Ellen called to let me know how much she and Mike had enjoyed last night's dinner.

It was a pretty short conversation, and I had just gotten back to taxing my brain to come up with a couple of interim plans, when Harriet phoned. “I haven’t talked to you in a while,” she told me, “so I thought I’d say hi.”

I was surprised to hear from her. “I expected that you and Steve would have gone someplace for the holiday.”

“No, we’re where we usually are — right across the hall from you. We’d intended to get away, but then Steve’s boss invited us to this barbecue he was having this afternoon — we just got home a few minutes ago, as a matter of fact. If you ask me, the man purposely scheduled it for today so his executives would be stuck in town for the Labor Day weekend.”

“The guy must be a real sweetheart.”

“That he is. But anyway, how are you doing?”

“So-so.”

“No luck with finding the murderer yet, huh?”

“Not really.”

“Listen, Steve and I are going to his cousins’ place in Queens tomorrow. And if you have nothing else planned, why don’t you drive out there with us?”

“Gee, Harriet, I —”

“Don’t tell me you’re too busy with work. We all need a break sometimes. And you’d certainly be welcome there. Steve’s already checked with them about bringing a friend — we were both hoping I could persuade you to come along. Anyway, Mel and Ramona assured him that they'd be delighted to have you."

Well, why not? I *could* use a break. I was all set to say yes when Harriet added, "They have a beautiful pool, too. So be sure to bring along a swimsuit."

Now, I'm pretty comfortable with my appearance. But still, I scrupulously avoid the kind of clothes that practically invite the world to count my dimples. (And I'm not talking about the ones I don't have on my face, either.) So, naturally, bathing suits would have to occupy a space at the very top of my "What Not to Wear" list. Although I admit that I did allow Jackie to badger me into buying a swimsuit that time I accompanied her to Aruba (which is a whole other story). The way you dress in the tropics is one thing, though. But to prance around in something like that in Queens, New York? I'd die first!

"That sounds wonderful, Harriet. And I'd love to go. But I have to follow up on a couple of leads concerning the poisoning, and it's not something I can postpone."

"I can't convince you to change your mind?"

"Uh-uh. I'd better not weaken. But thanks for thinking of me. And thank Steve for me, too."

I hope you realize that I hadn't lied to Harriet — not unless you insist on being really technical. After all, I did have a couple of leads. And I did intend to pursue them. The one *teeny* little falsehood to come out of my mouth was that I'd claimed I would be doing the pursuing tomorrow, when in actuality I hadn't the slightest notion yet how I should even go about it.

But anyway, I had to acknowledge that Harriet was right; I needed some time off from the investigation. And while I initially toyed with the idea of calling a friend and taking in a movie or even getting some last-minute theater tickets, before long I was derailed by a pretty heavy case of the guilts. Which led me to decide that I'd devote Monday to a project I'd sorely neglected since becoming involved with Bobbie Jean's murder: cleaning my apartment.

And I ask you, can you think of a more fun way to spend a holiday than scrubbing out your toilet bowl?

Chapter 36

On Monday I came to the conclusion — and not for the first time, either — that it really *isn't* fun to scrub out your toilet bowl. Or mop your floors. Or scour your tile. Or even polish your furniture, for that matter.

For a moment my mind leapt back a few years to the days when I could leave a lot of that nasty business to Charmaine, my every-other-week cleaning lady. Unfortunately, however, Charmaine wasn't around anymore. Oh, I don't mean that she died. You see, right from the beginning she just wouldn't show up half the time. And then eventually she stopped showing up any of the time.

At any rate, having spent over four hours that afternoon doing battle with grime and gunk, after supper I lay prostrate on the sofa, watching TV. It was almost ten when Nick phoned. His voice was an instant pick-me-up.

"I hope I didn't wake you," he said.

"Oh, no. I'm a night person. I'll be up for hours yet. How was your weekend at the beach with Derek?"

"Great. He's a terrific little guy." He laughed. "And I'm not the least bit prejudiced, I swear. What about you? Were you able to take some time off from your work to enjoy yourself?"

"Actually, yes — one evening anyway," I informed him, hoping this might cause the man to wonder what I'd been doing that night. And who I'd been doing it with.

But if Nick was engaging in any wondering, he covered it up quite nicely. "I'm glad to hear it. Uh, the reason I'm calling, Desiree, is because I'm going to have to break our date for next Saturday."

"Oh."

"I'm really sorry, but Tiffany is anxious to fly to Las Vegas with her boyfriend tomorrow. He's in a rock band — he's quite a bit younger than Tiffany — and the group's been booked at one of the clubs out there. She asked if Derek could stay with me until she gets back next Sunday, and I couldn't say no."

"Of course not. We can do it another time. How will you manage with your son, though? Being at work all day, I mean."

"Tiffany thinks of everything," he stated,

the merest hint of sarcasm in his voice. "She's arranged for a former nanny of Derek's to pick him up at school and bring him here. She'll prepare his dinner and look after him until I come home."

"Well, then, it doesn't sound as if there'll be any problem."

"Actually, I'm very happy that Derek will be with me for so many days. The only thing I regret is having to cancel with you."

"Like I said, we'll do it another time."

Nick thanked me for being so understanding and said he'd call me soon to reschedule.

Naturally, I was disappointed that I wouldn't be seeing Nick this weekend, but I managed to console myself. After all, it wasn't as if this thing between us — whatever it was — was over before it started. We'd be getting together again before long.

Nevertheless, it *was* something of a letdown, so to take my mind off it — and with the television blaring — I shifted my focus to Lorraine Corwin. And that's when this nagging little doubt took hold of me and refused to let go.

Yesterday I'd pooh-poohed all of Chief Porchow's objections to my explanation of the murder. But this evening, revisiting my conversation with him, I began to wonder if perhaps he'd made one point that I'd been too quick to dismiss.

And while I didn't actually consider it *crucial* to my theory, I found myself suddenly having second thoughts. And they were troubling.

In bed that night, a single word kept repeating in my head: *Why?*

It was a long time before I was finally able to drift off into a fitful sleep.

Now, my friend Barbara has always maintained that when you finally give up (consciously, at any rate) trying to figure out something that's been puzzling you — this is when your brain is apt to start operating at top efficiency.

And damned if my eyes didn't fly open at around three thirty A.M.

"Lucrezia Borgia," I said aloud.

Chapter 37

I had, of course, made a colossal mistake.

I'd tried to convince Chief Porchow (and myself, as well) that Lorraine's putting on the topaz ring that Sunday could be attributed to her ostentatious nature. Very likely because it was the only explanation that occurred to me. But as I'd come to appreciate last night, this really wasn't logical.

Listen, it was apparent that Bobbie Jean's murder had been carefully planned. And while Lorraine might be incredibly showy, she was also a very sharp lady. So why would she take the time to fiddle with that ring of hers while carrying out the serious business of poisoning her longtime enemy?

Which question is what led me to the sleep-induced realization that the ring had to be an essential element of Lorraine Corwin's plot.

I gave thanks to the powers that be that I'd paid attention in history class the day Mr. Fenstermacher told us about Lucrezia

Borgia, that devious member of fifteenth- (or was it sixteenth-?) century Italian nobility, who'd employed *her* ring to carry death to her foes. In fact, at the time, I remember thinking what a wonderful idea this was and lining up a few candidates for future consideration.

Naturally, having experienced this epiphany, it was impossible for me to fall back to sleep that morning. I was too wound up to even try.

Getting out of bed, I went into the kitchen and made some coffee. I stood over the glass container, watching it fill up but not really seeing it. What I *did* see was that enormous topaz ring, its secret compartment wide open and packed almost to overflowing with little shreds of monkshood leaves. I mean, shades of that Borgia woman!

At any rate, a couple of minutes later, coffee cup in hand, I sat down at the kitchen table to reconstruct the crime, making a couple of important changes to my original assessment.

I could now envision Lorraine emptying the monkshood from the hidden compartment in her ring into Bobbie Jean's salad. What quicker, more efficient way to dispense a poison? (And how that must have appealed to Lorraine's flair for the dramatic!) I then pictured her snapping the compartment shut and hastily mixing in the bits of leaves with the gloved forefinger of her left hand, just as I'd imagined before. This accomplished, she would have hurried across the hall to the powder room.

Naturally, I couldn't be sure of her next move. But since there was at least the chance — even if a minuscule one — that some tiny pieces of monkshood had found their way onto the exterior of the ring, it was hard to believe the woman would risk transferring it to her bare skin without first taking precautions. So in this updated version of my script, I had her slip the ring from her pinkie and wash it thoroughly with soap and hot water — keeping the gloves on for protection, of course.

And now I played devil's advocate. *But what if someone should happen to walk in on her while she was engaged in tidying up?* I put to myself. *Or suppose the powder room attendant should notice her scrubbing away like that?*

I decided this wasn't a problem. Lorraine could simply claim that she'd just handled this very sticky hors d'oeuvre.

On second thought, however, it was possible none of this was necessary. Maybe there was some kind of cleaning solution for the ring sitting in her handbag.

Anyway, the rest of the scenario remained pretty much unchanged from the original. In the privacy of a stall, she'd have removed the gloves and deposited them in the plastic bag she carried in her purse. After which she would have put on the ring again, this time transferring it to another finger — the third, as I recalled — where it no doubt fit better once the gloves were eliminated.

I leaned back in the chair at that moment, satisfied that I had it straight at last.

As eager as I was to provide Chief Porchow with this latest — and accurate — version of the homicide (plus, as a by-product, dazzle the man with the brilliance of my reasoning processes), I elected to wait until nine before trying to reach him. I mean, I considered it unlikely that the top guy in the department would have assigned himself to night duty.

Come eight fifty-five, however, I was too antsy to contain myself any longer. I lifted the receiver.

A funny thing, though. The instant I began dialing the Forsythe station house, my entire body turned cold. Suddenly I had the premonition that I'd find myself up against a brick wall again.

It required a major effort to ignore the invisible hand that was clutching at my chest. Certainly, I assured myself, Chief Porchow would determine that this new theory had to be explored. . . .

The chief wasn't in, I was told by the woman who took the call. A snap of her gum immediately enabled me to identify the owner of the voice.

"Is he expected today?"

"Yeah, at around ten thirty. You wanta leave a message?"

"Yes, thanks. Would you please tell him that Desiree Shapiro phoned and that it is absolutely *urgent* that I speak to him as soon as he gets in." I gave her my number, after which, at her request, I spelled out my last name — twice. "Desiree" required a third spelling.

During the next hour and a half, I put on my clothes, had some breakfast (which I could barely get down), and then tackled Sunday's *New York Times* crossword puzzle. And let me tell you, if I should ever feel the need to be brought down a peg, it's reassuring to know that the Sunday *Times* crossword can accommodate me.

Porchow returned my call promptly at ten thirty. "This is Chief Porchow. I understand there's something urgent you want to talk to me about." I don't say that he sounded unfriendly. But I can't say he sounded friendly, either.

"Yes, I do. And you were absolutely right," I announced, doing my best to pave the way for a favorable response to what I was preparing to lay on him.

"Well, that's a novelty," he commented dryly. "And just what was I right about?"

"You pointed out that it wasn't logical that Lorraine Corwin would put on the ring that day. And in spite of my attempts at rationalization, I finally came to agree with you. Well, then I started wracking my brain as to why she would have worn it." I paused long enough to convey to the man that he was about to hear something momentous.

"And your conclusion?" But Porchow seemed almost disinterested.

"The ring was the murder weapon."

"The *what?*" The man had become an instant soprano.

"It had to be. Why else would she saddle herself with it? And just consider the size of that thing — it was the perfect container for the monkshood leaves." And now I reminded him about the infamous Duchess of Ferrara, a.k.a. Lucrezia Borgia. Then before he could comment, I gave a short, amended account of the poisoning itself and the cleanup that followed it. I concluded with, "I don't believe I'd ever have figured all of this out, though, if you hadn't questioned the presence of the ring to start with."

"I'm not immune to flattery, Ms. Shapiro, and I thank you for the kind words. But I hope you realize that what you've just told me is, once again, nothing more than a theory."

"Well, yes, but —"

"And what, exactly, are you proposing I do about it, anyway?"

"Listen, I believe that there's a really good chance Miss Corwin is still in possession of the ring. I mean, she's probably pretty attached to it — in its own way, it's actually quite stunning — and as far as she's aware, no one's associated it with the poisoning. So why get rid of the thing? Also, I'm sure she figures she washed away any evidence of the monkshood."

"Your point being — ?"

"That there might still be *some* trace of the stuff inside that compartment. So if you obtained a search warrant, it —"

"Hold it, Ms. Shapiro. I can't ask for a search warrant on the basis of what you're suggesting. You don't even know if the ring *has* a secret compartment. And even if I were inclined to try and obtain a warrant, no judge of my acquaintance would consider issuing one."

"Look, you were telling me the other day that there wasn't any proof of Lorraine Corwin's guilt. But how am I supposed to get you that proof?"

"You aren't, remember? Obviously, you're not convinced of this, but the Forsythe Police Department is fully capable of apprehending the perpetrator. So just back off, and let us do our jobs here."

"But you could at least take a crack at getting that warrant," I whined.

"I was under the impression I'd made myself clear. You want me to do something that I'm simply not able to do." His voice became sterner. "Incidentally, Ms. Shapiro, I find it unbelievable that you'd have the gall to request anything from me at all, considering that you've been hampering this investigation from the very beginning."

"If you're referring to my telling you that Mrs. Lynton and I were constantly together at the shower, well, I know you think I was lying, but —"

"*Think* was the other day. Now I *know.*"

"What —"

"Good-bye, Ms. Shapiro." And Chief Porchow gently put down the phone.

* * *

It was past ten thirty when I got to the office on Tuesday. Almost immediately I was aware that I'd done the unforgivable: neglected to contact Jackie to inform her that I'd be late. I mean, experience has taught me that Jackie places such an oversight on a par with kicking a puppy or stealing from the collection plate.

Anyway, I was immediately confronted with a hostile expression, blazing eyes, and a "Where have you *been?*" uttered from behind clenched teeth.

"Don't be mad, Jackie. I should have phoned, but, well, I guess I forgot. Everything just seemed to get away from me today. I'd been up most of the night, and then this morning I had a very upsetting talk with the Forsythe chief of police, and —"

"Do you have even the slightest inkling of how worried I was?" Jackie demanded shrilly.

"I'm really sorry, but as I said —"

"I called your apartment twice, and no answer. I presume you must have already left by then. Another minute or two, though, and I would have contacted your friend Harriet and asked her to check on you." She thrust a pink message slip at me. "It's from

Allison. She called at nine forty-six. She wants you to get back to her."

I was tempted to remind Jackie that I could read. But plainly, this was not the time.

"I couldn't even tell the woman when you were expected," she grumbled. Which prompted me to engage in a little teeth-clenching myself. I mean, enough was enough. Then unexpectedly, Jackie's tone softened. "How was your holiday?"

I realized the question was meant as a lead-in to my inquiring about *her* holiday. But all she got from me before I walked away was a terse, "It was okay," followed by a peremptory, "See you later."

I dialed the number reluctantly. I was fairly certain I knew what Allison wanted to discuss with me, and I dreaded having this confirmed. Which it was — almost as soon as she answered the phone.

"Oh, Desiree." The catch in her voice led me to suspect that she'd been crying. "Chief Porchow was here a little while ago. Apparently he's located somebody — one of the shower guests — who saw me returning from the powder room alone not very long before we were all called in to lunch." And here Allison sniffled a few times, which removed any doubt that she'd been crying.

"Did you pass anyone in the corridor?"

"I don't think so. But anybody standing at that end of the Minerva Room might have noticed me coming down the hall."

"What did you say to Porchow?"

"I said the woman — whoever she is — was mistaken."

"Good."

"Umm, there's something I should tell you, Desiree. When Chief Porchow initially inquired about my movements prior to the group's entering the dining room, I said that I'd been with you the entire time. But I promise you this wasn't to deceive the man. That brief trip to the restroom just didn't occur to me. I imagine I sort of sloughed off the question, most probably because I had no idea I was a serious suspect — or, at least, that I soon would be. During their second visit, though, the police were a bit more specific. The chief wanted to know if I was certain neither of us had even gone to the ladies' room by ourselves during the cocktail hour. And that's when it came to me. But of course, I had just learned that I'd become the focus of the investigation. And while I'm hardly proud of myself, quite frankly, I was too shaken to admit the truth.

"However, I never meant to put you in the

position of lying for me. That's why, when I came to consult with you regarding my . . . my revised status with the Forsythe Police Department, I didn't bring up having given them misinformation. I was very concerned that you might consider any mention of that as an attempt to induce you to back me up. In actuality, though, I fully anticipated that when you were asked about this, you'd provide an honest recounting of the facts. And at the point that I was confronted with your version, I intended to claim that our short separation had simply slipped my mind. Which is, after all, precisely what happened — at first, at any rate. But I assume that, for some reason, the police have delayed interrogating you about my whereabouts."

"No, Porchow spoke to me about that last week. And I assured him that you and I had been like Siamese twins right up until the meal was served."

"God, Desiree. I didn't expect — I can't allow you to do this, you know. You have your professional reputation to think about and —"

"It's already done. And, listen, I didn't do it for you. I acted out of self-preservation. The thought of you sitting in prison, stamping out license plates, would have caused me nightmares."

Allison managed a laugh. But in a second or two she turned serious again. "This witness . . . how much weight do you suppose her statement will carry?"

"Look, it's just her word against ours. But even if it could be definitely established that you walked down that hall at what was approximately the requisite time, it still wouldn't prove that you committed the murder. You're in no worse shape than you were before Ms. Big Mouth came along."

"Do you really believe that?" Allison asked softly.

"Yes, I do." But my palms were moist when I said the words.

Chapter 38

I was brain-drained by the time I got home Tuesday evening.

After my talk with Allison, I'd spent the better part of the day trying to devise some sort of plan that would help me establish Lorraine Corwin's guilt. The best I could come up with — and I'm not claiming it had success written all over it — was simply to sit down with Allison and tell her all I knew. Maybe once I got her to accept her friend's culpability, she'd reveal something incriminating about the woman, something she either hadn't thought to or hadn't wanted to mention before.

Plus, I was still hoping that something would come of Dominick Gallo and friend. But it's not exactly as if this could be regarded as money in the bank, either.

At any rate, I had no sooner sat down to what remained of that dinner with Ellen and Mike than a skinny little man with a surly expression rang my doorbell and delivered a surprise: a stunning bouquet of cymbidium orchids.

Imagine!

Before placing them in a more appropriate setting, I had the orchids share the kitchen table with me while I ate. Not that I paid much attention to the food. I was too busy admiring the flowers and replaying in my head the message that came with them. The card really didn't say anything that special, simply, "I look forward to our spending some time together soon." But it was enough for me.

I phoned Nick at around eight, figuring he'd be home by then. And he was.

"Thank you! The flowers are gorgeous!"

He was obviously pleased. "I'm glad you like them."

"You didn't have to do that, you know."

"But I wanted to. Uh, Dez, I hope that by making and then canceling our plans for this Saturday, I haven't caused you to miss out on something else."

Now, I don't know for sure why I did it. I have a suspicion, though, that most women come into this world equipped with this special gene that prevents them from overlooking an opportunity like the one I'd just been handed. Anyhow, after a slight — but meaningful — pause, I proceeded to protest too much. "Oh, no. Don't give it another thought. Please. I assure you I didn't pass up anything important."

"That's good," Nick said evenly. But I have a feeling this was because there really wasn't much else he *could* say.

The conversation ended with Nick's promise to call the following week. He was anxious, he said, to set up another date as soon as he was certain his ex was, in fact, back in town.

The grin was still on my face when I curled up in one of the living room chairs with a mystery by a "highly talented" new author. One of the attorneys at Gilbert and Sullivan had insisted on lending it to me. "You *must* read it. It's absolutely wonderful," she'd gushed. I swear, the woman practically had it winning the Edgar. Less than an hour later I put down the book in disgust. I didn't object to all those dead bodies piling up, but the writer's throwing in a dead *animal?* Well, that's where I drew the line. (Okay, so I'm weird.)

I was about to switch on the TV when the phone rang.

"Ms. Desiree Shapiro?" an unfamiliar male voice inquired.

"Yes."

"There's something I need to ask you."

"Who is this?"

"I can't tell you that. Not until you answer a question for me."

"A question?" I repeated stupidly.

"That's right. Suppose I know something about what took place at Silver Oaks a couple of weeks ago. That's not to say I actually *do* know anything. But, for argument's sake, let's say that I do. Understand?"

"Uh, sure, I understand. What's your question?" My heart was pounding so loudly that I could barely hear my own words.

"If it so happened that I *could* provide you with that information, would you have to give the cops my name?"

Afraid of scaring the man off, I thought it best not to respond to this directly. "Are you in some sort of trouble with the law? Is that why you don't want to identify yourself?" I was making these little clicking sounds when I spoke, the kind that come from your mouth's being bone dry.

My caller was indignant. "For your information, lady, I've never gotten so much as a parking ticket."

"Well, why won't you — ? Wait. Are you in this country illegally or something? Is that it?"

"Do I *sound* like I am, for crying out loud?"

"No, but —"

"I was born in the good ole U.S. of America." This proud declaration was followed by a short span of silence. Then: "But . . . well, there could be a problem about my girlfriend, who lives with me — we've been together over two years now. She's an illegal. From Central America."

"Listen, I'll be honest with you. The police *would* require that I give them your name. In fact, they'd no doubt want to speak to you themselves. But they couldn't be less interested in your girlfriend's immigration status, honestly. Besides, I can't see any reason for them to even learn she exists."

"But if they *do* find out about Marisol, would they report her to the INS?"

"Only if she robbed a bank."

The man laughed halfheartedly. Following which there was another brief silence. Then he conceded with a certain amount of resignation, "I guess Dominick had it straight after all — Dominick Gallo, I mean. The two of us are waiters at Silver Oaks, and Dom's been on my case to do what he calls 'the right thing' since this happened. 'Maybe she put something in this Mrs. Morton's water glass or fooled around with her salad,' he said when I told him what I'd seen. But this was even before the police had any idea what caused her death. And then while he was away on vacation, Dom heard from one or two of the other waiters that Mrs. Morton really had been poisoned. And right away he got on the horn to bug me about spilling what I knew. But charity begins at home, correct?"

"Yes, but your coming forward won't affect your home situation. Anyway, I'm glad you finally got in touch with me."

"Hey, after you convinced my buddy that the dead lady practically walked on water, forget about it. He wouldn't let up. I used to be married to this incredible nag, Ms. Shapiro, but trust me, these last coupla days Dom's been making her look like a mute. Anyway, he kept yammering at me that I was worrying for nothing. And I did feel bad that, in a way, I was allowing somebody to get away with murder — particularly once I found out that the victim was such a good person. Dom finally persuaded me to at least give you a call and talk to you."

"I hope I've managed to reassure you."

To my surprise, there was no further hesitation. At this point the man simply went into his story. "On the day of the murder, I was just walking into the dining room with the condiments when I saw somebody ducking out the side door — the staff uses the back entrance. I didn't get a look at the woman's face, but she was tall — very tall — and she was wearing a black-and-white outfit with a real short skirt. And oh, yeah, she had on this huge black hat."

"And this was after the salads had been distributed?"

"Yeah. Maybe five, ten minutes later. To be on the safe side, though, I'd put the time I spotted her as between one o'clock, which is approximately when we finished laying out the salads, and one fifteen or even one twenty — that's about when everyone came in to lunch."

Hallelujah! I could have kissed the guy — whoever he was. Which reminded me: *Who was he?*

"Uh, I can't thank you enough for your help, Mr. — ?"

"Dreher. Frank Dreher. And listen, I'm really sorry for not leveling with you when you questioned all of us at the club that day. I didn't like lying like that, but well, there was the situation with Marisol and —"

"The important thing," I said, only too happy to give him absolution, "is that you made up for it tonight."

* * *

Well, here it was. The confirmation I needed.

I felt like singing at the top of my lungs. I felt like twirling around the room until I collapsed from exhaustion. But since I happen to be a tone-deaf klutz, I remained seated and picked up the phone instead.

It was very unlikely Porchow would still be at the station, but certainly somebody there could get in touch with him and have him contact me.

I laid the phone back down.

What if the chief didn't consider the evidence of that sterling American citizen Frank Dreher up to his standards, either?

I mean, he could always cite an innocent reason for Lorraine's having been in the dining room then. Like maybe she'd merely stepped in for a second to check on the seating arrangements.

And this is when I realized there was no other way.

I had to get my hands on that topaz ring.

Chapter 39

In view of the fact that I was about to embark on a mission, I didn't go into the office on Wednesday. I did, however, remember to notify Jackie of my intention to play hooky. (I like to think I reported in to her because this was the courteous thing to do — and not a result of my being just plain chicken.)

At any rate, I phoned Lorraine Corwin at her office at about ten, and she acted as if we'd been in touch on a regular basis.

"Hi, Dez," she said casually, "what's up?"

"I have to see you, Lorraine."

"Sounds serious. Can you give me a little hint as to what it's about?"

"Allison."

"I don't understand."

"I suppose you're aware that the police are now looking at Allison for her sister-in-law's murder."

But she wasn't. Aware, I mean. Apparently — and understandably — Allison hadn't been too anxious to disclose the reason she'd come under suspicion, not even to her closest friends.

"Oh, my God," Lorraine whispered. And then she all but bellowed, "How the hell did they come up with *that,* for Christ's sake! Never mind. When do you want to get together? I could meet you after work, say about five, five thirty?"

Well, that wouldn't do at all. "I can't make it then. I have an appointment that should last until eight o'clock. I could stop off at your apartment at around eight thirty, though, if that's okay with you."

"Then eight thirty, it is."

In the early afternoon I went down to the jewelry district on West Forty-seventh Street and canvassed the stores for a very large topaz ring. At the fifth shop I found one of fairly decent dimensions — although not quite in the category of Lorraine's colossus. But I figured that if a person wasn't really that focused on the ring, it just might serve my purpose. Anyhow, after a great deal of haggling, I got the price reduced to three hundred ten dollars.

When I left with my new acquisition, the merchant's thundering voice followed me out onto the sidewalk. "You're a thief, lady, you know that? You committed highway robbery here today!"

Sitting in the taxi that evening, on my quest to "borrow" the murder ring, I was about as nervous as I've ever been in my life. I patted my handbag. Nestled inside, ready for action (heaven forbid!), was my trusty little .32-caliber security blanket, which I almost never carry and would probably faint if I had to fire. Still, it was a comfort to know it was there.

I suppose it would have been smart to review my strategy. Only I didn't exactly have one. The extent of my plan had been, first, to gain access to Lorraine's apartment, which I was about to do. Then I'd have to learn where she kept her jewelry and somehow manage to substitute today's purchase for the real thing in order to delay the woman's discovering that her own ring was missing. These matters accomplished, I'd do my damnedest to persuade Porchow to submit Lorraine's weapon of choice to toxicology.

Now, as to explaining to him how the ring had come into my possession, the truth is, I hadn't an idea in my head. At that point I also refused to contemplate any of the other issues that, sooner or later, could be staring me in the face. Such as what I'd do if I was unable to locate the thing or if the good chief declined to have it tested or if the toxicologists failed to find any evidence of monkshood on it. I did concede, however, that in the latter two instances I'd have to dream up some sneaky way to return the ring — and, with any luck, before Lorraine realized that it wasn't the genuine article lying there in her jewelry box or drawer or wherever.

But I'd worry about all that stuff when I had to. I mean, that ring was my one shot at apprehending Bobbie Jean's killer. So I was going to get ahold of it — or die trying. (Although, hopefully, only in a manner of speaking.)

The cab pulled up in front of one of those stately old buildings on the Upper West Side that, with some help from Publishers Clearing House, I'm looking forward to living in one day. The doorman advised me that Ms. Corwin was expecting me and indicated the way to the wood-paneled elevator that would be delivering me to the twelfth floor.

When I exited the car Lorraine was standing in her doorway, a few yards down the hall.

Her height helped me identify her. I mean, I'd never seen the woman without a hat before.

Anyhow, I noted that Lorraine Corwin had really lovely light brown hair, which tonight she was wearing down — parted in the middle and turned under at the shoulder. She was decked out in red satin lounging pajamas — low-cut, of course — and matching sky-high mules. To jazz up the outfit a bit, she sported a ruby ring the size of a doorknob on her left hand, three smaller rings on the other hand, and a wide gold cuff on her right upper arm. That's not all, either. She also had on long, *long* gold earrings, and strategically placed to draw attention to her décolletage (which hardly needed drawing attention to), was a large gold-and-ruby brooch. All that was missing from tonight's little ensemble was a feather boa.

She bent down and gave me a hug. "Desiree, how nice you look!" she exclaimed. Which was baloney. My lipstick had to be pretty much gone, considering all the lip gnawing I'd been doing on the ride over here. Plus, my hair was practically begging for its periodic rehennaing, and I was wearing an old and not particularly flattering gray dress with the hem coming down. (Klutz-like, I'd caught my heel in it getting out of the cab.)

I followed Lorraine into a large, high-ceilinged living room dominated by a magnificent grand piano. And while the remainder of the furnishings appeared to be antiques, for as much as I know they were just as likely decent reproductions. The upholstered pieces were covered in exactly the type of fabrics I would have anticipated that Lorraine would choose: velvets and brocades and damasks with a touch of faux suede thrown in — each in a different vibrant color. Instead of clashing, as I would have expected, however, this hodgepodge of color imparted a sense of exuberance to the space.

"This is *such* a striking room," I remarked.

Lorraine beamed. "Would you care to see the rest of the apartment?"

I'd been spared the asking. "I would love to."

She walked me through the adjoining dining room, then led the way into what was a very decent-size kitchen (particularly when you compared it to you-know-whose). After this, she steered me down a short corridor. On one wall was the bathroom and facing us, at the end of the hall, the bedroom.

You would have had to see that room to believe it — it was *so* Lorraine. There was an ornate, king-size four-poster — the bedspread, canopy, and curtains of which were fashioned of the same purple chintz with enormous shocking-pink flowers. This same print was repeated in the window drapes and in the two pillows that adorned the pale pink moiré chaise longue. And while you couldn't really ignore décor like that, I didn't pay that much attention to it, either. There was only one item here that was of interest to me then, and it was sitting atop the mahogany triple dresser.

Lorraine's jewelry box.

I'd been counting on its being out in the open like this. I mean, it has been my experience that the majority of women do leave those things in plain sight — although they might hide their more costly pieces in a drawer or stash them away in a safe. From what I'd seen of Lorraine Corwin, however, I didn't figure that there would be much she'd choose to keep hidden, jewelry-wise or otherwise. (Her recent little foray into murder excepted, naturally.)

The one surprise was the jewelry box itself. Mahogany, like the bedroom furniture, with an inlaid mother-of-pearl top, it must have been over a foot high. And — get this

— it covered more than half the length of the dresser.

"My jewel box seems to have caught your eye," Lorraine commented.

I think I may have turned red, and I also forgot to breathe for a second. "I've never seen anything like it."

"You never will, either. I designed it myself and had it made up a couple of years ago."

"It's really something."

She smiled. "Isn't it?"

Lorraine had excused herself to get us some refreshments, instructing me to make myself comfortable in the meantime. Considering the state of my nerves, this was not as easy as it sounds. I took a seat on one of the armchairs (which was in the style of some Louis or other — I have no idea of his Roman numeral), positioning myself on the very edge as if poised for flight.

My hostess soon returned with a large silver tray that held all the items for our little repast — including an elegant silver coffee service and a platter filled with an assortment of pastries. Setting the tray on the marble cocktail table that stood between the couch and the chairs, she devoted the next couple of minutes to dispensing the coffee.

Following which she sat down on the sofa, her legs curled up under her. Putting her cup to a pair of very red lips, she took only two or three sips before placing the delicate porcelain cup and saucer on the cocktail table.

"Talk to me about Allie," she said, looking at me earnestly.

I chose my words carefully. "Not very long ago — earlier this year, I believe — she and Bobbie Jean had some sort of argument. I don't know what it was about — Allison didn't tell me — but anyway, right afterward, Bobbie Jean went to Hawaii on vacation." I helped myself to a baba au rhum now, merely to collect my thoughts (I swear!). But in spite of the pastry's being quite delicious, I barely managed to swallow a bite of it. Which should give you a pretty good indication of how tense I was.

"Well," I continued a moment later, "for some reason Allison wrote to her sister-in-law while she was away on that trip, kind of rehashing their dispute. They eventually straightened things out between them, but when the police were going through Bobbie Jean's things, they came across the letter."

"And *that's* why Allie's under suspicion?" Lorraine exploded. "Those ignorant bastards! Pardon my French. But after all, who *didn't* have something against Bobbie Jean, for Christ's sake!" She picked up her coffee cup and took a few more swallows.

"Chief Porchow evidently feels that Allison is the only one with a motive that doesn't date back years."

"Big effing deal."

"Apparently he puts a lot of stock in the fact that it occurred fairly recently. Plus, he has this witness. One of the guests spotted Allison coming down the hall that leads to the side entrance to the dining room — and this was around the time Bobbie Jean's salad must have been doctored."

Lorraine came close to dropping her cup. "Christ!" she shouted. "So what? So she visited the little girls' room." I winced. (*Don't you hate that expression?*) "Allie couldn't have been the only one who had to empty her bladder within those ten or fifteen minutes or whatever. My God! What do you have to do to become the Forsythe chief of police — pass a test to prove that you're the biggest dimwit on the eastern seaboard? Anyway, is that all the man's got?"

"As far as I can gather. But there might be more. I honestly couldn't say."

"I'm absolutely stunned that Allie's never

mentioned a single word to me about what's been going on."

"Most likely that's because she doesn't want to worry any of her friends."

"She talked to *you*, though," Lorraine reminded me, making it sound like an accusation.

"Only because I'm investigating the case, and it's necessary that I be informed of something like that."

"I presume I'm not supposed to let on that you repeated this to me."

"It would probably be better if you didn't."

Lorraine nodded. "All right." Then she said softly, "Allison must be terribly upset. And I can't imagine what this must be doing to Wes. Mike, too."

"Mike doesn't know anything about it, but Wes is . . . he's sick over it."

Lorraine looked so stricken that for a fleeting moment I got the feeling she might be about to confess all and save me the trouble I'd scheduled for myself that night. But then she remarked, "I'm pleased that you decided to confide in me, but I'm not clear about what your purpose could be."

"I'm hoping that if you have so much as the slightest suspicion regarding who really *did* poison Bobbie Jean, what's happening to

Allison will convince you to tell me about it."

"You think I might be protecting somebody? Honestly, Dez, I haven't a clue who messed with that bitch's food. But if Allie should ever be arrested — please, God, no" — and she held up two crossed fingers — "it wouldn't shock me if the guilty party came forward."

Was she speaking for herself? I wondered.

It was very possible. But I wasn't prepared to wait and find out if she'd deliver.

Well, I suppose I should just get it over with. I tried to keep my voice from quivering, and to some extent, I think I succeeded. "Uh, may I use your bathroom, Lorraine?"

"Of course," she responded, absently reaching for a pecan square.

Snatching up my shoulder bag from the floor, I went quickly down that hall. After noisily opening and closing the bathroom door, I headed for the bedroom — and Lorraine Corwin's jewelry box.

I took a fast peek in the top drawer. *Damn! Earrings!* But on the next try I hit pay dirt. The second drawer held the rings, each in its own little plush-lined compartment. I had no trouble spotting the one I wanted in the third row — it was so much larger than the rings surrounding it. With shaking hands, I fumbled in my bag for the surrogate topaz and made the switch. It really wasn't a bad replacement, I decided, taking a split second to appraise my purchase. And at least when the woman opened the drawer she wouldn't be confronted with an empty space.

And now I stealthily slipped down the hall to the bathroom. To authenticate my visit here, I hurriedly repaired my lipstick and combed my hair. I even flushed the toilet for good measure.

A short while later I was back in the living room. I had to make a concentrated effort to avert my eyes from the shoulder bag, which I'd plunked down only inches from my chair.

After spending the next few minutes fidgeting in my seat and listening to Lorraine heap impassioned curses on Porchow et al., I prepared to leave. "Thanks for seeing me, Lorraine. And if you should suddenly remember something . . ."

"You don't have to say it."

I stood up then, and in my haste (call it panic) to get out of there, tripped over my handbag.

I didn't wind up on the floor, but that would have been preferable to what did: half the stuff in the bag — including Lorraine's ring and my .32.

What followed next seemed to take place in slow motion. I looked at the aforementioned items in horror. Lorraine looked at them in shock. Then, coming to life again, I scooped up the ring — there was no possibility of retrieving the gun; it was lying practically at Lorraine's feet. And now I made a dash for the door. Yes, a *dash.* (It's amazing what a little adrenaline can do for your physical prowess.) But a loud "Hold it!" aborted my flight.

I whirled around. Lorraine's expression was grim — and she was pointing my own gun at me!

"Give me the ring," she said, oh-so-quietly. Approaching me, she held out her hand — the one that wasn't otherwise occupied.

"No," I responded firmly. It just came out, believe me. Listen, there is absolutely no possibility of my ever receiving a medal for bravery.

"Give it to me!" Lorraine repeated, more forcefully this time.

I was about to comply (I told you I wasn't very brave) when suddenly she peered down at the gun and shook her head. Then, to my amazement, she slipped the weapon into the pocket of her pajamas. "Shit. I can't do this," she muttered.

And now she stared at me in wonder. "I *thought* I saw you ogling that ring when we had breakfast together that morning. But I never imagined I had let a goddamn kleptomaniac into my home. All right, Desiree, take the damn ring if you like it so much. Although why you'd pick on the citrine when I have so many other pieces that are worth far more doesn't say a helluva lot for your savvy."

The citrine? I unclenched my fist and stared into my palm. Sure enough, I'd helped myself to the wrong ring! (Well, it wasn't as if I'd had all the time in the world, you know. And the bedroom light *was* pretty dim, and the two stones *do* resemble each other.)

Tossing the ring onto a nearby table, I ran to the door as fast as these seldom-tested legs would permit.

Chapter 40

It was past ten when I arrived home. The first thing I did was to pour myself some wine — for medicinal purposes. To give you an idea of the shape I was in, I could almost *hear* my nerves jangle.

I mean, it had been absolutely vital that I leave Lorraine's with what I'd come there for. But I'd managed to screw up. And it wasn't easy, either. No matter how poor the bedroom lighting was and how rushed I felt, I still should have been able to identify the right ring. Listen, even in that brief look I'd had of the citrine later on, I could see that it wasn't nearly as large as the topaz and, if I remembered correctly, it was quite a bit paler in color, too.

God! What good was I if I couldn't carry out a simple little crime like that!

I had to concede, though, that there was one amusing note in my confrontation with Lorraine: her assumption that I'd coveted the citrine ever since our get-together at the coffee shop. She'd been wearing six rings that day, for heaven's sake! Who could even sort them all out?

At any rate, it was imperative that I get in touch with Porchow immediately. But it wasn't until I'd drunk about half a glass of the merlot that I had the courage to make the call.

I assumed he was long gone for the day, but I dialed the station house anyway, hoping to get a message to him. And guess what? Either he was working overtime or the guy had assigned himself to night duty again.

"This is Desiree Shapiro," I said when he came on the line. "Uh, how are you, Chief Porchow?"

"Tolerable." And then, an ample helping of sarcasm in his tone: "Just what is it you'd like me to do for you this time, Ms. Shapiro?"

Now, I've already mentioned my concerns about using Frank Dreher's statement to induce the police to obtain a search warrant. But I had to give it a try. After all, in light of tonight's fiasco, what were the chances I'd be able to latch onto that topaz ring myself? "Uh, I wanted you to know that there's a witness who spotted Lorraine Corwin leaving the crime scene soon after the salads were put on the tables."

A long, drawn-out silence followed. "And who is this witness?"

"He's a waiter at Silver Oaks."

"Correct me if I'm mistaken, Ms. Shapiro, but I thought we'd agreed that you'd back off this thing."

What does he mean — "agreed"? Porchow was making it sound as if it had been a mutual decision, for heaven's sake. However, if there was a single worst moment to antagonize the man, this was that moment. "Oh, we did. And I have. But this one waiter was on vacation when I interviewed the staff at the club, so I left a message on his answering machine asking that he phone me when he returned from his trip. Of course, this was before you and I had our discussion."

"And this individual has now admitted to you that he can place Ms. Corwin in the dining room just prior to lunch?"

"Well, no. Actually, when he called back he convinced me that he hadn't noticed anything of significance that afternoon. But then we started to chat. And I got kind of preachy about how important it was that we all do everything we can to make certain that somebody who commits a crime like that is brought to justice. Evidently it struck a chord, because he badgered another waiter — his friend — into coming forward."

"The friend, I take it, *was* the actual witness."

"Yes."

"And he was obviously advised to contact *you*, rather than the law enforcement officials in charge of the investigation," Porchow observed sourly. "At any rate, I presume you have the fellow's name."

"Frank Dreher."

"Dreher . . . Dreher . . . That's familiar. Hold on."

For about a minute the only sound to reach my ears was that of papers rustling. Then the policeman got on the line again. "We spoke to Mr. Dreher shortly after it was determined that we had a homicide on our hands, and he denied seeing anything, hearing anything, *knowing* anything."

I responded to this with an empathetic expression and a shrug — until I realized that these didn't communicate too well over the telephone. "Initially he didn't want to get involved. I run into that sort of thinking on a pretty regular basis. I would imagine you do, too."

"Yeah. Listen, I'll have to question the guy myself to verify what you're telling me. But keep in mind that even if we're satisfied that Dreher saw Ms. Corwin on her way out of the dining room within the critical time frame, this doesn't prove she did the job on the Morton woman's salad." *See? That was exactly what I was afraid Porchow would hand me!* I almost fell off my chair when he added, "It should be enough to get us a search warrant, however."

Now doesn't that beat all!

"Just so you understand, though, Ms. Lynton was — and still is — our prime suspect. I'm proceeding with this not because I give your theory a helluva lot of weight, but because I feel that it's incumbent upon me as an officer of the law to explore every possibility. At any rate, I'll keep you advised."

"Wait! Don't hang up yet."

"Is there something else, Ms. Shapiro?"

"Yes, there is," I admitted sheepishly. "When you go through Miss Corwin's apartment? Uh, maybe you could keep an eye out for my shoulder bag and my gun. It's a thirty-two caliber and —"

"I don't believe this! Did you actually say what I think you did?" Porchow was speaking so loudly that I had to hold the receiver at arm's length. "I hope you have a good explanation as to how those things got into her possession."

As far away as that phone was, I was able to catch every syllable. "I . . . I left them at her place."

"When was this?"

"It was . . . before. That is . . . earlier tonight."

"*Tonight!* What in hell were you doing there, anyway?"

"I . . . umm, I thought that maybe I could persuade her to confess."

"So much for keeping your promise. But never mind that now. If you're right about Ms. Corwin, what you did was foolish and dangerous. You should be locked up for your own protection — do you know that?"

"Yes." I took another sip of wine at this point — I needed it.

"You still haven't told me how you came to leave your pocketbook and weapon behind."

"I was —"

"Never mind," Porchow broke in testily. "On second thought, I'd rather not hear it."

It was well after nine when Chief Porchow phoned the next evening. "Sergeant Block had a conversation with your Mr. Dreher this morning," he told me. (I'd had my doubts about Sergeant Block's even being able to talk.) "Dreher confirmed that he spotted Lorraine Corwin exiting the dining room some ten or fifteen minutes before the other guests went in for lunch. At any rate, we completed a search of her apartment about an hour ago."

I was one short step from hyperventilating. "And — ?"

"And I have your gun and your handbag — along with a second topaz ring that the lady maintains belongs to you, as well. Incidentally, I expected we'd turn up those white gloves of hers. Only that didn't happen. Ms. Corwin claims one ripped, and she had to toss them."

It was a maximum effort to keep myself from shrieking the next words. "But the topaz ring? *Her* topaz ring, I mean. Do you have it?"

"I was getting to that. It was right there in a jewelry box on her dresser. And you were correct about one thing — the ring does open. But if it was used in the commission of this homicide — and I still regard it as a very big 'if' — we can infer from its being left virtually out in the open that the woman was confident she was able to remove all evidence of the poison."

"Also, she wasn't aware that we had the slightest inkling as to what purpose that ring had served."

"Mmm," was the extent of Porchow's response to this. Following which he cleared his throat. "By the way, the suspect gave me an earful regarding what occurred there last night. But we'll leave that for another time — when you can also tell me what the hell a citrine is."

"Uh, when do you think you'll be getting the toxicologist's report?" I put this to him quickly, before he could change his mind and insist that I provide him with every mortifying detail of that visit then and there.

"I can't say exactly. Most likely the latter part of next week."

"You'll call me — one way or the other?"

"I will. But about your property — it's at the station house here. Aren't you at all interested in retrieving it?"

My God! What was with me, anyway? I was so consumed with seeing to it that Lorraine Corwin was apprehended that everything else was taking a back seat to this. I mean, that bag contained my Social Security card, my checkbook, my credit cards, my driver's license, my cell phone, and my wallet (never mind that inside of this was the grand total of eleven dollars and ninety-six cents). And what about that other absolute essential: my makeup case? (I'd had to rely on my skimpy supply of emergency backup cosmetics today, and I swear that one of the law clerks at Gilbert and Sullivan took one look at my face and actually shuddered.)

Also, let's not forget those you-never-know-when-you-might-need-it items that I always carry with me. Like cough syrup, Extra-Strength Tylenol, hairspray, a flashlight, a stapler (you'd be surprised at how often that's come in handy), a metal tape measure, my Ivoire spray cologne — and I don't remember what else. Plus, aside from the handbag, there was my gun. I certainly wasn't crazy about having it sit around in the Forsythe police station. I wanted it where it belonged: buried at the bottom of my lingerie drawer.

Well, it's fortunate that I enjoy a little train trip now and then. Because with my driver's license in temporary residence at the station house, that's how I'd be schlepping out to Long Island to retrieve my treasures.

"Would it be all right if I came by in the morning to pick up my stuff?"

"Of course. I'm off tomorrow, so ask for Detective Malloy."

It was four very long days before I got the news.

When the phone rang I was just returning from the ladies' room — one foot hadn't even made it inside my cubbyhole yet. Hurrying to my desk, I reached over and snatched up the receiver. "You got any bubbly at home?" Porchow hadn't bothered to identify himself, but it was hardly necessary anymore.

"Huh?" I responded, this not being one of my more intelligent moments.

"You have something to celebrate."

"And what's that?" I asked cautiously.

"The toxicology report is in. And there was evidence that the ring had contained monkshood. In fact, two tiny pieces of leaf were caught up in the compartment's hinges."

At that instant I was so overcome that I had to plop down on the visitor's chair alongside the desk, my legs no longer able to support me. I couldn't even find my voice.

"Ms. Shapiro?"

"I'm here," I managed to squeak.

"I'll bet you feel like you've got an elephant off your back, huh? Me, too. Listen, while I admit that I resented your interference, I suppose I ultimately have to thank you for it."

"Well, I'm certain you would have solved the thing yourself before long. Anyhow, I'm glad it all worked out."

"That makes two of us. Nevertheless, I have a favor to ask of you."

"Sure. What kind of a favor?"

"Next time, try to find yourself a murder in your own backyard. I realize I sound like an ingrate, but the truth is, Ms. Shapiro, you are a very trying woman."

Epilogue

It's been almost a month since I had that conversation with Chief Porchow.

Naturally, everyone concerned is relieved that the investigation is over. Nobody, however, is dancing in the streets to celebrate its outcome. I suppose that in some secret recess of their hearts, and against all logic, most of those involved in the case had been holding out a tiny sliver of hope that the perpetrator would wind up being someone out of left field. You know, like a psychotic chef or a vengeful busboy or something.

As for me, I don't deny that I'm pleased I was able to identify Bobbie Jean's killer. But I'm not too thrilled myself that it turned out to be Lorraine Corwin. The thing is, I'd developed a certain fondness for Lorraine — once I got over our initial meeting, when she'd made me feel like the Invisible Woman. Sure, she's eccentric. Listen, the very first thing out of her mouth when the police came to arrest her wasn't "I didn't do it" or "You've got the wrong woman." Nothing like that. She just demanded that someone tell her how to get in touch with Johnnie Cochran! At any rate, she may be a little over the top, but she's also warm and friendly and outgoing, kind of like a puppy. A very *large* puppy. Plus, I really appreciate her having elected not to shoot me.

As you might have imagined, though, it's Allison who is finding it hardest to come to terms with the fact that it was Lorraine who poisoned Bobbie Jean. I have an idea that of all her friends, Lorraine is the one she had most hoped would prove to be innocent.

When I'd called to notify Allison of the arrest, she exclaimed, "Oh, no, not Lorraine!" and burst into tears. "May I tell you something?" she said on regaining her composure. "You may not understand this — particularly in view of your profession — but when I contemplate all that Lorraine's been through courtesy of my sister-in-law, it's difficult for me to blame her for doing what she did."

"Murder is never the right solution to anything," I countered. The instant I uttered this pronouncement, however, I wanted to pull it back. I mean, I sounded just like Barbara at her most pedantic. At any rate, at this point I attempted to make it a little easier for Allison to accept her old roommate's being hauled off to jail. "Don't forget that Lorraine's actions put you in jeopardy, too," I reminded her. "The way the police had this doped out, you might have been the one to end up paying for Bobbie Jean's death."

"You're wrong, Desiree," Allison asserted quietly. "I don't have a single doubt that if it ever came to that, Lorraine would have confessed."

I didn't argue. The reason being that I figured this was probably true.

Well, at least things have recently begun to look better for Allison on the home front. A few days ago she came into the city to do some shopping, and we met for lunch. "How is Wes?" I asked soon after she joined me at the table.

"He's very grateful to you, Desiree. We both are. Although I wish —" She broke off here, and I could tell she was thinking about Lorraine. Then she repeated, "We both are," smiled wistfully and, leaning across the table, squeezed my hand. "Naturally, Wes is still very saddened by the loss of his sister," she continued. "But it appears that learning the truth has allowed him to move forward with his life." Two or three seconds later, to my surprise, Allison volunteered, "And Desiree? Our relationship, Wes's and mine, is much improved, too."

"I'm *so* glad to hear that," I enthused.

"Oh, I'm not claiming that suddenly everything is just dandy. Although he does his best to conceal it, I'm certain Wes is still hurt and angry — as he has every right to be. And perhaps he won't ever trust me again. For my part, that terrible feeling of guilt is always present, and I may never be able to shake it. But while things aren't as they once were, there's been a kind of *easiness* between us these last two weeks or so that hasn't been there since he discovered that I'd . . . since he found out about Justin."

Which brings me to my own situation with Nick. Sad to say, we haven't exactly been steaming up any mirrors. But that would have been tough to do, because I've only seen him once since that memorable meal at the Chinese restaurant. And this was a couple of weeks back, over breakfast at a neighborhood coffee shop — hardly the setting for indulging one's libido. But then, our options for socializing had been pretty limited. You see, Nick's ex-wife didn't return to New York that following Sunday, as promised. The fact is, Tiffany is still in Vegas with the boy rocker. And considering that she'd quit her part-time job at the tanning salon just prior to her trip, Nick suspects — and I'm reasonably sure he's got it pegged right — that she'd been planning an extended stay out there from the beginning.

Anyway, Nick had been reluctant to employ a baby-sitter, which put the kibosh on our getting together once the sun went down. He explained that because he had to leave Derek in the care of a nanny during the day, it was all the more important that he be there in case his son should wake up at night. (Something, by the way, that in all the weeks he's been staying with his father, the nine-year-old has yet to do.) Now, however, in view of a growing conviction that his ex won't be heading home until God-knows-when, Nick's decided to hire a sitter after all. And we'll be going out to dinner on Saturday. Which occasion, I believe, calls for a new dress — preferably something in blue that's incredibly flattering.

I'd like to share one last thing with you.

Yesterday afternoon Ellen called to inform me that Bobbie Jean left Mike a very handsome sum in her will.

I exhibited the proper amount of astonishment before asking, "And you just found out about this?"

"Yes. Mike had postponed telling me. He was concerned about how I'd react to what he has in mind. His own parents don't even know about that yet."

"What do you mean, 'has in mind'?"

"He wants to donate most of the inheritance to St. Gregory's and have the hospital name a wing for Bobbie Jean. He was extremely fond of her, Aunt Dez. Not that he condoned the sort of stuff she pulled — although he probably never realized the extent of it."

"His giving up so much money is okay with you?"

"Definitely. Mike said that he wouldn't do it without my approval, and I think it's a wonderful idea. He feels — and I agree — that it's the only way we can make something good come out of all this."

In spite of Ellen's news, I have to admit that like virtually all murder stories, this one doesn't exactly have a happy ending, either.

But thanks to Ellen's generous almost-husband — and to my big-hearted niece, as well — it's as close to one as you're ever likely to get.

Desiree's Wild Mushroom Croustades

For toast shells:
15 slices white bread
butter

Lightly flatten bread slices with palm of hand, then trim away crusts. Using a cutter about 2½ inches in diameter, cut 2 rounds in each slice. Coat cups of a mini muffin pan with butter, and press bread rounds into cups. Bake at 400° for 8–10 minutes or until shells turn a little golden. Set aside to cool.

For filling:
4T butter
3T shallots, finely chopped
2½ cups stemmed shiitake mushrooms (approx. 9 oz.), finely chopped
2 level T flour
1 cup heavy cream
½ tsp. salt or to taste
pinch of cayenne

1½ T chopped chives
1T chopped parsley
½ tsp. lemon juice
grated Parmesan cheese

Melt butter in skillet and add shallots. Cook, stirring constantly, for about four minutes without allowing shallots to brown. Add mushrooms and mix well. Cook for ten minutes, stirring frequently.

Remove from heat. Add the flour and mix thoroughly. Stir in the cream. Return to heat and, stirring continuously, bring to a boil. Allow to boil for a minute or two before removing from heat. Then add the salt, cayenne, chives, parsley, and lemon juice.

Transfer mixture to a covered bowl and refrigerate until shortly before serving time. Stir mixture, fill toast cups, and sprinkle with Parmesan. Bake at 350° for ten minutes. Serve hot.

NOTE: The toast shells freeze well for filling at a later date. The filled, baked croustades can also be frozen. Reheat these at 350° for 10–15 minutes just before serving.

Makes 30

The employees of Thorndike Press hope you have enjoyed this Large Print book. All our Thorndike and Wheeler Large Print titles are designed for easy reading, and all our books are made to last. Other Thorndike Press Large Print books are available at your library, through selected bookstores, or directly from us.

For information about titles, please call:

(800) 223-1244

or visit our Web site at:

www.gale.com/thorndike
www.gale.com/wheeler

To share your comments, please write:

Publisher
Thorndike Press
295 Kennedy Memorial Drive
Waterville, ME 04901